FAST AS YOU
BIJOU HUNTER

Copyright ©2019 Bijou Hunter

No part of this publication may be reproduced, distributed or transmitted in any form or by any means, including photocopying, recording, or other electronic or mechanical methods, without the prior written permission of the publisher, except in the case of brief quotations embodied in critical reviews and certain other noncommercial uses permitted by copyright law.

Publisher's Note: This is a work of fiction. Names, characters, places, and incidents are a product of the author's imagination. Locales and public names are sometimes used for atmosphere purposes. Any resemblance to actual people, living or dead, or to businesses, companies, events, institutions, or locales is completely coincidental.

<u>Cover Design</u>
Photo Source: Depositphotos
Cover Copyright © 2019 Bijou Hunter

<u>Dedication</u>
Thanks to my personal Bubba, Butch, and Buzz;
My mom for listening to me babble;
My betas—Sarah, Debbie, Sheri, Carina, and Cynthia;
&
Judy's Proofreading

THE CHAPTER WHERE THE STORY BEGINS

NIKOLAS "BUBBA" DAVIES, AKA THE RUNAWAY

I'm too old to be waking up in a stranger's place with only vague memories of how I got here.

Not everything from yesterday is a blur. I remember arriving at my cousin's two-story recently remodeled house after midnight. With Audrey owing me a favor, I figured she'd keep her mouth shut about my crashing at her place for a few days.

On Sunday, I woke up around noon to find Audrey, her husband, Cap, and their crawling kid, Keith, in the living room. My dark-haired cousin and her darker-haired man make an odd couple with her barely over five feet tall and him well over six and a half feet.

When Audrey asked what I wanted to do that night, I said drink beer and get laid. She hadn't been thrilled with going out on a Sunday, claiming only alcoholics got wasted on the Lord's day. Cap laughed at her fake high-mindedness before suggesting they drop off their kid at his parents' place and take me to a bar in the town over.

"We don't have trashy places in White Horse," Cap insisted. "If you want loose women and cheap booze, you'll need to visit Hickory Creek Township."

I didn't care where we went. I only wanted to blow off a little steam, go wild for a few hours, and regain my confidence for when I returned to my town, family, and motorcycle club.

My usually savvy cousin—whose father is the president of the Reapers Motorcycle Club back in Ellsberg, Kentucky—decided to take me to Salty Peanuts. Also known as the clubhouse for the Serrated Brotherhood Motorcycle Club.

"You do realize we're in less than friendly territory," I mentioned when we gained the leery attention of a table full of local bikers.

"Don't be dramatic," Audrey said. "The Rutgers have been to Ellsberg plenty of times."

"Yeah, back when the Memphis guys backed our clubs," I pointed out. "Things have changed since then."

"Whatever," she said, waving off my concern. "I don't know any other trash-holes around here."

"Doesn't he?" I asked, gesturing at her giant husband.

Cap Hayes is the heir to the crime family running White Horse. Despite his connections, he only shrugged like a big doofus in response to my question. I suspected he didn't want me stinking up his precious hometown.

"My boy, Keanu, hangs out here," Cap said as we arrived at the honkytonk. "He even has a drink named after him. This bar is friendly-enough territory."

Minutes, after he promised we were safe there, a few long-haired bikers wearing Brotherhood patches started trouble with Cap.

"No deal. You need permission to be here!" shouted the shortest of the three club dicks.

Audrey ignored the argument and walked to the bar top. I followed her, but my mind remained on an outnumbered Cap.

"Should I help him?"

"What can you do, cousin?" she snickered. "Cheer on my giant hubby while he stomps those stupid bikers into the ground?"

The grizzled bartender gave us a dirty look, but Audrey only smiled wider. "I'm more important than you," she told the guy and then added, "Don't spit in my drink."

"How about a little piss?" he asked.

"Not in my drink, no, but feel free to take a whizz in his," she said, gesturing toward me. "He's from Kentucky and won't be able to taste the difference."

Audrey laughed at my expression while the amused bartender seemed less inclined to use her drink as a toilet. As tempted as I was to point out how she was also from Kentucky, I didn't care enough to get into a sparring match with a full-fledged bitch. Blood-born Johansson women refuse to lose arguments. Even when they seem to be defeated, they've actually laid a trap to lower their opponents' guards. I wasn't falling for that again.

"I've arrived!" yelled an Asian man from the door. Wearing a slick black suit in a place filled with jeans and leather and being the only non-white person in the bar, the guy probably should have seemed out of place. instead, he sported the swagger of a made man. "I've come to rescue you, Iron Giant!"

Audrey laughed at his comment while the man ran over to the long-haired bikers and playfully karate-chopped them in the necks. The men chose to humor him. It was all fun and games until one of the guys ruffled his thick black hair. His next karate-chop took the biker to the ground.

Laughing harder, Audrey applauded. "Never fuck with a black belt."

Cap and his friend left the bikers—who lifted up their injured brother—and joined us at the bar top.

Audrey wore a relaxed smile, and I like seeing how settled she was into her life in Tennessee. "Keanu Slater, this is my cousin, Bubba Davies."

"I'm sorry," Keanu told Audrey.

"We all are, but I owed him, and here we are."

"Owed him how?" Cap asked.

Audrey shrugged. "I don't remember."

The men looked at me, but I only smiled. If Audrey chose not to mention the time that she knocked over a line of Harleys at her father's clubhouse, who was I to rat her out? Of course, she didn't take the hit that day. After watching the domino effect play out and seeing how terrified my cousin was, I accepted the blame.

I was a nice guy back then. Growing up with two younger brothers—one freakishly shy and the other wildly reckless—made me sympathetic to the fuckery happening in people's heads. I was an honest-to-goodness fucking saint back in the day.

I also seemed as if I had my shit in order. That was the main reason I decided to ditch Conroe and visit White Horse. I needed a break from the illusion of being in charge.

Not that I shared my problems with Audrey, knowing she'd eventually blab to her family back in Ellsberg. Once she told her mom and pop, they'd be on the phone to my mom and pop. Then before I had a chance to get comfy in my mini-vacation, half of the Johansson family would be up my ass with questions and demands.

I kept crap simple with Audrey, telling her only that I needed a place to crash and that she should keep her mouth shut about it. I suspected her promise to remain quiet would last two days max.

Yeah, I remember ending up at Salty Peanuts as clear as day. I also recall Audrey and Cap dancing like two drunken sea lions to "Whiskey Glasses." The long-haired bikers took turns glaring at us from their table. Then around nine, Keanu ordered me a Korean Kickass.

"If you want to relax," he said, flashing a sly grin, "this is your friend."

Wary of the colorful concoction in a chimney-style glass, I nearly turned it down. Fruity drinks aren't my thing. Back at the Reapers' bar in Conroe—Morty's Pub—I wouldn't be caught dead drinking something so festively bright.

But last night, I wasn't Bubba from Conroe. A free man, I downed the sweet brew and ordered a second one.

Taking off his black suit jacket, Keanu smiled wider. "You're going to feel that tomorrow."

And he was right.

Now I'm in a stranger's bed, barely able to recall how I got here.

My bare feet are pointed at the wall while my head rests at the open end of the mattress. I realize the wall is a slanted roof that I no doubt would have slammed into if I was sleeping in the opposite direction. Based on the lump near my temple, I already suffered a run-in with it.

From the night before, I vaguely remember this house is shaped like a triangle. Pinned to the slanted ceiling/wall in front of me is a colorful tapestry. My brain takes nearly a minute to organize the orange, blue, red, and green swirls into an identifiable shape.

"An elephant," I babble, choking on my dry throat.

The chick who owns this place isn't at my side. I run my fingers over my body to find no shirt or jeans, but I am wearing my boxers. Turning over, I scan the room to find a six-foot partial wall blocking me from wherever music plays. Rolling out of bed, I pause to allow my head to stop spinning. The urge to piss is the only reason I make it to my feet. Stumbling out of the walled-off section of the house, I spot a tiny bathroom to my right.

After pissing for what feels like ten minutes, I splash water on my face over the bowl sink. In the mirror, I spot fresh bruises on my face. On Saturday, I traded punches with my brother Butch. Apparently, I went a round with someone last night too.

Just in case I lock lips with the chick, I swish mouthwash I find in a wire hanging shelf.

My mind is fuzzy on a lot of details from last night. The girl's name starts with an "S," and I'm certain she's hot, and I possibly love her. That last part is likely from the booze, but I remember she was a good kisser, and I think she sucked my cock at one point. The rest of last night at Salty Peanuts and back here at her triangle house remains a painful blur.

Leaving the bathroom, I walk past the bedroom and into the open section of the house where I find the woman's ass sticking in the air. I watch her for a long time before realizing she's exercising. Not aerobics but that stretchy type.

Despite her loose-fitting cotton beige shorts, I easily detect a perfect heart-shaped ass. Her legs are long and leanly muscled. I'm very curious about the rest of her since I woke up feeling as if I'm in love. The chick must be something special despite her New Age music grating my hungover nerves.

Appearing on the arm of the low-sitting, orange couch, a tiny dog—popular with chicks and old people—yaps at me and alerts the blonde to my presence. I notice her swipe a shiny object from the ground and shove it in her pocket. She turns to look at me with smoky, almond-shaped eyes. Her straight blonde hair rests around her shoulders, and her pale pink lips begged to be kissed.

Memories flood back from last night. Not images as much as feelings. I wanted this woman in my arms. Despite earlier remembering sex between us, I now feel as if she remained out of reach.

Most of all, I recall swearing to myself how she was the woman I planned to marry.

Now if I could only remember her name.

CALYPSO "SOSO" RUTGERS, AKA THE BOHEMIAN

I don't know why I'm at Salty Peanuts on a Sunday night. There's no reason to tempt fate. Except I'm sick of hiding.

It's well past time I reclaimed this honkytonk. This is the clubhouse for the Serrated Brotherhood Motorcycle Club, and my dad is their vice president. I've been coming here since I was a kid. Instead of a mojito, I'd get an ice cream sundae.

Back then, I was my father's shadow, and this was his favorite haunt. Salty Peanuts even held events for the children of the club. Yet for the last few months, I've avoided the place entirely, and now I have to hide in the corner if I hope to sip my mojito in peace.

My brother doesn't seem to notice me in the corner as he torments the men our father considers family. They wear Serrated Brotherhood patches on their vests, but Keanu Slater is a man on the outside, and he's content to remain there.

I wish I could so casually torment the members of the Brotherhood. Years ago, I was able to tease them and laugh easily in their company. Then I grew tits, and they got boners, and everyone got awkward. My father isn't the kind of man who shrugs off someone jacking it to his daughter's rack. He won't kill these men, but on more than one occasion, he's made them hurt enough to think they might die.

I shouldn't be here at the clubhouse. Not since Griff claimed me as his main bitch and decided I was an extension of his will. The problem is I just wanted to fuck him. Nothing personal. He had a fuck-me body and a decent-sized dick, and I was looking for something to stick in my vagina. How my lust transitioned into him swearing off all other women—only when I was looking, of course—I will never know.

Sure, we got serious eventually. Griff had all the similar stats as my dad, and I'd always assumed I'd fall in love with a biker.

But I never did. Now, to avoid drama—and I don't do drama—I have to hide in my own damn town while Griff has free fucking rein. It's a damn shame that I managed to foul up things for myself. Tonight, though, I'm taking a stand. While hiding in the corner like a wuss, of course.

When I showed up and realized Griff wasn't around, I took a spot in the corner near the toilets where no one wants to sit. My blonde hair is covered by the hoodie on my sweater. My usual loose-flowing skirts are replaced with dark jeans. I blend in easily without my signature bohemian attire. Though the waitresses might recognize me, they know better than to snitch out my disguise.

Around ten, Keanu's best friend—and male soul mate—starts dicking around with the Brotherhood guys. Cap Hayes thinks he's top dog in this part of Tennessee. Some days, he's right. Other days, he might be wrong.

The Hayes family in next-door White Horse and the Serrated Brotherhood in Hickory Creek Township don't throw down. For as long as I can remember, we've been either friendly enemies or hostile allies. This arrangement is important since Cap and Keanu bonded hard as kids. A war between our families would put them in a tough spot.

Whenever Cap fucks with the Brotherhood, my big bro is right there with him. I absolutely love when he unleashes his badass self. While the rest of these men are buffed-out white-bred meatheads, who use their size rather than any finesse to win, Keanu's exotic and trained in martial arts. They're sledgehammers; he's a scalpel.

Around eleven, after I've sipped to death my mojito, Keanu stops screwing around with Cap once the giant decides to dance with his tiny tot wife. My brother then stops by the bar where he chats with a hunky stranger.

Lonely from hiding in the corner too long, I mentally summon Keanu to join me. He senses my wishes and struts in my direction. What I don't expect is for the hunky stranger to follow Keanu like a boisterous puppy.

"Nice getup," Keanu says, sliding into a chair across from me.

The sandy-haired hunk drops into the spot next to Keanu and smiles at me like a dope.

"Who's this?" I ask.

"Audrey's cousin from Kentucky."

"Is this your girlfriend?" the muscled, tatted stranger asks Keanu.

"No, man. I told you that my girlfriend was visiting her family in Indonesia. I swear it's like you can't remember anything while drunk."

"What's he drinking?"

"A Korean Kickass," Keanu says, smirking.

"Does he know about the absinthe?"

My brother's smile grows. "I believe in allowing life to surprise people, Soso."

"Huh?" the hunky stranger asks, tilting his head in the most puppy move ever.

Smiling, I ask, "Huh, what?"

"Is Soso code?"

"It's my name."

"I'm Bubba."

I shouldn't laugh, but he announces his name as if he's just so blazing proud. His smile falls away.

"It's stupid. I'm stupid."

"Was he like this before the Kickass?" I ask Keanu.

"I suspect booze makes this one on the sad side."

"I'm on vacation," Bubba says and leans close enough for me to admire the perfect symmetry of his gorgeous face. "You're so fucking beautiful."

Keanu and I share a smile. "He's wasted," I mutter.

"Well, you are hot."

Bubba's face twists into a stony glare as he growls at Keanu, "Don't you dare flirt with my woman."

"Uh, that's my sister, dumbass."

"No," Bubba says, doing his confused puppy head tilt again.

"Yeah."

"Was she adopted?"

"No, why?" Keanu asks, fucking with the out-of-towner.

"She's not Korean."

"You know, I did notice that fact but never felt it was my place to mention anything."

"Did I just say something racist?" Bubba whispers.

Keanu tries not to laugh. "Yes, and we're very disappointed in you, Kentucky."

"I don't know if you're messing with me now."

"We have the same mom," I explain when Bubba's confused expression wears down my resolve to ignore his babble.

"Oh. Is she beautiful like you?"

"Yes, but she's taken. Tough luck."

"You're not, though, right?"

"Would it matter?"

"I don't know," Bubba says, leaning closer. This time, I realize his eyes are a striking green. "You're so beautiful that I might break up your marriage."

"Not married."

"Good. You can do better."

Keanu leans back and chuckles at how far Bubba spirals into the rabbit hole. I sip my drink while wondering if I should steal what's left of his Korean Kickass before he destroys what's left of his brain.

"Why are you hiding your hair?" Bubba asks, reaching over to push back my hoodie.

I nearly smack away his hand. If he tugs a single strand of hair, I swear I'll kick his blotto ass. Well, Bubba's size means I might need to ask my big bro for help.

No one needs to kick anything, though. Bubba's touch is careful, gentle even. Not bad considering he's sloppy drunk.

"I want to know you," he says, sounding sad. "But I'm not anyone worth knowing."

Before I can console him, my attention shifts to the entrance where Griff, aka Heartbreaker, and Andy, aka Toymaker, eyeball Cap dancing with his tiny wife.

Then I'm spotted by the man who didn't break my heart—though he did steal my fucking smile and ruin this bar as a social spot. The sinking sensation returns to my stomach. If only I could invent time travel and return to the moment when Griff first flirted with me. I would, without a doubt, vomit in his face.

"I'm weak for hot men, and they're weaker for me," I mumble, and Keanu nods.

"I'm sorry," Bubba says and runs his fingers over my knuckles.

It's a small, tender gesture. He's obviously hot for me, but I also suspect he'd be hot for anyone with the right parts. His glassy eyes tell the story of a man far past his booze limit.

"Who the fuck is this cunt?" Griff rages behind Bubba.

I flinch at the sound of his rage while Keanu doesn't react at all. Without a doubt, my brother is ready to attack if Griff decides to spill blood.

"Audrey's cousin," Keanu says.

"Who the fuck is Audrey?"

"Cap Hayes' wife."

Griff glances back at where Audrey and Cap pretend as if they don't notice what we're saying. This is an old drill. Cap feigns a relaxed demeanor like the happiest giant fool in the world. Then trouble breaks out, and he turns into King Kong tearing up the joint.

It's no shock to watch my ex-boyfriend's raging expression falter at the thought of becoming a smudge on the floor. His gaze returns to me. Where anger lived just a minute ago, longing now rules his blue eyes. I see such pain in them. I can only hope he finds cold indifference in mine.

"Who is this fucker?" Bubba asks as if awakening from a dream. "Is he hassling you?"

I look at Keanu who struggles not to laugh at Bubba's bravado. I'm not nearly as contained. My giggles end as soon as Griff gets in the face of the now-standing Bubba.

"You don't belong here," Griff growls, full-on pompous biker asshole.

Bubba doesn't back down. Both men are over six feet, staring eye to eye. The hunky puppy is far prettier, but he's also sporting a bruised right eye and a fat bottom lip. Very recently, he threw down with someone who put up a decent fight. No reason to think he won't fuck up Griff to defend my honor.

No way am I sticking around for Griff to whine his way into a fight.

"Later, tater," I tell Keanu. "I'm heading out."

My brother only allows a curt nod as his black eyes focus hard on the table. He's hyper-alert, waiting for the impending violence. If it breaks out, he'll crack a lot of ribs. It's his favorite move lately.

Griff hears I'm leaving and decides to stop his staring contest with Bubba. Reaching out for me, his hand gets smacked away by the hunky puppy who's now growling like a wolfman under a full moon.

Griff charges Bubba and their collision sends the entire bar into an instant violent frenzy. I swear everyone's been sitting around all night, aching for a brawl. Those hoping to stay safe duck and cover or flee. Those wanting a piece of the action rush to where the two men bash into each other.

I don't run, hide, or join in. Freezing up, I'm not sure how to handle what's happening. Keanu is gone from his chair, disappearing into the crowd of men. I never think to worry about him. He's so much faster than any biker. If they're lucky, he'll only play with them tonight.

Cap must be in the mix too. I spot Toymaker go flying like a ragdoll. The only one massive enough to do such a thing is the giant from White Horse.

Once Bubba ends up on the ground, Griff staggers toward me. His bloody mouth says my name, obsessed with owning me. I stare into his eyes and wish he were dead. If it didn't cause issues in the club, I'd have asked my dad to end this asshole months ago.

Like a missile, Bubba tackles Griff to the ground. Snapping out of my fear, I race for the door, dodging the bikers stupid enough to try to take down Cap. Audrey crouches under a table, talking on the phone. The Brotherhood better hope she isn't calling the Hayes family. The last thing this township needs is for Cap's father and brother to show up, swinging bats and breaking crap that can't be fixed.

The damp spring air reinvigorates me, and I nearly run to my Chevy truck parked on the farthest end of the lot.

"Soso!" Griff hollers.

I spin around and can't believe he's still coming. The guy is like the Terminator, unable to accept no for a blazing answer.

"Leave me alone!" I scream and throw open my truck door.

Shaking as I start the engine, I think of the gun in my purse. I could put a bullet in Griff and stop worrying about him around every corner. Except nothing is that easy.

Griff ends up on the ground again as Bubba barrels out of the bar and takes down the obsessed dickhead. I pull my truck out of its spot, ready to disappear into the night.

Bubba and Griff remain in a tangle of flying fists on the ground. Out here in the almost empty lot, the asshole could easily kill Kentucky. I see a flash of Bubba bleeding out on the ground just because his ego demanded that he protect a pretty girl from a stupid fathead.

Even hating myself for being a sap, I still stop the truck next to the men and scream for the Kentucky hunk. He reacts to his name by popping to his feet. The booze has made him both hyper-vigilant and easily distracted. He nearly ends up on his ass when Griff kicks him in the leg.

Eventually, he notices how I've opened the passenger door. Bubba catches the hint. I don't wait until he's entirely in the truck before I peel out of the parking lot. He manages to get the door shut by the time I'm screeching around a corner and blowing through a stop sign on the empty road.

"I couldn't let you die," I say despite him not asking me why.

"I couldn't let him touch you."

Shaking my head, I fight a smile. "Fucking idiot."

"Are you talking about you or me?" he says, sounding tired now.

"Why not both?"

I race home, thinking if I'm behind the walls of my A-frame house that I'll be safe.

Only a few blocks out from my house, I'm struck with the realization that Bubba might be a danger I'm inviting into my sanctuary.

Then I catch him in the darkness wearing that dopey smile. He watches me like he's where he needs to be. In a way, it's the same needy gaze Griff gets. I should be nervous, but my heart wants to believe he's a good guy.

I just hope Bubba from Kentucky doesn't turn my bad taste in men into a habit.

THE CHAPTER WHERE THE RUNAWAY AND THE BOHEMIAN OFFICIALLY MEET
THE RUNAWAY

The word "awkward" doesn't do justice to the feeling I suffer while staring into the eyes of a woman I'm already soft on, yet whose name I can't remember. Her soft brown eyes hold amusement. Does she know I don't know? Or is she happy about last night and thinks I'm happy too? *Hell, I'd be plenty happy if I knew her fucking name.*

"I'm going to go on a limb and guess you're having trouble remembering how you got here last night," she says, standing in her living room while I remain stuck in the kitchen.

"Yeah, it's a little foggy."

"Do you remember meeting me at Salty Peanuts?"

"A little," I lie.

"Do you remember me driving you here?"

"A little less."

Her soft smile makes my heart beat a little faster. My dick voiced its approval back when she was stretching, but I'm starting to remember why I thought she was "the one" last night. There's something intoxicating about the way she looks at me.

"Seems like Bubba from Kentucky wasn't ready for so many Korean Kickasses."

Her distance from me makes me doubt my memories from last night. If we fucked like rabbits, why is she still standing so far away and watching me as if I'm a possible threat? *Was I rough? For fuck's sake, did I hurt this woman?*

"We fucked, right?" I ask before realizing some things need to be left in my damn head. Or at least, worded better.

She bites her smiling lower lip and fights laughter. "No, Bubba, we just talked, and you fell asleep."

"Why was I in your bed?"

"Because you're too big to fit on the couch."

"No," I say, rubbing my pounding head. "I remember us doing stuff."

"Then, you must have enjoyed one helluva dream. Or more likely, the absinthe gave you a hallucination."

Staring at her like a dipshit, I'm not usually this incompetent with women. I don't know what I said or did last night. I mean, it's probably best we didn't fuck. Sloppy drunk people are notoriously bad in bed. When I get between this woman's legs, I want her to forget every other man exists.

First, though, I really should learn her name, but how the hell do I ask that question?

THE BOHEMIAN

Bubba staggers onto my front porch and stares in awe at my house. He remained mostly quiet in the truck on the way over. He only spoke when I stopped at a red light and texted my brother, who worried about my disappearance. I mentioned Bubba was with me, and I'd return him safely to his cousin tomorrow. You know, assuming I wasn't forced to gut the asshole.

While Keanu doesn't demand to check on me, I bet he'll keep his phone close just in case I need him. My big bro takes his job very seriously.

"It's a circle," Bubba says as I unlock the front door. "No, wait, that other shape."

I shouldn't smile at his drunken babble, but he sounds so young. I think that's why I'm trusting him to behave. He doesn't act like a grown man looking for pussy, but a lost child needing safe passage.

However, I nearly chicken out. Standing in my house, I watch him still outside, staring slack-jawed at the shape of my house. I could lock him out and let him sleep off his stupor on the porch. The weather's chilly, but he'll survive. I could even call Keanu to get his bestie to pick up the hunky puppy. These options flash through my mind, but I still allow Bubba to stumble inside.

"I'm too soft," I mutter.

Bubba stands next to me, his wide eyes taking in the sight of what's not that interesting to a sober person. It's a small, A-frame house. On the righthand side is a kitchen along a short wall. The living room sits directly in front of us. Before reaching the double doors at the back, there's a small detour with a bedroom and bathroom created by a set of half-walls.

My cousins, Lincoln and Lennox, put them up after I moved in. Though the only other owner of this house hadn't worried about modesty, I want to be able to take a crap without an audience.

"Your house is all wrong," Bubba says, but there isn't the anger in his voice like when Griff saw this place.

My ex wanted me to be fun and different but never too fun and different. I don't know if I'm fun at all really. Different, yes, but that's only because I grew up seeing Keanu stand out in a crowd. Why wouldn't I want to do the same?

"Listen up, Kentucky," I say, refusing to use his name now that I'm reminded of his massive size. Back at the bar, he was tall at a few inches over six feet and wide in the shoulders. He was reasonable there surrounded by other large men. But in my small house, I'm getting that Godzilla-about-to-tear-up-the-place vibe.

His gaze finally leaves the ceiling he's fascinated by. With the amount of absinthe that he ingested, everything is awe-inspiring.

"I'm letting you stay here tonight as a thank-you for helping with Griff, but you and I will not be fucking," I say in my hardest voice. "If you touch me, I will hurt you. Do you understand?"

"He shouldn't touch you," Bubba says in a somber tone that would probably be intimidating if the words weren't so slurred.

"Yeah, and neither should you. Don't make me regret bringing you here."

Bubba nods like an obedient child, and I struggle not to smile at the earnest expression he's wearing. I instruct him to remove his jacket and shoes and to put them in the front armoire.

"There are no closets in the house," I say when he only stares at first.

Turning my back on him to open a kitchen drawer, I find the gold and blue switchblade that my father bought me for my eighteenth birthday. I'm probably paranoid, but I worry Bubba could be another Griff, and I don't want to end up wishing I had a weapon if things get iffy.

"A dog," Bubba says, now sitting on my low, wide couch.

I smile at the sight of his long legs struggling to make sense of the small space. He looks at Freki as if he's never seen a dog up close before. Then again, maybe he hasn't. I don't know jack shit about this guy.

"He's nervous around men," I say without explaining why.

Bubba doesn't reach out for my skittish black and brown Yorkie. He leans back on the couch and smiles in that dopey drunk way. "My family has a dog named Frenchie. Wanna hear why he has such a stupid name?"

"Sure," I mumble while removing my shoes.

"My pop adopted the mutt from the shelter, and we planned to name him something tough like Magnum or Big Dick. That last one was my brother Buzz's idea. But then Mom had a dream where the dog wore a beret. She said he looked French, so Pop started calling him Frenchie."

"That's cute," I say, choosing those words because I find the story sweet and I'd also like to poke at his ego to see if he gets nasty. "Here's an ice pack for your face."

Bubba doesn't respond immediately. I freeze, thinking he's about to get angry. Then I realize he doesn't understand what I mean about the ice pack. Either the booze dulled the pain, or he was so banged up from his first fight that he doesn't feel what Griff did to him.

I press the ice pack to his jaw where I witnessed an elbow make contact earlier. He catches the hint and takes it from me. His gaze holds mine, and I can't deny there's something sexy about being the only thing he sees.

"I'm on vacation from being me," he says, and his shoulders sag, making him look like a giant disappointed kid.

I sit on the other end of the couch and carefully slip the knife under me. "What's wrong with being you?"

"My brother hates me, and I hate him," he says between gritted teeth. "I always took care of him, and he was my best friend, but that's all shit now."

"Is he the one that beat you up?"

"I kicked his ass too," Bubba growls and then deflates. "I'm not a smart man. I fucking suck."

"Why don't you just tell me what the deal is with your brother and then maybe you can crash on the couch for the night?"

Bubba's gaze searches the house, again fixating on the ceiling. "Why do you live here?"

"Someone has to."

"But it's a triangle."

Smiling at his comment, I pick up Freki and set the dog in my lap. "The man who built this house might have been mentally ill. He lived in the woods for decades. Then a relative of his died and left him money. Nylon Dolphy went from homeless to buying half an acre on what was then just an empty road. Rumor has it that he feared the Illuminati and thought if his house was shaped like a pyramid that he would be safe. He lived here for over twenty years. After he died, no one wanted such a small, odd house. They also thought it was haunted."

"But you live here now," he says, stating the obvious as if he's discovered something profound.

"I wanted a small place for me and my birds," I say, wishing I would shut up. Swallowing the grief burning in my chest, I sigh. "I used to have two parrots, and their noises can bother some people, but the neighbors here aren't so close. Plus, they're all old and can't hear well. This seemed like a nice starter home."

"Is it haunted?" he asks, watching me intently now. I want to believe he noticed my sadness and feels pity rather than he just remembered a hot chick is within reach.

"I don't know. I never feel anything."

"Do you believe in that stuff?"

"My mom does, but she thinks if Nylon still roams the earth that he would return to the woods where he felt the freest. I like that idea," I say and swallow the sadness threatening to rise in me. "I imagine him in the woods with my birds."

"They died?" he asks, sounding heartbroken.

His concern makes me want to taste his lips. Not a complete moron, I keep my ass put.

"I don't know. Someone tore open the atrium when I wasn't here. I don't know what happened to my birds. They probably just flew away, and I guess they could come back, but it's been months. If they're alive, I assume they've found a new home."

"I'm sorry."

"Thank you," I say, hating how easily I fall into trusting men. I'm already convincing myself that this banged-up hunky puppy is harmless. He's probably sweet as sugar and only a little rough during a good fuck. No reason to stab him tonight. "Are you going to tell me about why Buzz hates you?"

"Buzz?"

"Isn't that your brother's name?"

"Yeah, but that's not the one. No, Buzz is the nice brother. The fun one. He's so fucking reckless, though. As a kid, he was always jumping into pools without anyone around or running into the road without looking. He's impulsive. Like one time, he climbed onto the roof because he thought a cat was up there. Then he decided the best way to get down was to jump. He broke his arm and ankle, but it didn't scare him," Bubba says and then mutters, "Scared the shit out of me."

"If Buzz doesn't hate you, who does?"

"Butch."

I take a moment to wonder why his parents punished their children with such faux manly names. Yes, I'm Soso—well, Calypso actually—but my brother has a very respectable cool name. One goofy name choice is understandable, but three?

"Why?"

Bubba turns so suddenly toward me that Freki flinches and I nearly pull out my blade. His intense gaze forces me to lean away. My instincts demand I flee.

"You won't understand if you don't know my brother," he says in a dark voice. Then he blinks, and his melancholy returns. "You'll think I'm the asshole, and I need you to see me right."

"Help me understand then," I say in a voice stuck somewhere between curious and fearful.

Everyone knows about the two main reactions to fear: fight or flight. But there are three others: freeze, friend, and flop. I tend to react in those three ways. Like I froze at the bar. I tried to "friend" Griff when he started acting like a psycho a few months ago. Now I do the same with Bubba. I believe if I'm approachable, these men will act less threatening. As if it's my job to keep them from becoming violent.

Despite knowing this viewpoint is bullshit, I still fall back into the habit of trying to make nice to avoid running or fighting.

Even so, I keep my blade at the ready while wondering why I ever allowed Bubba into my house in the first place.

"Butch is weird," he whispers in almost a hiss. "Fucked in the head." Bubba taps his temple and nods. "My parents thought maybe he was autistic because of how Butch didn't want to talk to anyone and got rigid when in crowds. The kid threw up at school like every day because the teacher would talk to him or the kids would get loud. He couldn't handle anything."

"But he's not autistic?" I ask, based on his wording.

"No. He has some kind of mutism. Selective might be the word. I don't remember exactly. I was a kid when all that went down. Once I grew up, I didn't care what was wrong with Butch. He was just weird. He talks when he wants. Keeps people at arm's length, but he can get close. It didn't matter what was wrong with him. I'm his big brother, so I needed to watch out for him."

Even still nervous about Bubba's slightly aggressive demeanor, I smile at his need to watch out for his little brother. Keanu always protected me growing up. I wanted to be a boy. Well, maybe not have a dick, but I craved to be as tough as my dad.

Except I wasn't tough. I'd get hurt and cry every single time. But I still wanted to be a badass. It was a stupid cycle—much like Buzz's need for impulsive adventures, I guess.

Keanu always helped me up when I was down. He dried my tears and talked trash about people in Korean, so only we'd understand. Keanu made the world less scary, and he did it with style.

"Do you like your brother?" I ask Bubba.

Nodding with too much enthusiasm, he leans back into the couch, and I loosen my grip on the knife. "He's funny sometimes. We were best friends, and I liked him, but I never really knew if he liked me. Butch isn't easy to read. Since I didn't make him vomit from stress, I figured that meant I was someone important to him."

"Then what happened?"

"She happened," Bubba hisses. "Sissy Mullen. That name doesn't mean anything to you because you don't know Ellsberg, but her family's trash. Fucking nasty evil bastards."

"And she screwed with your brother?" I ask when he stops talking.

"No, Sissy's got a good heart. She's not like the rest of her family. I guess her brother's okay too. He's harder to like than her. Sissy finds a way to smile even when life gets rotten. She's always humming and singing, and she's as dumb as a box of rocks, but she's got a light to her."

"And you liked her?"

"Yeah, but Butch loved her. See, she was in Ellsberg, and we'd moved to Conroe. Those are places in Kentucky," he says in case I'm confused. Wearing a smile, I nod at his helpfulness. "Then she moved to Conroe with my cousin. That's Audrey's sister. I can't remember her name for some reason."

Bubba trails off for a few seconds until I tap him with my foot. Regaining his focus, he shrugs. "When Sissy visited our house for the first time, I was totally going to hit that hot ass of hers. I mean, she's an attractive chick. But then I saw the way Butch was acting around her. It was so fucking

23

obvious how much he wanted her. I'd never seen him act like that with a chick before. Ever. He can barely tolerate women long enough to get laid."

"He sounds like a charmer."

"No, see," Bubba grumbles, wagging his finger at me, "you say that because you don't know him. Like you think he's just a jerk, but he's got wires messed up in his head. Like with Sissy. She's dumb, but not because she wants to be dumb. Some people don't care if they forget shit or fuck up stuff. They're selfish but not her. She just can't remember crap. And Butch can't be close to people. They want too much from him, and he gets rattled and closed off and then sulks in his room."

"But not with Sissy?"

"Well, he still acts like him, but he was always hanging around her place. I knew he wanted her, but I realized he wasn't going to do anything about it."

Bubba stops talking and stares at me for like a minute before I wonder if the absinthe has finally shorted out his brain.

"You're going to think I'm an asshole," Bubba says and literally pouts.

"I already do, so why not finish your story?"

His laughter startles me. He sounds so damn happy. Finally, he tires himself out and smiles. "You're too beautiful to be with me. I'm a loser, you know? Everyone knows. Even Butch."

"Finish your story before I rule on how much of a loser you are."

"Fine," he sighs and loses his smile. "I asked out Sissy. Just to rile up Butch. He can be competitive with me. We're close in age. We look a lot alike, and people often get us confused. I'm not really competitive with him because he's fucked up in the head, and I don't want him to puke from stress. That's all I'm aiming for with him, so keep that in mind when I look like an asshole later in my story."

Hiding a smile behind my hand, I wave for him to continue.

"So, I asked Sissy out. I didn't expect her to say yes. I got the sense she was into Butch. He was always fixing shit at her house, and she would stare at him. Sissy does stare at people a lot. I wasn't a hundred percent sure if she liked him because of her staring habit, but I figured asking her out would answer some questions."

"But she said yes."

"Yeah," he says in a quieter voice. "She did, and I thought maybe she didn't like Butch. I knew Butch wanted her, though. I wasn't sure what to do after she said yes."

"What did you do?" I ask when Bubba falls silent again.

"This house really is a triangle."

Rolling my eyes, I don't know why I'm trying to have a conversation with Mister Blotto over here. I stand up and walk to the fridge, where I pour him a glass of mint-flavored water. At the very least, he'll stay hydrated, and his breath ought to be better.

"Thanks."

"Let's skip ahead to where you fucked your brother's dream girl, and he hates you."

"I didn't fuck her. I didn't really want to date her at all, but then Butch was acting like a cocksucker to me after I asked her out."

"I wonder why?" I ask, struggling to keep my sarcasm in check.

"He didn't know I knew he wanted her," Bubba says, spilling water on himself as he tries to handle the complexity of a glass. "Butch could have come to me and said, 'Brother and closest friend, could you kindly step the fuck away from the chick I want to bang?' Did he say that? No, he acted like I was a cocksucker."

"And you dated her to get revenge?"

Bubba wags his finger at me again and returns to his sexy pouting. "See how you think I'm the bad guy?"

"Dude, I'm going to be square with you right now. I have no emotional attachment regarding how your story ends. Like if you set fire to your brother and are on the run,

I'll feel about the same as if he tried to set you on fire and you're in hiding."

"No fire was involved," Bubba says as if letting me in on a secret.

"But you fought?"

"Yeah. Sissy and I dated a few times. We didn't even kiss. I kept going because Butch pissed me off. I also thought I'd hurt her feelings if I ended things. When it was finally over, I was relieved. But like twenty-four hours later, my cocksucker brother humped her in public. I looked like a fucking loser, and Butch knows no one respects me. But does he try to protect me like I've protected him his entire fucking life? No, and he didn't just disrespect me. He proved he doesn't care about me either."

Despite the anger in his words and tone, I see only hurt in his expression. I hope he doesn't cry. Booze can turn the toughest men into crybabies under the right circumstances.

One time, my father cried over his dead mom despite her being very much alive and ten feet from him. Dad was so upset over never telling his dead mother... Well, we never really understood what he wanted to tell her because his sobs made his words incoherent.

This incident is why my father no longer drinks moonshine.

"I'm sorry your brother hurt you," I say because I don't know what else to tell Bubba.

The anger drains from his face, and he gives me a crooked smile. "I've never met a woman as beautiful as you. I think I'd be fucking shy if I wasn't a little buzzed."

I smile at his compliment and his far off-the-mark analysis of his drunk level.

"I'm the president of the Conroe chapter," he says, sounding tired as he rests the empty glass on the table. "No one respects me. My mom calls the shots, or my uncle calls them. The Dogs think I'm a joke. Now I know my brother does too. I'm not even sure why the fuck I should go back there? It's not like any of them would miss a beat without me."

"Then maybe don't go back," I say, not really caring about his club's internal workings. "Be your own man. Do what's right for you. If that's going back, then do it. If it only serves other people, fuck them."

With his head resting on the couch and his body sagged half off it, Bubba watches me with sad eyes. "My mom will raise holy hell if I don't pretend to be president."

"You're not a little boy, and your mommy isn't your master."

"No, she's not, but I feel like she is sometimes."

"Then make a change," I say, sliding off the couch and gesturing for him to stretch out. "Or don't."

Bubba rests his head on the arm, and I smile at the sight of his feet dangling off the other end.

"You smell good," he says, and I immediately tense at the horny implications.

Bubba's expression is more goofy than predatory, and I suspect he'll be asleep soon.

"This isn't going to work," I mutter. "Since it was my idea for you to crash here, you can have the bed. Come along before I change my mind."

I try to sound edgy, intimidating even. "I'm just so apathetic toward you" is the vibe I'm going for, but my voice is too soft, and I'm already wondering what Bubba's like when sober. Is he half as sweet as when plastered?

Bubba doesn't really understand where we're going, but he shuffles after me. I warn him to duck as we enter the bedroom section since the ceiling is lower, but he still conks his head.

"Sorry," he mumbles, yanking off his damp shirt before flopping onto my bed.

"You're on a roll with the head injuries, pal."

"I'm sorry I don't fit on your couch."

"Stop apologizing. You're making me want to start a charity in your honor."

Bubba chuckles as he rolls onto his stomach and stretches out. I'm relieved to see he understands how I'm not sharing the bed with him. With his back to me, he whispers,

"I'm going to make you love me so much that no other man will do."

I smile at his words despite having no idea if he's even talking to me. Bubba hasn't said my name once all night, and I suspect he doesn't remember it.

Leaving him to crash, I walk to the living room and cuddle on the couch with Freki under a colorful afghan. I worry about sleeping with a strange man in the house. Letting down my guard isn't an option, but I don't think I can stay up all night.

What have I gotten myself into with Bubba?

THE RUNAWAY

I study the triangle house and the woman who calls it home. Flashes from last night fill my throbbing head. The fight at the bar involved Keanu. I remember that much. Who started it? Were he and I on the same side or fighting each other? Did I beat a black belt? Did watching all those "John Wick" movies make me a martial arts master? *No, that's stupid, and I might still be a little drunk.*

Around the room are hints of this woman's personality. She has a fluffy dog, but he isn't wearing any clothes, so she's not a total nut. I don't see a TV anywhere. She listens to New Age music—Celtic-Arabian-sounding crap that fortunately she turns down once we start talking.

The floors are cedar, and I suspect the cabinets are too. Everything is scuffed up and lived-in. I feel surprisingly comfortable in this odd house despite worrying I'm going to bang my head.

I spot a bowl of what looks like granola on the freakishly small circular kitchen table. From this, I surmise she doesn't host company much, and she eats like a squirrel. I smell a mixture of flowers and plants, but not a fake scent like from perfume. The odor reminds me of my visit to a botanical garden.

I scratch my chest and realize I never put on my shirt. When I left the bedroom, I saw it on the compact, scratched-up dresser. I assumed I'd want to be as close to naked as possible when I met up with my last-night fuck partner. Now, I'm standing shirtless in front of a chick who didn't even kiss me. "Wait, did we kiss?"

"No," she says when I ask as she brews a small pot of coffee.

"Did you want to kiss me?" I ask, and she glances at me over her shoulder.

"At times, but I don't kiss strangers."

"But you bring them back to your house."

She turns around and crosses her arms in a way that makes her tits jut out. Even wearing a baggy flowered shirt, I can tell she's got ample flesh to nuzzle my face between. Too bad her expression is full-blown cock block.

"I should have left you in the parking lot with Griff, but I suffered a moment of weakness. I guess you implying I'm a slut is my reward."

"No," I mumble, feeling like an asshole. "I think I remember you were nice to me last night."

Her shaming frown fades. "You were sad."

Oh, crap, please, Lord, tell me I didn't cry in front of this gorgeous woman! I don't know how I can walk back such a display of ball-less wonder.

"I wish you hadn't seen me acting like a punk. I'm not usually like that," I admit, shoulders sagging from a lack of confidence.

"I liked your sweet side."

Her praise immediately inflates my balls. "Well, in that case, you saw the real me that I hide from others."

She quietly laughs, and I'm now the badass motherfucker who made her smile. It's a good feeling.

"Wait, who's Griff?"

"An asshole I used to date. He thought you were making eyes at me at the bar and got his tighty-whities in a twist. He tried to get handsy, you threw a punch, violence broke out. I tried bailing, but he followed, and you two acted out Wrestle Mania in the parking lot. That's when I made the fateful decision to save you."

"My hero."

Smiling wider, she flashes a look that makes me think I won't suffer from blue balls for long.

The sound of an approaching motorcycle kills her grin and my boner. There's nothing sexy about the worry on her face. I tense up and stare at the front door where her gaze is also focused. Nothing in this world matters as much as protecting and soothing this woman.

My role as protector would be a helluva lot easier if I knew her damn name! For fuck's sake, why can't I remember?

The motorcycle's engine shuts off right outside the house. Her breathing quickens, and I notice her reach into her pocket. Is that a weapon I see?

The dog yaps at the person on the other side of the door while his owner's breath catches, and I prepare to beat the shit out of someone. Then a booming voice calls out the name I've been willing to sell my left nut to know.

THE BOHEMIAN

Last night, I sneaked by the bedroom to reach the bathroom, hoping to avoid any detection from Bubba. That's when I heard him mumbling in his sleep. I should have kept going, but I was highly paranoid at that point.

What if he choked on his vomit and died at my house? After resting on my couch under my tattered afghan, I came to the realization that this man is important to the Reapers Motorcycle Club. If he dies in the home of the daughter of the VP of the Brotherhood, does the passive hostility between the clubs get personal? Which side would the Hayes family take? Fatigue was likely the reason for my sudden hyper-concern for my dad. Whatever the reason, I kept checking on Bubba.

I also leave on the white bulbs strung up around the bedroom to provide faint lighting. If he wakes to pee, there's no way he'll avoid crashing into everything in the dark. The first few times I check on him, he's dead to the world, stretched out on his stomach and less prone to gagging on any potential upchuck,

This time, though, he's still asleep but whispering about someone doing him wrong,

"I'm always sorry," he mumbles against the pillow, "but you never are."

Warily, I reach out to rub his head to encourage him to stop sleep-ranting. Bubba sighs when my fingers stroke his hair, and he murmurs his approval when I caress the last few days' worth of damage to his face.

I keep waiting for him to grab my wrist as if the entire sleep-babble is a ruse to get me closer so he can pounce. But Bubba just returns to sleep while I rub his head and wish I could sleep comfortably now that I'm stuck on the couch.

Managing only a few hours of rest, I keep waking up certain that I hear someone at the door—mainly Griff—or I feel a presence standing over me—Bubba. Neither proves to be real, but I'm nervous.

I also worry I'll panic, trigger my switchblade, and either kill myself or, worse, my dog. No, maybe me dying would be worse. After all, who'd believe I was stupid enough to kill myself? Wouldn't they just blame Bubba from Kentucky?

I don't stab myself, and no one attacks me. As soon as the sun is up, though, I get off the couch and start my day. If I keep busy, I'll remain alert. First off, I return texts from my brother to say I'm fine. I also ask if any of those rednecks got blood on his shirt? He assures me he dodged their blood as well as their fists.

I text my mom with my usual morning message. I love her. I love Dad. I love Keanu. I'm just a big bouquet of love flowers. XOXO

My mood improves until I imagine how Bubba might be less appealing when sober. He could get violent, expect me to service his oversized body. A fight would break out. I won't go down easy, but I saw how confidently he challenged Griff who is far from tiny or weak. *Ugh, why do I have a stranger in my house!?!*

I'm sure meditation and yoga will settle the insanity brewing in my head. I need to remain calm and stop assuming the worst.

Eventually, Bubba is bound to wake up from his drunken stupor, and I want to put my best face forward. He likely won't remember much from last night, and I'm rather curious about the sober version of Bubba.

Except he's from Kentucky, and I can't stand the state. There's no logical reason to be curious. But I'm already sweet on the hunky puppy, assuming he's the guy I met last night and booze didn't provide him a winning personality.

Things don't have to be complicated. Life can be easy. *Yeah, sure.*

Then to set the awkward mood for our first sober conversation, Bubba appears while my ass is in the air. I see he hasn't put on his shirt, leaving his broad, ripped, tatted chest for all the world to enjoy.

Last night while he slept, I couldn't help studying the dragon tattoo across his lower back. That bastard must have taken hours and a skilled artist to create. Should I ask a question about his tattoo to break the awkwardness? Or will he realize I've been checking him out and increase my embarrassment?

And, of course, he thinks we fucked. Why would any woman bring a hunky puppy home except for the sole purpose of molesting his hot body? I can't really explain why I brought him here when I never intended to do anything. He was too drunk to fuck. I doubt he even remembers my name.

Our current awkwardness makes me nostalgic for Drunk Bubba, who was easy to talk to since his brain cells were dulled by the hard liquor. Now he's awake and sober enough to wonder what my deal is yet still buzzed and hungover enough to make an easy chat tricky.

I'll feed him! Or offer a cup of coffee! Help him locate his shirt! Yes, talking like ordinary people will be so much less complicated if I don't have to stare at his bare chest. The tanned skin, the perfect ink on his arms, the thick patch of hair down the center with a line that keeps traveling south of his jeans. *Too much visual information!*

Is liking him even an option? That's a Reapers club tattoo on his left arm. I can't swoon over an out-of-town biker when swooning over an in-town one already ended catastrophically.

Fucking Griff cost me my birds. Will riding this guy's dick mean the death of Freki? Or maybe he'll just burn down my house or steal my truck? No, I'm sure he's completely sane and not at all like Griff. Sure, sure.

The sound of an approaching motorcycle awakens me from my internal dialogue and the need to study every inch of Bubba's bare flesh. How is he so fucking hot? I noticed he was handsome last night. His drunken babble was beyond cute. But I wasn't prepared for his level of buffed madness in the bright light of day.

And now my troubles deepen at the arrival of a biker. No one drives by this house or down this street on accident. I live on a rural road with only a few neighbors, and none of them are buddies with bikers.

I am, of course. My dad could be outside. Or maybe a random member of the Serrated Brotherhood just decided to show up at my place. Could totally happen. I know the sound of my brother's Benelli. What's parking in front of my home is a chopper like the Brotherhood guys drive. Including Griff.

I shove my hand into the pocket of my shorts and find the switchblade. It won't help if Griff goes homicidal. My handgun is under my couch. A shotgun is stashed in the umbrella rack. I'd been worried about Bubba, but not enough to walk around the house locked and loaded.

My heart begins to race when the chopper's engine shuts off. I shouldn't be this nervous. I've dealt with the asshole nonstop for months. This isn't new.

But Bubba is, and I don't know what happens if the men fight again. Does Griff end the hunky puppy? Does Bubba kill a member of the Serrated Brotherhood? I know I've got a lot going on in the hot chick department, but that doesn't mean I'm worth starting a damn war over.

I side-eye Bubba to find him bracing himself for whoever's on the other side of the door. He's got his macho thing happening. Usually, I'd admire how his chest puffs out, and arms flex into a fighting stance. Just like how my dad gets when preparing to beat down someone. This isn't a normal situation, though, and I'm unbelievably nervous about what happens next.

The knock on the door goes unanswered. I can't move. I'm so fixated on what could happen next that I'm unable to react to what is actually taking place. Then I hear his voice.

"Soso Rutgers!" yells Dayton Rutgers—aka my father.

Relief floods through me until I remember the shirtless member of the Reapers standing nearby. Yeah, I'm not sure that'll go over well with my dear old dad.

"Hey, Daddy," I say through the door. "Come back later. I'm shaving my legs."

Somehow, my ace lie doesn't persuade my father. Bubba's edgy demeanor drops a few notches after hearing who's at the door. Or maybe he likes the leg shaving thing.

"Open up, Num-Num, or I'll use my keys," he says in his fake-patient voice.

"I changed the locks."

"I got a copy of the new keys."

"Go away," I say, fighting laughter as my fear turns into wary embarrassment. "We don't want any."

When my father unlocks and opens the door, I immediately hug him. "Oh, Daddy, I'm so glad you're here. I've missed you."

"Save the lies for the man about to die," he says, glaring at Bubba.

"He's a made man, Daddy. I heard he's got lots of connections."

"Who told you that?" Dad asks, still shooting hate-daggers at Bubba.

"The tall man from Mayo Pony."

Dad gives me the quickest of glances before asking, "Do you mean the elderly one or the fat one?"

"I don't think Cap's fat."

"Oh, but you think Hayes is elderly?" Dad says and frowns at me. "Well, I'm telling him you said that, Lil Miss."

Freki decides I'm under threat and barks protectively. The dog doesn't jump down from the couch or even get up from his spot next to his favorite pillow. No, my tiny defender feels his bark is terrifying enough to put my father in his place.

When Dad isn't properly frightened, I stumble back to act as a barrier between him and Bubba.

"Put a shirt on," Dad mutters, giving Bubba a disgusted frown.

Bubba's earlier edginess is gone. My gut says he realizes the score. Rather than fearing my badass

Brotherhood VP dad, he just smirks and mutters, "It's hot in here."

Dad forgets whose side he's on and says, "I told her to get an air conditioner, but she won't listen."

"You raised her well, sir."

"Are you talking smack, boy?" Dad asks, moving closer.

"Little bit, yeah."

"Daddy, this is Bubba Davies. He stayed here last night, but we didn't, you know, swap any kinds of fluids."

"No," Dad says, shaking his head and causing his shoulder-length blond hair to bounce. "I can't have my only daughter shacked up with a hillbilly."

"I come from strong redneck stock, sir," Bubba says, still wearing his smirk. "Not a hill-folk in the entire family."

"He sounds weird. Is he drunk?"

Unsure how buzzed Bubba might still be, I blurt out, "He's from Kentucky."

Dad instantly growls, "The home state of illiterates and inbreds."

"But he's a biker like you, Daddy. See how much I love you?" I say, hugging him.

"Stuff it, Num-Num. I know exactly who he is, and I know he threw down with my brothers last night."

"Wait," I grumble, stepping back. "You're not here to defend my honor but to clean up the mess created by your stupid biker friends."

Dad doesn't fall for my feigned offended stance. "He shouldn't be here."

"Why are you really here?"

"I heard about the fight and needed to make sure you were okay."

"Bubba stopped Griff from manhandling me."

Dad doesn't take the bait here either. Wow, my father has got me pegged completely. I find this fact oddly heartwarming.

"From what I heard, your brother was sitting right there, locked and loaded to break Griff and anyone else who gave you trouble."

"That's a lie, Daddy," I say, tossing Keanu under the bus.

My brother will understand. He once blamed me for breaking something that his woman dropped because she was too scared to upset my parents. I just nodded and declared that my clumsiness was a sign of wisdom. Sure, it didn't make any sense, but Dad was so busy wondering what the fuck I was talking about that no one questioned the broken Big Foot figurine. Yeah, Keanu will totally be cool with my current traitorous move.

"He was so busy watching Cap's back that I think he forgot I even existed. You know how those two are," I say, and Dad's murder-frown shifts to his WTF-frown.

"Doesn't matter. He shouldn't be here," Dad tells me and then lies to Bubba in his best growl, "She has no money if that's what you're looking for."

Bubba shrugs. "I have plenty of money."

"Bullshit. You don't even have a shirt."

"Why don't we dial things down a bit?" I suggest. "Daddy, would you like homemade beef jerky?"

"No."

Just then on the kitchen counter, my phone chimes a familiar ringtone.

"She cannot help you," Dad warns me, though his gaze never leaves Bubba.

"We'll see."

Answering, I put my mother—the gloriously unfazed Harmony Slater Rutgers—on speakerphone. "Has your father murdered anyone yet?"

"No, he's still stalking his prey, which is weird since Bubba is standing perfectly still. I think Daddy doesn't really want to attack. Aww, he's sweet on Bubba too."

Mom laughs, which makes my father roll his eyes. "You're encouraging her."

"It's called good parenting."

"He's half-naked, Harmony."

"Which half?"

Bubba chuckles, which pisses off my dad even more.

"Mom, I'm a grown woman with grown woman needs. If Daddy doesn't leave soon, I might have to list out those needs in great and gooey detail."

"You heard her. Just chill out and meet me for lunch. We'll devise a game plan to break up the lovebirds," Mom says and hangs up.

"Ha!" Dad cries and snaps his fingers at me. "She's on my side. You're screwed, Num-Num."

"Well, then you best hurry along, so you can begin plotting," I say, pushing him—gently of course—toward the door. "Bye-bye now. Love you. Drive safe."

Dad glares at Bubba and then softens his gaze—just a little—for me. "I'm letting this happen because I know Johansson men are pussies. If he proves to be the exception to the rule, shoot him and call me to help with the corpse."

"Message received."

"This isn't over," he growls at Bubba suddenly. "Put on a shirt, pervert."

Bubba only smiles wider while I nudge my father away from the shirtless hunk. "Though I'll no doubt submit to your will, we're not there yet. Until then, so long."

Finally giving in to my subtle hints, Dad storms out of my house and to his Harley. He leans on the throttle, revving the engine dramatically. I laugh at my father's always entertaining dick-wagging.

"He's very macho," I tell Bubba after Dad roars off and the door is shut.

A sly smirk warms his face. "I noticed how small and feminine I felt in comparison."

"I'm short on breakfast options," I say, walking to the kitchen where I sip my coffee, "but I can fix you something quick before driving you to Audrey's house."

"Tell me more about this asshole Griff."

I freeze up, staring at him over my cup. Our gazes hold, and I realize I was wrong about his eyes. They're blue rather than green. Or his eyes might change colors. Not that it matters. Nothing about him is more than a passing curiosity.

"That's old business and none of yours," I say. "Your shirt is in the bedroom. Watch your head."

Erasing the space between us, Bubba now stands too close. "I want to be here with you." His sudden bravado makes me wonder if knowing my name reignited his ego. Or does he think fucking the daughter of Dayton Rutgers will give him bragging rights back in Kentucky?

"Why do you think I have nothing better to do than babysit you?"

Bubba's steely glare falters. "I don't know anything about you, but I woke up thinking I need to know everything. I can't do that if you ditch me at Audrey's. If you have places to go, I'll tag along. If that's not an option, I'll sit on the front porch and wait for you."

"You sound pathetic," I spit out, wanting to piss him off so he'll stop tempting me. I don't know where my power went. This is my house. He's on my turf. My family rules this fucking town. He's no one here, so why do I feel like he's holding all the cards?

"Look, maybe I acted like such a fucking loser last night that you can't see me any other way. That makes sense, but you said my bullshit last night was sweet. Girls say that when a guy hits the right notes for them. I know who you are now. Like I don't know all the family connections in Hickory Creek, but I know that was either Dayton or Camden Rutgers, and that makes you royalty around here."

My father and his brother are twins. They're technically identical, but decades on the planet branded them with enough individual scars to make them distinguishable to most people. Not a stranger like Bubba, though. He just heard the name Rutgers.

"That was Dayton," I say, feeling hurt over—? Why am I upset? Is it that I'm sweet on this guy and I know he's going to ditch me to go home in a few days? Why do I care? I used to date casually. I know how to be that girl, but now I'm heartbroken that a guy who does not own my heart might possibly break it in the near future. I decide fatigue has made me super girly hormonal.

"My father is not the nice twin," I say, narrowing my gaze and unleashing my inner-Rutgers. "That man will be back to fuck with you. You might think you're safe because of your bloodline, but in this area, my family name is all that matters."

"I know," Bubba replies, never missing a beat.

It's like my angry routine doesn't affect him at all. I'm seriously losing my mojo.

Bubba's gaze holds mine, searching for something in my eyes. "I'm fully aware I didn't make a great first impression. I thought I could hold my liquor, and I just pray I didn't cry like a bitch in front of you. Even if I did, I still think there's something here."

"For you, but I don't get squat."

"What does that mean?" he says, his expression darkening and jaw clenching.

"You're lost, Bubba. People back in Conroe treat you like shit or like a baby or something. You don't know your place in the world. I do, though. Let's say we hang out and have fun. Well, you get an ego boost by fucking me, and I get to be the stupid bitch you brag about to your buddies back in Shithole USA."

"This isn't about fucking. I woke up feeling something for you before I could even remember what you looked like. You did something to me inside," he says, tapping his chest, "and I need to know what."

Sighing, I remember how goofy sweet he was last night. The tension in me relents, and I reach up to pat his cheek. The coarse hairs on his several days' worth of stubble feel both inviting and threatening against my fingers.

"There's no secret to unlock. I was just nice to you, Bubba. You needed to vent, and I listened. There's nothing magical about what you're feeling. It's just the need to be heard after feeling dismissed back in Conroe."

Bubba's expression is unreadable. Feeling on the spot under his gaze, I realize I'm pinned between the kitchen counter and his hard body. If he moves even an inch closer, I won't be able to escape. I think to the switchblade in my pocket and the coffee cup in my left hand.

If push comes to shove, I'll slam my "Be Wild and Free" mug into his gorgeous face. Yes, then I'll run out the back door and into the woods behind my yard. No, wait, I'll need to grab Freki on my way out, but then I can disappear into the lush forest while he—

Wait, what exactly will he do if left alone in my house? Trash the place? He can't leave the property without some kind of transportation. Maybe he'll call his cousin. Sure, that's it.

Okay, I've got my plan just in case the look he's giving me isn't grateful submission.

THE CHAPTER WHERE THE RUNAWAY MAKES A PLAY
THE RUNAWAY

Soso Rutgers is the last woman I ought to crave a kiss from, but she's literally all I can fucking see.

Unfortunately, she's looking at me as if I'm a threat. The only reason a powerful woman retreats into such wariness is that someone hurt them in the past. I suspect the asshole is Griff. No doubt I'll need to kill the motherfucker.

"If I told you my problems last night," I say, stepping back despite wanting her in my arms, "then you know I'm in Tennessee to figure out some things. I don't want to hang out at Audrey's, and she doesn't really want me there."

"Doesn't she like you?" Soso asks, and I notice the wariness in her dark eyes lessens the more distance I create. This fact is a kick in the balls, but I can be patient.

"Audrey's a new mom and wife. She and I aren't tight either. She just owed me a favor, and I needed somewhere to hide out where I could think."

Soso's mouth opens, and I bet she wants to know why Audrey is in my debt. She doesn't ask, sighing instead. "I have work to do at the sanctuary. If you tagged along, I'd be willing to have lunch with you," she says and then grunts, "And that's it."

"What sanctuary?"

"Are you allergic to birds?"

"No."

"Well, if you don't mind helping me there, then I'd be free for the afternoon. Just two sober people talking."

"And that's it," I say, wagging my finger at her. "Don't get any dirty ideas about me."

Soso rolls her eyes, but my efforts also win me a smile. She walks out of the room and returns with my shirt.

"I need to change. Stay in here. Do not try to catch a peek. I'm not even kidding."

"Man, that Griff asshole really did a number on you."

Soso doesn't like this response, but she says nothing before gesturing toward an armoire where I find my black boots and jacket.

I get dressed in the living room while she hurries off to the snug bedroom. The dog watches me from his spot on a fluffy pillow on the couch. Little dogs creep me out because they look very breakable, but I still reach out and pet his head.

Returning after only a few minutes, Soso wears a long, multi-colored skirt and a loose white shirt. She reaches into the armoire to find a pair of strappy sandals. While she looks gorgeous, there's no way she's trying to seduce me with these clothes. The skirt is frayed at the bottom, and the shirt looks a decade old. Her lack of seductive strategy makes me doubt I'll get laid today, yet I'm harder than I was before she walked out in her new outfit.

This babe just does a number on me without even trying.

My inability to take my eyes off her clearly puts Soso on edge despite her faking like she doesn't notice. I'm not fooled. Her lips turn into a straight line, and she dodges my gaze.

Before we head for the door, Soso fills a satchel with snacks. The granola doesn't interest me, but that homemade beef jerky sounds good. After she says goodbye to her dog—whose name I can't quite catch despite her saying it three times—we leave the triangle house. I want to ask about why she picked this place, but I'm sure she told me last night. *Man, what I would give to have those memories back.*

Her truck feels familiar. I don't really understand why she owns such an old vehicle, though, when her family has money. Her grandfather—Adam "Mojo" Rutgers—was the original Serrated Brotherhood president. Her grandmother—Clara—is the youngest of three Hallstead women who own the nice half of Hickory Creek Township.

Yet Soso drives a battered truck, wears clothes better suited for a woman twice her age, lives in a tiny house, and even her satchel looks older than her. Is she ashamed of her wealth? I can't remember the details regarding her parents. I think maybe her mom didn't come from money. That might be the parent she identifies with more. Buzz wants to be our dad, who pinches every penny. I'm more like my mom, who enjoys indulging.

"The work at the sanctuary should only take an hour. What are you in the mood to eat?" Soso asks after we twist and turn down many long, rural roads.

"Anything that's filling. I'm starving."

Giving me a quick glance, Soso smiles. "I saw you eyeballing the beef jerky. Have at it."

I smile like a fucking fool because I need Soso to warm up to me. So far, I've enjoyed only glimpses of the gentle woman, who listened to me without laughing while I whined last night. Back in Conroe, I'm always playing a role. Last night, I was me, both good and bad, throwing punches one minute, sharing private shit to a stranger the next.

Somehow, this gorgeous chick with plenty of options didn't blow me off as soon as I woke up. Hell, she even gave up her fucking bed to me. There's no way she did that without seeing something worthy in the drunk fool I was last night.

That's why I give her my best smile while savoring every bite of the beef jerky. Soso pretends not to notice, but I catch her fighting a grin.

Arriving at our location, I don't care what's awaiting me at the Alice Hallstead Memorial Bird Sanctuary or where she wants to eat afterward—even if it's hippie crap with kale. My only concern is that Soso and I get to know each other while I'm sober enough to remember the details.

THE BOHEMIAN

Twenty years ago, my aunt Alice Hallstead built a 30-foot-high sanctuary with a vet station and visitor center on several acres in the boondocks. I grew up visiting the birds—mostly abandoned parrots and cockatiels—and then took over management when I was eighteen, and Alice had passed away in her sleep. My cousin, Layla, helps along with a few part-time employees and a handful of volunteers.

I park in the side lot and discover bags of feed ready to be carried inside. Glancing at the obedient hunky puppy following me, I realize Bubba's buff body will come in handy. On the downside, I don't think I'll hide my attraction to him as well once he's sweaty.

For every bag I carry into the storage area, he manages two. Bubba doesn't complain about working. In fact, physical labor seems to be in his wheelhouse.

"I work on construction at home," he says when I hand him a bottle of water. "If I didn't have Johansson blood, I'd stick to straight renovations and improvements."

"I fixed my toilet once," I babble. "Right after I moved into the house, I wanted to prove I had mad skills and didn't need my dad saving me." When Bubba smiles too widely, I feel like a liar under his gaze. "It was leaking within weeks again."

"You have other mad skills, I'm sure," he says, magically closer to me. Did he even fucking move or is my attraction making me dumber? "Look at how you run this place."

"We take in birds ditched by their owners. Many domesticated birds can't survive in the wild," I say, and a lump grows in my throat when I imagine my missing parrots. "Aunt Alice loved birds, and I fell for them too. My first one lives here."

Bubba glances back at the habitat where the birds squawk and scream. "Are they upset?"

"No. Parrots are just loud and have a lot to say. Odin is out there somewhere. He likes hiding up high, but he'll come down if I call him."

"Why is he here?"

Without thinking, I pull back my shirt to reveal a deep scar on my shoulder. Something about Bubba's gaze acts as a truth serum, and I can't avoid sharing info I ought to keep to myself.

"Parrots can get very attached to their owners, and Odin loved me the most. But one day, he got startled when like a dozen Brotherhood guys showed up with their choppers. The noise set him off, and he bit me."

Bubba, of course, runs his fingers across the scar. The man is dying to touch me. I see the need on his face no matter what we're doing or talking about today. I wonder if he sees the same desire in my eyes.

"Fuck," he murmurs. "I can't believe a bird did that."

"A macaw's bite can be as powerful as a large dog's. They'll fuck you up."

"I see," he nearly whispers, leaning closer to study the size and no doubt touch me a little more.

"Dad found me covered in blood, and he freaked out. I'm lucky he didn't kill poor Odin. He said the parrot had to go. I begged him to let me keep Odin, and my dad is fairly easy to push around when I cry, but he put his foot down after I needed ten stitches. That's why Odin lives here now. After I got my house, I didn't have the heart to make him leave the sanctuary for me. He's the king of the east end."

Bubba's fingers finally leave my shoulder, and I let my shirt slide back into place. His blue eyes study me in the oddest way before he reaches out to wipe a tear from my cheek. I rub away the wetness, shocked to find I've gotten choked up about something I'd long accepted.

"Odin was my best friend," I mumble. "I talked to him about everything, and he called me Soda."

Bubba laughs, looks guilty for doing so, and then sighs. I smile, though. A normal man would likely think I'm nuts for crying over a damn bird. Griff refused to understand my love for them.

"They're not loyal like a dog," he'd say despite not really liking dogs either.

I never tried to explain to Griff why birds fascinated me. Perhaps, I knew deep inside he wasn't worth sharing with. Then there's Bubba who tempts me to blurt out my entire life story.

"I have a few things to do before we go to lunch. Want more beef jerky?"

"By more, do you mean all of it?" he asks like a big hungry kid.

On cue, his stomach growls, and I fight giggles as I hand him the rest of the beef jerky. I'm so taken with the way he enjoys the food that I don't immediately notice Layla's arrival.

My cousin stands at the main entry, wearing a blue and black flannel dress, black leggings, and heavy combat boots. Her long blue hair shines in the spring sunlight, making her look like a troubled pixie.

Leaving Bubba to eat, I join Layla in the office where we watch him wander into the primary habitat. I consider warning him to be careful but feel silly talking down to a grown man. I bossed him around last night without a second thought, of course. But since then, he's snuck his way into my heart.

"What the ever-loving fuck?" Layla asks as soon as we're out of earshot. "Are you trying to shatter what's left of Griff's sanity?"

"It's not my job to keep Griff from freaking out."

"Bringing that Reaper here is like throwing blood in the water and expecting sharks not to be bothered."

"Don't be so dramatic. Griff's an eel, but he's all bluster."

"You bailed on the fight at Salty Peanuts too soon. It was a mess."

"That was most definitely not Griff doing the damage. He was on the ground in the parking lot when I left with

Bubba. If anyone tore up the bar, it was Cap Hayes. Probably did it as a mating dance for his woman."

Layla allows a tiny smile. "He's so stupid over her."

"Big men fall harder, I hear."

I allow myself to glance at Bubba and find him looking up at a green macaw. Has he already finished the beef jerky? Lord, I forget how much a man his size eats.

Before I can return to Bubba, my cousin grabs my arm. Her eyes are so thickly lined with black makeup that I have trouble reading her emotions. Layla likes to hide under all her goth, rocker girl facade. It's her armor, leaving me and everyone else unable to tell what's happening in her head.

"Are you messing with this Kentucky guy to make Griff jealous?"

"Why would I want him jealous?"

"To fuck with him because he killed your birds."

I feel as if she slapped me. Layla knows she shouldn't have said aloud what's been obvious all along. My girls are dead. Griff killed them. They died because I let a violent man close without worrying if he'd become violent when I pushed him away.

"I'm sorry," Layla says.

"I like Bubba. He's sexy as hell, and he was sweet last night. He's also hot."

"Yes, I noticed the hot thing."

I glance back at where Bubba listens to Grinch talk trash. The parrot's former owner taught the bird cuss words along with more than a few racist, homophobic, misogynistic phrases. Naturally, the hateful asshole didn't make a suitable caretaker and ditched the bird when Grinch got too expensive.

"Bubba wants to kiss me so badly," I whisper to Layla. "But he hasn't made a move. It's killing him."

"And you like torturing him?"

"No, bitch, I just want him to prove he's worth wanting."

"Don't call me a bitch."

"Ula and Bjork agree that I shouldn't call you a bitch," I grumble, thinking of my poor birds.

Layla and I are close, but we often get on each other's nerves. "I said I was sorry."

"Yeah, but every time you want to win an argument, you bring up my birds."

"You're trying to distract me."

Frowning, I hadn't expected Layla to pick up so quickly on my diversion tactics. She's usually easily sidetracked.

"Bubba's only in town for a few days, and I like him."

"You said you wouldn't date another criminal after you ended things with Griff. You said you'd learned your lesson after the only men you dated turned out to be super douches."

I suspect Layla would hate all men if she didn't have a cool father and two doting big brothers. However, every man she gets near romantically ends up being a psycho. She clearly has a type. And it's obvious I do too.

"Most of those guys were regular-level douches. Only Griff was a douche king."

"I don't know. I've met douchier douches."

"Let's agree that there are many douches in this world, but I really don't think Bubba is on the uglier end of the douche spectrum. And if he turns out to be an undercover super douche, who cares since he'll be back in Kentucky soon?"

Layla doesn't like my answer because it didn't involve me ditching Bubba and hanging out with her for the day. Sighing, she mutters, "I still can't believe you brought him here to do manual labor."

"I wanted to see him around the birds. Look at his face whenever Grinch cusses at him. Bubba's gorgeous, and that's a face I want to sit on."

Layla gasps as if she's turned puritan when I wasn't looking. "Oh, wait, I thought you meant you wanted to suffocate him with your vagina."

Snickering, I wonder if she's stoned. "No murder plans. With him being the president of the Reapers' Conroe chapter, killing Bubba might be a problem."

"No way he's the president. He's fucking with you. Like how that guy told you he was royalty," Layla says, smiling nostalgically.

"Yeah, and I could sit on his throne and suck on his crown," I mutter, rolling my eyes. "Such a charmer, but Bubba's the real deal. He told me the president thing when he was too drunk to lie."

"Booze is a great lie detector. Remember when Cap admitted he was a virgin after pretending he'd gotten so much pussy?"

"Yeah, and we laughed and laughed, and then he burped so loud the waitress nearly cried."

"It was a horrifying sound," Layla says, losing her smile.

"He's a freakishly large man, and those Mayo Pony weirdos make freakishly large noises. I bet Bubba's burps are normal like our dads make."

"Uh-oh. You're comparing him to your dad. Bad sign," she says, crossing her arms and sighing dramatically. "Tragically misguided sign."

"Where do you think I should take him to eat for lunch?"

"Nowhere in the H.C. unless you want to piss off Griff."

"Don't call it that, and I don't care about Griff."

"Don't you care about Bubba's poor face? After another run-in with Griff, maybe Kentucky isn't so pretty anymore."

"Fine, then we'll eat somewhere in White Horse. Ooh, I know. I'll get him a Houdini at the Dove Tail Pub."

"Big men need a big meal, but he won't last that long if you don't get him away from Grinch."

Without thinking, I ditch Layla in the office and hurry to where Bubba leans a little too close to the cussing parrot.

"Bubba, carefully back away from him."

I make a mental note of how well he listens rather than demanding to know why first. He's a tatted, muscled hunk, but he's no meathead. Bubba takes a few steps away from Grinch, who shuffles on the branch and calls me fat.

"That bird said that I was a shit-eating whore. Am I not allowed to ask how he knew my secret?" Bubba says once I have him outside the bird area.

His answer might be the sexiest fucking thing I've ever heard. Or I'm just in a state of arousal that makes every word he utters panty-wetting.

I reach up and wrap my fingers around the back of his neck. Tugging him lower, I lift my lips to meet his. The kiss starts so gently. He's in complete control. I don't expect much. A quick peck to thank him for being adorable with Grinch. I need only a tiny taste.

But Bubba has other plans.

THE RUNAWAY

Soso offers her lips and then hopes to steal them back before I'm finished tasting them. I can't imagine she thought such a tease would satisfy me. My hands demand more—one on her hip, the other cupping her jaw. I hold her still, just enough for me to savor what I've hungered for since finding her this morning. I'm sure the drunken version of me wanted to kiss her too, but he was too fucking stupid, and she was too fucking smart to let it happen.

Now I know her flavor, and I can't imagine enjoying the taste of another woman. Soso intoxicates as much as a Korean Kickass. I'm stoked by the way she makes me feel. Was I ever this fucking alive before? I've never felt as powerful as when I wrap her in my arms and deepen the kiss.

Soso slides her arms around my waist and gives into what we've been dancing around all morning. Even wanting to devour her, I pace myself. This isn't some babe that I'm planning to bang and run away from while my cum is still hot. Soso needs to forget that any other man ever kissed her. I'm officially branding these lips as the property of Bubba Davies.

"Cunt!" a voice cries out, and Soso pushes me away.

Her expression is pure panic as her gaze searches for the aggressor. My hands ball into fists, and I'm ready to punch someone's fucking face.

Soso's anxiety deflates, and she chuckles embarrassed. "Oh, Grinch," she says, pointing at the bird who calls us an asshole. "We've tried teaching you new words, but you just love cussing."

"Whore!" the bird yells, shuffling back and forth on the branch.

Despite wanting to kick the bird's ass for cock-blocking me, I only mumble, "He looks happy."

"He loves it here. He wouldn't cuss so much if he didn't."

I smile at how proud she looks when gazing at the bird. She's in her element. That's why I'm suffering from serious guilt, and my smile fades. I want this woman so fucking bad that I'm sporting a hard-on, talking to birds, and wondering how I can convince her to leave her life and join mine. What kind of asshole am I? Soso can't give up this sanctuary and her family and her home for me.

But I'll make her do it. No way can I leave this town without Soso. We're still getting to know each other. I have so much to learn, but there's no denying she's the one for me. I can't take my eyes off her, and my heart is set on this one woman. My dick's a huge fan too.

A petty part of me hopes she pisses me off, and I lose this feeling. It's inconvenient wanting the daughter of the Serrated Brotherhood's VP. Plus, I'm not ready for the emotional drama of wanting her to ditch everything she clearly loves about her life.

Long ago discarded, Conroe ain't a fun town. Mom talks about it growing into something cool like Ellsberg, but that crap takes time. I'll be asking Soso to leave a place where she's powerful and comfortable for a town where I'm not even powerful and comfortable.

Yeah, maybe we'll go to a restaurant where I'll learn stuff about her that pisses me off. Maybe she's gross or weird or does something so out-of-bounds that my dick will get soft and my heart will stop beating so fast every time she looks at me.

Sure, that's going to fucking happen.

I catch Soso eyeing the blue-haired chick from earlier. They're both wearing frowns. I bet that has to do with me—an out-of-town biker rubbing up against local royalty.

Once in the truck, Soso mentions the blue-haired chick is her cousin and the daughter of the local club president. Family's going to be an issue between us.

Mine won't stop nagging me. Hell, so far today, my mom texted me ten times to claim she thinks someone's trying to break into the house and I should come home to save her. I don't respond. She's well aware my father and brothers can handle an intruder. Shit, even Mom can handle one without breaking a sweat.

But she keeps texting anyway. I finally respond as Soso drives us to lunch. Just a quick message about how I'm unable to help with her now seven-hour intruder situation. Within seconds, Mom texts to ask if I'm being held against my will.

"Only by a woman's tight pussy," I message back. Even over a hundred miles away, I feel Mom rolling her eyes.

"Girlfriend?" Soso asks, sounding hopeful that I'm a cheater and she can kick me to the curb.

"Why would you text me when I'm sitting right next to you?" I ask, making clear how I'm not going any-fucking-where.

Soso sighs. "What's a dog?"

"Is that code for something?"

She refuses to smile, but I see her wanting to. "You said the Dogs don't respect you."

"Don't you have anything more interesting to ask me?"

"What sexual position do you prefer?"

A smile flashes across my face, and my dick struggles to free itself from my jeans. "With you? That's a tricky question. On the one hand, you bouncing on my dick would give me a fantastic view of your tits. On the other hand, if I'm on top, pumping my dick into you, I gotta believe you'll have a harder time running away."

"What about doggy-style?" she asks with complete seriousness. "Is that what the Dogs prefer and how they got their names? Oh, and who are they again?"

"It's Reapers' business, and you're not in the club."

"Is it a secret?" she asks, smiling at my attempt to dodge the subject.

"No, it's just not information that'll make you hot for me."

"Nothing you say will make me hot for you. That kiss was disgusting. You make me sick. Now, who are the Dogs?"

I think to mention how her nipples remain rock-hard since our kiss. I could also point out how her pussy is no doubt hot and wet right now. Then again, why should I rub in her face what her body's already screaming at her?

"Where are we eating?" I ask rather than answer her question.

"A place in White Horse where you can get a monster-sized sandwich."

"Why can't we eat close by?"

"Are you that hungry?"

"Yeah, and I want to know if you're hiding me from your family?"

"No, not my family. Just the Brotherhood," she says, keeping her gaze on the road. "Besides, I'm dropping you off at Audrey's house after lunch."

My mood sours immediately. I don't want to leave her side. Why is Soso ready to get rid of me? I saw the look on her face before she kissed me. That wasn't a nonchalant peck of a woman who hands them out like candy.

Doesn't matter if she wants me, though. Soso plans to ditch me after lunch. Nope. Not happening. I refuse to be okay with walking away. I mean, hell, if we lived in the same town, I might be able to take my time seducing her into my bed. But with her here, there's no time for patience.

"Don't sulk," she says after we arrive at Dove Tail Pub and we've suffered through ten minutes of silence.

I climb out of the truck without responding. Soso's fucking with my heart. Why the hell not? I screwed with Butch's and then made a fool of myself last night. I deserve for Soso to nail me in the balls a few times.

But after my humiliation, I want Soso with me.

And I refuse to accept no for an answer.

THE CHAPTER WHERE BUMPING UGLIES IS GOOD FOR THE SOUL
THE BOHEMIAN

I've hurt Bubba's precious boy feelings. Good! Screw him! How dare he be so tempting when we both know he's got one foot on his way out of town? Cocksucker! Vile peckerhead!

If only I could hate him. Why did he have to be so fucking cute with Grinch? Or kiss me so thoroughly that my pussy hurts with disappointment? He knows exactly what he's doing too.

Bubba's insecurities last night gave me temporary amnesia about who he is. Johansson men never need to worry about anyone's feelings. They come from power and money. They take what they want from women and move on when they're bored. Sure, the same could be said for Rutgers men. That doesn't mean I want to be Bubba's ex-hookup, one of many for sure.

That's why when Bubba asked if he could meet Odin before we left the sanctuary, I pretended we were in a hurry. It'd be a mistake to share my avian best friend with a guy I plan to fuck a few times and never see again.

Now I know I should just walk away without any fluid swapping. But not sleeping with Bubba would be a terrible waste of a gorgeous man. Besides, I'm too emotionally invested in feeling him inside my body now. I'd take him home for sex today if I didn't need to worry about a painting party at one of the club guys' new house.

"I'm good at painting," Bubba says after we arrive at Dove Tail Pub.

Hurrying to open the door before he can, I hold it for him and smile. "I'm sure you're good at a lot of stuff."

Bubba reaches over me and grips the door. "After you."

"Gentlemen first."

Leaning down, he whispers, "My dick is so hard right now. Why don't you scoot your ass inside so I can jack it in the bathroom?"

"Jack what? Your dick or my ass?"

His intense gaze holds mine. "I need to feel your pussy."

Mouth instantly dry, I feel all my sassy boldness disappear. I'm suddenly petrified to be discarded by this man. *Where did my confidence go?*

"But fucking you fast and hard just to get off won't cut it," he says in a husky voice that I feel between my legs. "Now stop screwing around with the door and get inside where we can have a conversation that doesn't involve what I want to do to you."

"What else is there to talk about?" I ask, gripping his shirt and pushing him away before walking inside.

Bubba follows me to the hostess stand and places his right hand snugly around my waist. I don't know if he's about to pass out from the lack of blood to his brain or he just wants everyone to know he's staking a claim on my body. If it's the latter, I don't think anyone gives a crap. This is White Horse, and people here tend to react to tattooed men by turning into those monkeys who see, hear, and speak no evil.

The hostess tries to seat us at a table, but Bubba insists on a booth so he can slide next to me.

"I'm not giving you a handy," I mutter when he groans and tries to get comfortable. "Just go jack it in the bathroom."

"I don't want you thinking of me in there."

"I don't care. Really."

"Come on, babe," he says, relaxing his arm behind me. "What kind of man finds pleasure in a toilet stall while his woman sits alone and horny?"

"I'm not horny," I angrily whisper.

"You're not fooling anyone, Soso. I can smell your wet pussy."

Gasping, I feel my face flush scarlet. Bubba kisses the side of my head while I struggle with embarrassment.

"I can't even," I mumble.

"Don't ditch me at Audrey's house. Take me back to your place, and I'll eat you out until you can't spell your name," he says, nudging me. "Get it? Because your name is really easy to spell."

Still bright red, I shake my head and fight a smile. "It's too fast."

"You're the one who brought me home last night."

"Just doing my civic duty."

"Bullshit," he says, nuzzling my temple. "If I looked like a dog, you'd have left me to die in the parking lot. You wanted my hot bod, but that's okay. I want your hot bod too. Though I admit, I wouldn't leave you to die in the parking lot even if you were a dog. My mama raised me to give a shit about the ladies."

"Yeah, you're a fucking gentleman. No denying that, jackass."

Bubba throws his head back and laughs even after the waitress arrives to take our order. I tell her to bring two Houdinis and a pitcher of lemonade.

"Any issues with my choices?" I ask Bubba, who rests his lips against my head.

"I don't care what we eat. I just want you to let me stick around."

"I can't. Not today. If you're still around tomorrow, we can meet up around noon. Unfortunately, I might not want you by then."

"Doubtful," he mumbles. "What's one day going to change?"

"It's just attraction, and that can fade with a little distance."

"It's more than that," he insists.

"You can't share anything with me about the Dog people, and I can't take you to a painting party without starting a riot. We have nothing connecting us except for the attraction. Not that I'm naïve. You and I will probably feel terrific naked together. Let's just not waste time pretending it's anything bigger than you and me wanting to take the pressure off our genitals."

Bubba whispers, "No."

"No, what?"

"You'll see."

I twist to look him in his now green eyes. Bubba's expression is a mess to understand. His lips hint at a smile, but tension lingers in his gaze. He's a man on the edge. Maybe a good fuck is all he needs to fix what ails him. It works for my mom when my dad is in a piss-poor mood.

I consider stopping somewhere for a quickie before leaving him at Audrey's house. As I willing to get him off quickly and tell him goodbye now rather than relish his body for a few days and suffer more when he says goodbye?

I didn't use to be so scared of flirting and fucking. Life was breezy before Griff. Now, I know what men can turn into and how I'm not nearly as strong as I want to believe.

THE RUNAWAY

Soso ain't kidding about the sandwich. The oversized sixteen-incher is overflowing with steak, onions, mushrooms, and peppers. I lose a shit-ton taking my first bite, but I'm so hungry that I can't worry about making a mess.

Soso spies a dropped red pepper and goes for the steal. "I'm a notorious food thief," she says, wearing a sly smile that makes me want to keep her forever.

Is this what Butch feels for Sissy? Why the fuck didn't he come to me day one rather than act like an asshole and let me hang around his babe? Fuck! If Butch sniffed around Soso even once, I'd confront him until he understood that brotherly love only goes so far.

But Butch isn't me. Talking is too hard for him. Better to act like a cocksucker than let down his guard with a person he's known his entire fucking life.

"What's that look mean?" Soso asks after stealing one of my mushrooms.

I reach over and snap up one of her dropped chunks of steak. She watches me pop it in my mouth. I notice how her gaze lingers on my lips before she blinks a few times and returns to eating.

Wanting her to share information with me, I decide to answer her earlier question. "Conroe used to be controlled by a seven-man motorcycle club called Midnight Dogs. When my uncle Cooper wanted to expand, he gave the men a choice to either move out of town or be absorbed into the local chapter of the Reapers. They chose to remain."

"And they don't respect you?" Soso asks, sounding more curious than judgmental.

I think her tone shorts out the common sense part of my brain. Rather than stick to explaining the Dogs' situation, I get way too honest by saying, "No one does."

"Why?"

"I don't do anything," I say, shrugging as my hard-on deflates. Nothing makes my dick less excited than thinking about what a shitty president I am.

"What do you want to do?"

"Kill the Dogs and build a club with new people."

"Why can't you?"

I don't answer. Soso means too much for me to piss away a chance at her heart by proving I'm not worthy. Except I've done just that by admitting I'm not my uncles or grandfather. I'm not the Rutgers either. I'm a boy on a leash his mommy holds.

My earlier confidence is out the fucking door. I just eat in silence, wishing I hadn't mentioned the club at all.

Soso takes the hint and eats quietly. The entire mood from when we arrived is gone. I fucked it up. *Why not?* I figured I'd share what she wanted to know, and she'd trust me more. It was dumb. I just can't seem to do anything right anymore.

It's a tasty fucking sandwich, but I've lost my appetite. I probably couldn't finish it even on my best day. The thing is enormous, and the sauce is heavy. When the waitress dropped off the sandwiches, she claimed, "You'll need to be a magician to make it disappear." Well, I'm not Houdini, and I get the other half to go.

Soso doesn't even eat a third. She's annoyed now. Or bored. I don't know. There's too much space between us despite us sitting in the identical positions as when she craved me with her every breath.

The walk to the truck is surreal. I was in this same place not long ago, and our connection was electric. Now there's only dead space. Maybe I was wrong about us. I'm wrong a lot lately. I fucked up with Butch. Why not crash and burn with Soso too?

I don't know White Horse and have no idea how close the restaurant is to Audrey's house. I could check on my phone, but I don't care. My mind is on Soso. She's the most beautiful woman I've ever known, and she was in the palm of my hand. Now she's a million miles away and closing the door on me.

Soso drives through an adjacent lot to a local park before heading down a tree-covered road. Is this a shortcut? Before I can ask, she puts the truck in park and turns off the engine. Leaning over, she reaches into her glove compartment. Her hair spreads out across my lap as she searches for something.

Is it a weapon? Will she off me and dump my body here? I can't imagine that'd turn out well for her. My mom's a psycho when it comes to protecting her boys. It's why I'll never really be the chapter president. Mom refuses to allow me enough power to possibly fail. Better for her to keep my training wheels on forever than to see me crash and burn.

Finding what she's looking for, Soso sits up and reaches under her seat to move it back. I have no fucking clue what she's doing until she climbs across the middle spot and straddles me.

"Suit up," she says, flicking a condom at my chest before planting her lips on mine.

Her kiss holds the answer to my questions. She's sure about what she wants. I don't know—or currently care—if this is a pity fuck or she's still aroused from earlier.

Ignoring the condom, for now, my hands reach under her skirt to find her soft, warm skin. I've wanted access to her body since this morning. There isn't much room to stretch out, and she grunts disapproval when I try to remove her shirt.

"No nudity in case a stray dog walker comes peeping," she says before returning her lips to mine.

I don't argue. Her loose-fitting top and skirt hide her curves, but they're a godsend as my hands roam her body. I don't even know what to touch first. My fingers stroke her thighs—first outer, then inner—before brushing across the damp cloth covering her overheated pussy. Barely skimming her flesh through her panties, I hear her whimper with need.

"You poor thing," I murmur.

Soso's gaze narrows. "Shut the fuck up."

Smiling bigger, I reach down and pop the button on my jeans. "My dick knows your pain."

Anger gone instantly, Soso returns to sucking at my busted lips and then my tongue. She barely catches her breath even when lifting her hips to make room for me to shove down my jeans and free my pissed cock.

Her soft touch against its hot flesh soothes the angry beast. I'd teased the damn thing all day with this gorgeous woman and the promise of relief. Then I shut down our opportunities again and again. Now my cock purrs as she strokes it with one hand while fondling me under my shirt with her other.

The woman has an outstanding plan. I can multitask too. My left hand emerges from her skirt and slides under her top. Soso moans into my mouth when I pinch her nipple. Her skin turns blazing hot once I roll the rigid flesh between my fingers.

"Bubba," she groans, making my dick twitch in her hand.

Between her legs, my fingers tease her pussy through her panties. Then the fabric is pushed aside as I slide a digit between her slick flesh. She whimpers again, sounding fragile despite her dominance over my cock.

Soso holds my gaze when she asks, "Will you come if I do because I'm so close?"

"I have no idea what the fuck will happen."

"Then wrap up your dick and put it inside me."

I tear open the condom and cover the head of my cock while Soso strokes my balls. Does she want me to come before she does? Is this a sick trick to make me leave her unsatisfied so she can blow me off without guilt?

The look on Soso's face is the only answer I need. No plan necessary. She just can't stop touching me. Her lips suck at my throat. Her teeth nip at my shoulder.

I nearly apologize for thinking she was fucking with me. I'm so damn horny right now that I get a momentary glimpse into Butch's brain. Words are hard. Life is overwhelming.

Then Soso reaches between us, lining up her sweet pussy with my throbbing cock. There's no time to slowly adjust, to savor every inch of my dick entering her. She drops down on my cock with a grunt and immediately rolls her hips. I see her close to coming and don't waste time teasing her clit. She's already at the finish line. My hands disappear under her shirt and bra, filling my palms with her soft flesh.

I watch her face flushing from pink to red as she rides my dick. Her dark eyes reveal the kind of vulnerability I've never seen before with a woman. Or maybe I never paid attention until now. I only know she looks afraid as the pleasure builds.

I don't know what to say. Smart words remain out of reach. I'm not a guy thinking with his brain. It's primal need right now. The only words I can manage are, "My Soso."

My brain might currently be stuck in neutral while my dick runs the show, but it knows I sound like a fucking caveman. Soso doesn't laugh at my words. I see only relief from her fear and then the physical relief of coming after too long in a state of heat.

I demand my dick keep working. No way do I want to cut short the incredible feeling of Soso's pussy sucking wildly. Her lips find mine, thanking me for making her come so hard. I wrap my arms around her as she bounces on my cock.

Every thrust into her body makes relief so much closer, but I'm not ready to let her go yet. I want to feel this way forever. I'm unleashed, commanding, and confident. This is the man I need to be, and I'm afraid to let go and lose this power.

I'm convinced Soso is the key to what I've been missing. But once I come, she'll drop me off at Audrey's, and I might never find my way back to this moment again.

THE BOHEMIAN

Bubba goes full lost hunky puppy on me during lunch. He shuts down when I ask about killing the Dogs. I can't tell what the problem is, but I sense he's stuck between being a kid taking orders and a man making them. I remind myself he's only twenty-two. There's plenty of time for him to break free of the expectations of others.

Despite the Johanssons always lingering in the background of conversations when I was growing up, I don't know his family's story beyond the basics. They were the charmed ones from Kentucky. Grampa was a badass. His sons were softer. According to my family, anyway. Cooper was the smarter brother; Tucker was the meaner one. I don't remember anything about Bubba's mother and father.

In fact, I don't think I heard anything of value about the family until Audrey hooked up with Cap. And all that info came from Keanu, who was mostly interested in teasing his best friend for being whipped by a tiny woman.

Without the details, I can't be sure why Bubba's running a chapter of the Reapers at twenty-two. As a Johansson, he probably didn't need to jump through hoops like a regular member. The blood running through his veins offered him shortcuts. Maybe that's his problem. Bubba never had to earn his patch, let alone control over his chapter. I wonder if he's ever even killed anyone.

I honestly don't care if he's taken a life or can't run his club. None of that involves me. Bubba's life in Conroe is his problem. Here, though, he's my lost hunky puppy, and I want to make him feel better.

And if in the process of helping him, I'm able to fix the pounding heat between my legs, well, then I'm not going to complain.

I never plan on stopping at the Baltazar Memorial Park. The silence at lunch left me stuck in my head. Running on autopilot, I let my heart take the wheel.

Now Bubba's balls deep inside me while we fuck like teenagers. His arms keep me pressed against him. My hips refuse to relent until I know he's come. I already got off, and it felt fantastic. I'd forgotten how incredible a dick-involved orgasm could be. It's been so long, and I don't want it to end.

But Bubba and I can't remain attached forever. His balls end our fun, but, hell, if they didn't give it their all. I expected maybe two minutes of fun after how long he'd been sporting an erection. I even manage a second orgasm before he loses the fight.

Eventually, Bubba hides his face in my hair, catching his breath. I stroke his head in the same way I did last night when he mumbled in his sleep.

"Soso," he whispers, and our gazes meet.

Then he just stares without speaking. But I get it. Men can be quite skilled with the sweet talk when getting laid is on the line. After their balls empty out, they just grunt and need a nap. Well, assuming they aren't busy running for the exit.

"Thank you for making my pussy hum," I murmur while cupping his face.

Bubba's smirk is back. "I did good, huh?"

"I've not had better."

"A lot of competition?" he asks, getting that possessive glint in his eyes.

"I'll tell you how many, if you'll list all the ladies you've blessed with jizz."

Bubba's smile widens. "I was a virgin before this particular fuck."

"Me too," I say and kiss his forehead before brushing my lips across his. "Yet despite my virginity, I can say that was the best fuck of my life. As such, I will allow you to spend time with me tomorrow."

My pussy gives his sated dick a farewell squeeze before I lift my hips and return to my seat. "Good thing I changed into a skirt."

"You knew."

Sharing his smile, I murmur, "Yeah, I think I did."

Bubba removes the condom with the kind of skill that makes me suspect he might have been lying about that virgin thing. Soon, his jeans are back on, and he rids himself of the used rubber.

"Why can't I hang out with you today?" he asks, shifting closer while I start the engine.

"I have the painting party tonight."

"And I said I could paint."

"It's club business, and you're not in the club," I grumble since he's making me want to ditch my responsibilities just to play with him more.

"Don't get mad."

"Well, then, don't beg like a bitch and make me feel guilty."

"That would be more intimidating if you didn't start laughing in the middle."

Giggling, I back out of the park and head for Audrey's house. "You'll be here for a few more days, right?"

"At least."

"Then you can hang out with me tomorrow. Then if we aren't sick of each other, you can hang out with me the next day. And if you ever get bored at home again, you can visit me for more truck sex."

"I want you spread out in bed."

"Well, we haven't done it missionary-style yet."

Bubba smiles while his hand plays with my hair. All his earlier tension is gone. Orgasms are nature's drug.

"I don't want this," he says when I pull up to Audrey's house.

"You're wearing the same clothes as yesterday and starting to stink up my truck. Get out."

"Can I come over tonight after your party?"

"No."

"Why?" he grunts, losing much of his post-coital glow.

"I don't want you sleeping over."

"Why?"

"I'm worried I'll get attached to you. That or I'm worried you'll hog the bed. Could be either one."

His fingers still twirling my hair, Bubba studies me. I stroke his cheek and smile. "Thanks for the wonderful fuck, Bubba Davies. Now get the hell out of my truck."

"When can I see you tomorrow?"

"We'll meet for lunch and see how things go."

"Don't push me away."

"Don't tell me what to do."

"I can't help myself," he says and kisses me before I can complain.

Our lips part once. Then his return. Again, they part. His linger over mine. I worry he won't leave, and I worry even more that I won't make him. He'll tag along to the painting party and cause trouble that I'll need to clean up after he returns to Conroe. Plus, his gorgeous face might get banged up more.

But Bubba does get out of my truck after one more kiss. He doesn't look happy, and I don't feel happy, but it gets done.

I tell him we'll meet up around noon and I'll text him with the specifics tomorrow. He just nods, seeming as if he doesn't believe me.

After I smile big enough for him to feel guilty for not returning the gesture, he grins. As soon as I pull away, I check the rearview mirror to find him pouting. It's a sexy look on him, for sure.

Tomorrow can't come soon enough.

THE CHAPTER WHERE FAMILY DISTRACTS FROM WHAT THE HEART WANTS THE RUNAWAY

Soso's scent is on my skin—a floral, earthy aroma like a summer evening. I don't want to leave her side, but here I am standing on the curb in front of Audrey's house. Based on the empty driveway, I might be stuck outside for a while.

Audrey, though, opens the door when I knock. She sizes me up in the same way she did when I showed up on her doorstep Sunday night.

"You have caused me trouble, Nikolas."

"I need to wash off my dick. Can I come inside?"

"Use the hose," she says, ruining her bitch persona by laughing. "So nasty."

I walk into her house to find it quiet. She locks the door—so many bolts—and follows me to the kitchen where I stick my leftovers in the fridge.

"What's in the to-go box?" she asks.

"Houdini sandwich."

"Couldn't finish it, huh, lightweight?"

"Look, kid, I get it. Your man is huge and eats like a pig. Whatever."

"I can't believe you ran off with Calypso Rutgers," she says, leaning against the kitchen table.

I nearly ask, "who" before realizing Soso is a nickname. Ah, so she knows the pain of a silly nickname becoming your official moniker. We're kismet.

"I don't even remember last night after I started my second Korean Kickass."

"I probably should have warned you about that drink," Audrey says, flashing me a smile.

"How can that little guy drink it with no problems?"

"Keanu has mystical powers."

"No, really."

"I think he started young and built up a tolerance. I don't know. Ask him yourself. Unless you're planning on heading home today."

"Nope. I'm here for the night, and then I plan to shack up with Soso until it's time to bring her home to Conroe."

Audrey's dark eyes widen, and she looks ready to yell. Then she remembers her kid is sleeping and controls herself. "For fuck's sake, you can't be serious. There is no way that woman would leave Tennessee for you."

"You ditched Kentucky and your family for Cap."

"Hey, I see them twice a month."

"You ditched everything you knew for a man. Why can't Soso?"

"You barely know her."

Smiling, I wag my finger at her. "I noticed how you changed the subject there."

"She's trouble. All the Rutgers are. Those Hallstead sisters were evil."

"Yeah, yeah, and our family's full of saints. Look, I'm going to take a shower and change my clothes. Afterward, you can talk more shit about people you barely know. I'll listen and nod since you were nice enough to let me crash here."

"And how long are you planning on staying?" she asks with her hands on her hips.

"I told you that I'm shacking up with Soso starting tomorrow."

"Does she know that?"

When I only smile, Audrey rolls her eyes. But she doesn't give me any more trouble while I get cleaned up.

Her house has a small guest room tucked behind the kitchen. Though I barely fit in the shower—and I bet Cap would suffocate in the small space—the hot water feels good against my battered body. Butch got in plenty of shots on Saturday night, and that asshole managed a few more last night.

Deciding to relax in bed after my shower, I think of Soso's tiny house. Is that what she needs to be happy? I can't imagine myself surviving long in such a tight space. Back in Conroe, I live with my parents, but the 5000 square foot house has more than enough room for our family. When

Mom and Dad designed the place, they made sure to give each of us a section to roam.

"Grown men need privacy," Mom said, wanting her boys to remain home for as long as possible.

Of course, she didn't respect our privacy. I often caught her rummaging around my room or checking my phone. Needing to protect us, Mom doesn't believe in boundaries. If we're smothered in the process, so fucking be it.

I wonder what Mom will think of Soso. My guess is she'll hate her in the beginning and treat her like crap. Then she'll warm up to her and become fiercely protective. I just hope she manages to take it easy on Sissy.

Conroe feels far away as I doze on the guest bed and think of Soso. I can't imagine her in Kentucky or living in a non-triangle house. What about her birds? I could put together one of those sanctuaries. How hard could it be? For Soso, I can listen to New Age music and live in a weird house and learn how to engage with birds. Whatever it fucking takes to keep her in my life.

THE BOHEMIAN

Years ago, my parents built a brick and wood siding home on five acres. The style is very retro since my mom and aunts have a running contest to see who can cream their panties hardest over the 1980s. Meanwhile, Dad triumphed with a four-car garage and workshop where he tinkers, drinks beer, and listens to old man rock and country.

I park my truck in the driveway, hear a Willie Nelson song playing in the nearby garage, and sneak inside through a side door into the kitchen. I'm not ready to engage with Dad yet.

Once my leftovers are in the fringe, I go searching for Mom. Instead, I find Keanu stretched out on the couch in the rec room.

"Sorry about last night," he says and glances at me through half-closed eyes.

"Why are you sorry?"

"I should have protected you better from Griff. That way, Kentucky wouldn't be forced to jump in. I can't imagine you found any pleasure in rewarding his penis as a thank you."

"Apology accepted," I say, smiling at his wording. "Is missing Lottie why you're vegging on the couch in the middle of the day?"

"Yeah, and I can't even play with Cap," he mutters and then adds when I frown, "He got grounded for the fight at Salty Peanuts. Poor sonovabitch is stuck in a giant corner, thinking about what he did."

Grinning, I sit across from him in an overstuffed, green chair. "'I'm sorry my drama got your boy stuck in a time-out."

"I caught Mom and Dad plotting to get you away from Bubba. I pointed out how the guy was from Kentucky, and they realized you'd get rid of him on your own. I guess I was right, but at least you got laid first. That's what I'm smelling, right?"

"I refuse to understand what you're implying," I mumble, standing up. "And now for an unrelated reason, I will take a shower. Farewell and feel free to finish my sandwich in the fridge."

"I'm timing you. Mom says no more than three minutes in the shower unless you're suffering from full-on summer stank."

I hurry to my old room, grab spare clothes, jump in the shower, skip washing anything that wasn't sexed-up, and then get out with a minute to spare.

"Killed it," I tell Keanu when I return to the couch where he now gears up "Halo." "Are you waiting for Cap?"

"Yeah, he'll play during his lunch break."

"I sometimes forget he's a father. Then I remember and feel sad for his kid."

"Shut up, Num-Num," Keanu says without malice.

"Your words sadden my heart," I express in Korean.

"My fondest apologies, sister." Keanu puts down the controller and hugs me. "I still smell Kentucky jizz on you. Color me flabbergasted to learn you hooked up with another biker."

"Flabbergasted," I snort. "Did your boyfriend teach you that big word?"

"Yeah, just before he went King Kong on Salty Peanuts."

"Was it that bad?" I ask, having assumed the entire thing died down as soon as Griff and Bubba's fight moved outdoors.

"It was a whole lot of nothing. Cap did his stompy thing. I had his back, of course. The meat and potatoes of a few bikers got kicked. Everything was fine, but a few chairs were smashed, so Uncle Camden called Angus to complain about his son's colossal feet."

"I'm sure the Imperial One got a good laugh from that."

"No doubt, but now Cap's grounded to White Horse for a few days."

"Are you sure it's Big Hayes that's keeping your boy locked away? Maybe Little Audrey wants Cap to herself."

74

"That bitch is always keeping us apart," Keanu whines dramatically. "I remember when I wanted to go bowling, and she had to ruin my good time by giving birth to a giant baby."

"She's just jealous of your love," I say, ruffling his black hair.

"I'm babysitting Keith later this week, so Cap can pound Audrey's vagina at a hotel. I don't know why that needs to happen, but it's probably related to how married people get bored with sex."

I study my brother, wondering if he and Lottie will ever make their love official. She believes people will think she's only marrying Keanu for citizenship. I don't know who these "people" are that care about her romantic life. I'm sure there are those in the club who don't approve of her, but Keanu isn't in the Brotherhood, and he doesn't give a single fuck what any of them—except Dad of course—think.

"What if Lottie didn't or couldn't come back from Indonesia?" I ask.

"Are you trying to make me cry?" he asks, flashing me a frown. "Do you get a reward if I shed tears?"

Hugging him, I sigh. "I'm sorry. I was just wondering if you'd move there to be with her."

"I don't know," he mutters. "Now, you have me worried."

"Don't stress. If she couldn't return legally, we'd get her in somehow. You know our family's motto is 'Laws are for suckers.'"

Keanu's tension lessens, and he rolls his eyes. "Is this about Kentucky?"

"Whatever do you mean?" I ask, standing up and walking away. "I don't understand. What? I can't hear you."

Keanu laughs behind me, but I'm sure he's relieved I'm gone so he can play with his grounded buddy.

My mood is all over the place while I look for Mom. I enjoyed my time with Bubba. I know he can't stay in Hickory Creek. I understand it'll be over soon.

Regularly, I can keep my emotional baggage in order as long as I look at a problem logically. People think I'm a hippie and assume I'm ditzy too. Much like Keanu, I don't really give a fuck about the opinion of most people. Let them think I'm a dumb blonde, pot-smoking hippie. It doesn't matter because I know me. I get how I work, which is why I'm bothered by how bothered I am at losing Bubba.

Unable to locate Mom, I finally end up in the garage where Dad drinks beer and listens to his music.

"Does the song choice mean you're sad?" I ask him.

Dad allows a lazy smile. "I listen to country on Mondays. Glad to see you finally got rid of Kentucky," he says and then scowls darkly. "Tell me that redneck isn't wandering around my house."

"No, I dropped him off at his cousin's."

"Good. Johanssons are trouble, Num-Num. Trust me. I've known that family since I was a kid."

"Why is trouble always so sexy?"

"No," he grunts, shaking his head. "I'm telling you that boy is going to crush you and laugh about it to his friends."

Jumping up on the worktable he's leaning against, I sigh. "Dad, did you have to give up anything to be with Mom?"

"Pussies that didn't belong to your mother."

"Was that difficult for you?" I ask, patting his shoulder sympathetically.

"Not really. I'd fucked enough pussies to know I locked down the best one."

"You should put that in a greeting card for your next anniversary."

Dad's dark brown eyes—that I inherited—narrow. "Don't you dare give up anything for that Johansson."

"But is he really a Johansson? Like isn't his dad a school administrator or something?"

"Doesn't matter. His mama is Bailey Johansson, and she's evil. I heard she cut off a man's dick, cooked it up with some Worcestershire sauce, and served it to the guy."

"Why would he eat it?"

"She starved him until he was insane with hunger."

Smiling, I poke him. "That's not true."

"No, probably not. Mojo and Playboy used to make up stories about the Johanssons. They claimed Kirk actually had six kids, but he killed one of the boys for wetting the bed and sold a girl to another club for gambling money. Shit like that."

"Why?"

Dad smiles wider. "For the same reason they made up stories about Angus Hayes. Talking trash about the competition is fun."

"But back to my question about giving up something for the one you love. Did you have to give up much to be with Mom? Besides, you know, the other pussies."

"I had to give up my carefree lifestyle. Your mom came with a brat who cock-blocked me left and right. Hated him."

"He's playing videogames if you want to join him."

"Fuck that," Dad hisses. "He and his stupid bitch friend always kill me."

Laughing, I hug Dad as he offers me a beer. "Booze makes me sad, and I'm already feeling down."

"Did he hurt you? I can drive over to White Horse and cut him a second asshole. It'll make us even for what he pulled last night."

"He defended me against Griff."

"Yeah, but chairs were broken, Num-Num. Gotta keep shit in perspective," he says, winking.

"I really like him," I mumble, feeling sad. "But he's from Kentucky."

"Exactly, and you're so fucking young. You need a few years of random dicks before you settle on one."

"What did Mom have to give up to be with you?"

"A life without orgasms."

Laughing again, I wish his bullshit made me feel better. I just hope I could have with Bubba what he has with my mom.

"Did you love anyone before Mom?"

"Fuck no."

"Did Mom love anyone before you?"

"Of course not," he says and then adds, "Wait, what did she tell you?"

"Nothing. I just thought maybe Keanu's dad."

"Pointless hookup. Let's move on."

"Not pointless. The swapping of fluids created my beloved brother."

"I like to imagine I was the one who created him, but I was talented enough to use another man's spunk to get the job done."

"You are very talented, Daddy," I say, leaning my head on his shoulder. "Where's Mom?"

"Is that your subtle hint that my advice ain't cutting it?"

"No, I think I want to cry."

"You don't look like you want to cry."

I scrunch up my face and close my eyes tight. My internal melancholy struggles to rise. Despite the storm in my heart, no tears show up.

"What's happening?" Dad asks, now pulling out his phone. "What am I looking at?"

"I think I'm going to cry."

"You think, or you know?"

"Sometimes, a good cry empties out all the bad feelings."

"Don't force it."

"I'm not."

"You look like you're trying to force it. That's not healthy," Dad says and then raises his phone and snaps a picture,

"You're trying to make me smile, but I can't," I say despite grinning. "I'm too heartbroken over what can never be."

"Yeah, I can tell. My heart breaks, watching your heartbreak."

"Am I human?" I ask my father, who shrugs. "Am I part monster? Is that why Mom studies cryptozoology?"

"Might be. While I like to believe you're mine, we never did a DNA test. You could very well be half monster and half Harmony. You're awfully blonde to be a Sasquatch, though."

"Why can't I cry?" I ask, trying again to squeeze a few tears from my eyeballs. "Was I not raised right?"

"I wasn't there for much of your childhood," he lies. "It's possible your mom did a piss-poor job."

As if summoned by Dad's bullshit, my blonde goddess mother appears from what I assume was a brisk walk around the property.

"What's happening here?" she asks, entering the garage.

"She's broken, Harmony. Shattered on the inside and possibly an alien. You'll need to get that fixed."

"Did that Johansson boy hurt her feelings?"

"Why do you assume he dumped me?" I ask Mom.

"Yeah, my baby girl dumps other people. They do not dump her."

"Thanks, Daddy," I say, jumping down from the workbench as Mom chuckles at the picture Dad took of me trying to cry. "I just thought crying would fix what troubles me before we do this painting party thing. Do you think Griff will be there?"

My parents share a frown. "He's on house arrest," Dad says. "Something like that. I don't remember what Camden was trying to convey because his words were slurred behind his lumberjack beard."

"Poor Daisy," Mom sighs, pitying her sister married to Dad's brother. "I can't imagine kissing that face."

"This is the better one, right?" Dad says, gesturing at his smiling mug.

"Always," Mom murmurs. "I scored."

My parents' love warms my heart. They're still into each other after all these years and two kids and no doubt enough sex to make the actual process rudimentary. I was in such a hurry to have what they do that I grabbed on to Griff without worrying about the consequences.

Am I doing the same thing with Bubba now?

THE RUNAWAY

Audrey does her best to entertain me on my second night in Tennessee. She chooses to watch action movies, feeds me mountains of pizza, and offers gallons of beer. Despite approving of my cousin's efforts, I can't settle down.

I ought to be worried about Conroe or how my mom keeps texting with cataclysmic concerns about the town's well-being.

"We might get tornados!" she messages all night. Having checked the news reports, I know Mom is full of shit.

Mostly, I spend my evening wishing I was with Soso. Is her ex-boyfriend at the painting party? Will people talk shit about me there? Worse is the worry that she isn't as obsessed with me as I am with her.

And I *am* obsessed.

Around midnight, I nearly take off for her place. I'm convinced I can push my way inside and make her accept me as her man.

But what if Soso isn't there? I don't know Hickory Creek Township well enough to track her down. If she's off with someone else, I'm fucking positive I can't control what happens when I see that man.

It's unacceptable that Soso's made me crazy while she might not be thinking of me at all.

I only sleep out of boredom. The next morning, I check my phone immediately. More rambling messages from Mom—tornados, intruders, a strange smell coming from the basement. There's also a quick hello from Pop. But nothing from the person I need to hear from the most.

Audrey invites me to join her, Cap, and Keith for breakfast at a Waffle House. Agreeing, I'm desperate for a distraction from thinking about Soso or the endless texts from my mom.

Despite knowing their office is next door, I'm startled to find the compact restaurant filled with the Hayes family.

Like literally no one else is in the fucking place except them and the staff.

There's the big man himself at the counter. Even three times my age, Angus Hayes remains intimidating with a head full of black hair that I'm reasonably sure he doesn't dye. Next to the giant sonovabitch is his curvy, blonde wife, Candy. Neither of them takes notice of me, but I know they're aware I've joined the party.

The rest of the Hayes clan sit in a line of booths at the back windows. Brunette Cricket relaxes with her husband whose name I never remember, but I do recall he's a member of a biker club in West Virginia. Their boy-girl twins are nearly teenagers, while their youngest son is a toddler.

In the next booth sits Cricket's blond twin brother, Chipper. His wife holds their pink-cheeked daughter while their uber blond son sits in his lap. Like with Cricket's kids and partner, I have no memory of any of these people's names.

Cap and Audrey take the open booth at the end and set Keith in a high chair. Sliding in across from the couple stuffed on one side, I keep an eye on the rest of the group. Then, without checking the menu, I order a waffle and coffee.

"He's still in town," Hayes says to no one in particular.

Without hesitation, Audrey announces, "My cousin is free to stay as long as he wants."

There's something damn precious about such a petite woman giving grief to a man as huge as Hayes. It's been a joke in my family that Audrey and Cap make no sense. How is she not endlessly intimidated by these people? *Because she's a fucking Johansson. That's how!*

"I thought you were screwing one of the twins' daughters," Hayes says, and I assume he's speaking to me about the Rutgers twins rather than any of his own.

Before I can respond, Candy asks, "Layla?"

"No, the one with normal hair."

"The blonde," Cricket adds.

"Which twin is her father?" Hayes asks.

Candy stops fiddling with her hash browns and frowns at her husband. "You know the answer."

"Remembering goes against my religions."

"Now you have more than one?" Candy asks.

"I'm a large man, which means I need more than one of everything," Hayes says and then smirks. "Except for wives. One is enough."

Even without knowing what Candy whispers to him, I suspect they'll be fucking after breakfast.

"I heard the blonde one is a whore," Chipper says, covering his son's ears before uttering the final word.

Before I can punch anyone, Cricket shoots a dirty look at her twin brother. "She's just doing what her father did before settling down."

"True. He was a whore then, and she's a whore now. Poor Bubba probably caught something."

Eyeballing Chipper, I mutter, "I don't want to break your face in front of your kids, but if you talk shit about Soso again, I'll have no choice."

Everyone gets very quiet—except for the small children who seem to be louder—and I wonder if I'm about to have my ass kicked by the giants. Then Candy snorts, and they all start laughing.

"Adorable," Cap says and nudges Audrey. "He's hooked on a whore."

"That's it," I say, standing up and coming at him.

"Stop!" Audrey cries. "Don't make Cap kill you in front of the children!"

Everyone laughs again, but I can't let it go. Since violence isn't an option with Keith staring directly at me with his dark, Johansson eyes, I knock over Cap's orange juice and soak his lap.

"I'll allow that to happen because you're family," says the big man, tossing a napkin in his lap while Audrey laughs wildly and takes a picture.

I return to my seat and grumble, "Uh-huh. Stop talking shit about Soso."

"She's probably fucking someone else right this minute," Chipper announces, but I barely understand the final words since he's laughing so hard.

Cricket and Tatum giggle at how he asks for trouble. Then his sister stands up and walks to my table.

Handing me her glass of juice, Cricket growls, "Punish him."

Nodding, Tatum reaches for her son sitting on Chipper's lap. "Just let me remove our child from the splash zone."

Cap leans across the table and whispers loudly, "Do it. My shame will be lessened if I share it with Chip."

"It's not as fun when you want it," I mutter before spilling the drink in Chipper's lap. "But it's still fun."

"For fuck's sake," Hayes grumbles. "My sons are idiots."

Candy pounds the counter and grabs for her drink. "Don't you criticize my boys."

"You made them this way."

"No, all the good stuff was from me. You gave them all the shitty stuff."

"Chipper isn't even biologically mine. How—"

Chipper, Cricket, and Cap gasp in unison.

"Father, is this true?" Chipper asks, blinking wildly as if about to cry. "Why was I never told before?"

Cricket gasps again. "Wait, we're twins, so does that mean I'm not from his seed either?"

"No, I don't think that's what it means," Cap says, sipping his coffee.

"Oh, good," Cricket mumbles and starts eating again. "Carry on."

Hayes sighs loudly, sounding like a dying locomotive. Candy, though, keeps tilting her glass of juice threateningly. He glares at her. She glares right back.

"I will never fucking bow," he growls at her.

"I will spill this shit in your fucking lap," she growls back.

"Why the fuck are we fucking fighting?" he snarls.

"I can't remember, but I want to win more than I've ever wanted anything in my fucking life."

Their staring match goes on for far too long for me to pay attention, so I take a bite of my newly arrived food and assume Candy will win. After all, Hayes no doubt wants to remain dry more than he needs to triumph over his wife.

"You don't really think Soso hooked up with another guy last night, do you?" I whisper to Audrey once Cap is in the bathroom cleaning up with Chipper.

The two men must be fighting because we hear a bang against the wall from that direction followed by laughter.

Audrey rolls her eyes while feeding Keith from a jar. "Well, I assume you wore her out, right? If so, she won't be in the mood for another cock."

"You're not helping."

"Let me try it again, and I'll lie this time," Audrey says before reaching for my hand. "I sensed something very beautiful between the two of you, and I can't imagine her ever feeling that way about someone else."

"I appreciate that," I say.

Audrey winks at Keith. "Crushed it."

"I don't know you," Cricket says, suddenly standing next to me. Her twins flank her, staring with crazy eyes that I'm sure they worked tirelessly to perfect. "But you should know Dayton Rutgers will never allow his daughter to leave Tennessee. He loves her too much to let her go."

"Hey," Audrey grumbles with her mouth full. "My pop loves me as much as any man could."

"Clearly not since he let you move here."

"He didn't *let* me do anything. I'm the boss of me and no one else."

Hayes says something to Cap as the brothers return from the bathroom. Their laughter only irritates Audrey more.

"You're ganging up on me."

"Now, you know how I feel when we visit Ellsberg," Cap says and slides into the booth. "What are we doing here, Cricket?"

"I'm trying to mess with Bubba's head."

"Is it working?"

"I don't know him well enough to tell. Thoughts, Audrey?"

My cousin studies me and sighs. "He's very bothered by your words. Mission accomplished. Now, go away."

Cricket smiles while her twins still stare like horror movie kids. "If you want to take Soso Rutgers out of Tennessee, you'll need to be sneaky about it. That's all I will say." Then instead of returning to her table, she adds, "But I sense you're just the latest in her very long line of hookups, so I can't imagine she'll want to go with you anyway."

"Look," I say, staring into her eyes, "I get how you're trying to upset me or intimidate me or whatever, but my mother is Bailey Fucking Johansson. She once knocked over one of those displays at the grocery store because she thought a group of old ladies was talking shit about her. They weren't, by the way, but she never apologized, and she didn't help clean up the mess either. To this day, she claims her only mistake was not chasing the women out of the store. That means, if you want to bother me, you'll need to amp your bitch level to an eleven."

"Well said, Bubba," Cricket coos and pats my head.

"No," growls her husband, who snaps and gestures for her to get back to their table.

"He's very good in bed," Cricket shares with me. "That's why I allow him to boss me around."

Chipper snickers. "Her pussy calls all the shots."

"Shut up."

The twins then proceed to talk shit about each other for ten minutes until my plate is empty and I'm finished waiting for Soso to call me. She claimed we'd meet for lunch, but I haven't heard anything, and I refuse to play hard to get with her.

Whether she's home or not, I'm driving my ass to her house. If she has a problem with my behavior, well, I hope she plans to amp her bitch level to an eleven too because I won't take no for an answer.

THE CHAPTER WHERE THE RUNAWAY TURNS INTO A BULLET
THE BOHEMIAN

Staying busy last night kept my mind off Bubba. I picked up Freki and returned to my parents' place. We spent a few hours painting at Rick and Leah's new house. I felt watched the entire time. Not that I was shocked by the sense of isolation.

Many of the club's old ladies haven't been my fans since I dumped Griff. Can't I see how sexy he is and how much he loves me? *Why am I so selfish? Do I think I'm too good for a biker?* No doubt hooking up with Bubba only made me more obnoxious in their eyes. Poor, poor Griff, they likely whisper.

Fortunately, he doesn't show up at the house, and I actually have fun since Mom and Dad might be the worst painters I've ever seen. She paints the same sections over and over again while he's sloppy as hell.

"They put the tarp on the floor for just that reason, Num-Num," he explains after making a mess.

I consider sleeping over at my parents' place, but I've missed my bed after spending last night on the couch. Despite the urge to text Bubba all evening, I crash early and sleep late. I want to be rested for today in case he breaks my heart, and I can actually cry.

Waking up groggy after sleeping for far too long, I enjoy strong coffee in the backyard while Freki explores. I used to come back here and talk to my Caique parrots. I'd shut the outer door on the back porch and open the atrium so my girls could fly free inside the house.

I adopted the birds when they were tiny and even housetrained them. They were sweet goofballs, but I left them vulnerable.

"Now, I can cry," I grumble and wipe my cheeks.

I hear a motorcycle approaching, and soon there's a knock on my front door. My protective little Freki bursts into a yapping fit. He doesn't actually head toward the threat, of course. Smiling, I pick him up and walk inside where I rest him on the couch where he yaps while cuddling with his pillow.

"Such a badass," I taunt.

Checking my teeth for gunk in a small mirror near the door, I want to make sure I'm presentable for Bubba.

Except when I throw open the door, I find the antithesis of my hunky puppy.

Standing on my porch and shifting from foot to foot, Griff looks like a restless kid waiting for the last bell at school.

I consider shutting the door, but he's already positioned to stop me.

"Why are you here?" I finally ask.

"You're killing me."

"Is that it?"

"How can you be so cold?" he whines, wearing the pained expression of a man wronged.

"We've gone over this before."

"I want to talk."

"I've told you nicely, and I've told you cruelly, but what I say is always the same. We're over, and nothing will ever change that."

Before I can shut the door, he pounds hard enough to send it flying at me. I take one step back before standing my ground. Griff looms in the doorway, blocking the light.

"Yes, nothing proves you're worth a second shot like breaking my damn house, you fucking bully," I growl.

"If you weren't such a bitch," he growls back, lowering his face until it's inches from mine, "I wouldn't have to resort to being a bully."

"If I'm such a bitch, why do you want me?"

"I love you despite your flaws, and I know you love me despite mine."

"If I loved you, I wouldn't have ended shit. Now, get out of my doorway."

"Not until we talk."

"Well, at least, get on the porch."

"I want to talk inside."

Knowing us alone wouldn't be safe, I lift my chin and force eye contact. "Get out, or I'm calling my dad."

"He won't take your side. Everyone knows you made a mistake leaving me."

"Fuck you," I say, yanking my phone from my pocket.

Backing down, Griff steps out of the doorway and onto the porch. I grudgingly follow him outside to avoid him breaking more of my stuff. He stands over me, refusing to allow any personal space. He's always been like this. I used to think his need to possess me was a sign of devotion. Now, I just find him creepy.

"Are you fucking that Reaper?" he asks, staring at me with heartbroken blue eyes.

Crap, is he going to cry again? Beg for another chance? Demand I love him like he loves me? *Ugh, I'm sick of everything about Griff.* Rather than feeling pity when I see his sad eyes, I want to punch him in the face.

"It's none of your business and hasn't been for months."

"That guy's a fucker. I heard he raped a chick."

I fight the urge to roll my eyes at his lame attempt to turn me against Bubba. "Thanks for the info. I heard you tried shoving your dick up some chick's ass even after she said no. Kinda sounds like you both need help, huh? Now, get off my porch."

"Is he here?" Griff asks, shuffling closer, erasing the oxygen between us, smothering me again.

"If he was, do you really think he'd be cool with you pounding on my door and crowding me?"

Growling in frustration, Griff kicks a planter off my porch. "You only care about things. That's Queen Soso. The selfish bitch who loves a fucking door more than a man."

Despite the urge to scream at this motherfucker, I'm aware he isn't entirely sane. He proved that with Bjork and Ula.

Rather than speak, I shove my hands into my pockets—one of which holds my switchblade—and wait for him to get to his point.

Griff still stands too close, but I've gone through all this before with him. Crowding me won't work. Breaking my stuff won't work. Reminding me that he's protected by the club won't work. I'm past falling for his tricks.

Trying a new tactic, he leans down and growls, "If you're going to spread your pussy for some diseased fucker, then I want my dog back."

"Fuck that!" I yell, forgetting all about my "cool as a cucumber" act.

Griff smirks angrily at my rage. "I only gave him to you because you were my woman. If you're sucking off other guys, I want him back."

"One, fuck you," I snarl at him. "Two, you can't take back gifts. Three, I didn't even want the dog, but you threatened to dump him at the pound if I didn't take him. Four, Freki is afraid of you because you're an asshole. And five, fuck you."

Griff leans over me, wanting to emphasize his size over mine. He growls deep in his chest, gritting his teeth, full psycho animal crap. "I want that fucking dog."

"Haven't you stolen enough from me already?" I hiss as my mind imagines his huge hands crushing my sweet birds.

"I gave you everything, but you're a selfish cunt, and it was never enough."

"You're dead inside. All fucked up and rotten. You used Freki to make me feel like I owed you. You never cared about him or me. You just wanted to fuck Dayton Rutgers' daughter."

"I'm taking my fucking dog," he says, pressing his forehead against mine and giving it a shove.

I should call my dad or brother. They'd rush over to settle things, but then what? Griff could kill Freki with his bare hands before either of them arrives. Would the club care if my dog died? No, he's one of them. Dad would care, and he'd make a mess, and then there'd be hell to pay.

"If you touch that dog, I will fuck up your ride."

"Bullshit."

I rush past Griff, hoping to draw him away from the house where my little guy minds his own business. On my way to the street, I grab a can of old paint I used on a table I refinished. Griff storms after me. I reach his chopper first and rip off the top of the can. There's very little paint left, but the dipshit doesn't know this fact.

"If you fuck with my stuff, I'll fuck with yours," I threaten while swinging the can over his Harley.

"Do it, cunt."

I don't mind the name-calling, but this asshole trashed my atrium and garden. Best case scenario, my birds flew away. Worse case, he killed them. Either way, I've spent the last two months hating him for taking away my babies.

Only a cup's worth of green paint plops onto the fender of his biker, but Griff roars as if I gutted his mom before his very eyes. I consider hitting him with the can still swinging from my hand. I doubt he'd feel it much.

There's something in his eyes beyond anger. It's a primal desire. He wants me. Someone else fucked me. He's got to fix what Bubba broke.

I back away and think to run to a neighbor's house. No, he'll either grab Freki or scare the hell out of one of the elderly women who live on this rural road.

"What's wrong with you?" he screams as if I'm the one who showed up at his house with the plan to use an animal as leverage. "Where's your heart? Your soul? You said you loved me!"

Face red, Griff screams all his usual insults—cunt, bitch, slut, whore, and variations of those four. I reach into my pocket as I back away. We make a circle in the yard as he whines about how he just wants to love me. Even after everything I've done to him, he could forgive me if only I'd pull the stick out of my ass long enough to see what I gave up. He then lists off all the crap he's supposedly done for me. *He got me a dog I didn't want. He bought me a shirt I wouldn't wear. He painted the atrium a color I hated. He did every-fucking-thing, and I just wanted more and more!*

"It's never enough!" he yells so loud that my ears ring.

Time stands still while also feeling as if an hour goes by. I'm so focused on watching his every move, dodging his hands, avoiding getting cornered, and making sure I have an exit route that I don't notice the approaching Harley until it jumps the curb and races at us.

The front tire clips Griff, sending him backward. I'm easily out of the way, staring in shock at the sight of Bubba sliding off his still moving bike. The chopper roars into the bushes while he steadies himself before tackling Griff who's returning to his feet.

I want so badly to run back into the house, lock the door, and let these two macho men fight it out. Except Bubba is, well, my hunky puppy, and I'm not leaving him with the psycho.

Their fists fly wildly. I hear the crack of bone against bone. I don't know whose blood is whose.

Without thinking, I swing the paint can at Griff and nail him in the temple. He reaches for me, but Bubba punches him in the stomach. Griff instantly pukes up his breakfast, and I think maybe he's had enough.

Inching toward the door, I consider calling Bubba's name, so he'll follow. Griff won't react well to hearing me inviting his rival inside, though.

I grew up hearing stories from my mother about how she calmed her clients. Many of them are autistic and can get aggressive when stressed. She taught me how to handle agitated people. Deescalating this situation would be ideal.

But Griff takes one look at me, and I know nothing short of the threat of death will get his ass off my property. He was already in a rage, but Bubba's arrival threw fuel on his insane fire.

I take off for the house, leaving the men to beat on each other again. Bubba might win with another few punches. He's already got Griff rattled and puking. Yes, he could easily win, but he could also end up dead. I can't take the chance of losing him.

Returning with my shotgun, I cock it to get Griff's attention and then point the muzzle at his head. "Leave now, or I'll put you down."

He spits blood on the ground and hisses, "You'd kill me for this fucker?"

"In a heartbeat. Or you can leave, and we'll let my dad sort shit out later."

I suspect hearing me mention my father more than his fear of the shotgun is what finally gets through to Griff. He feels safe in the knowledge that the club will side with him over an interloper like Bubba.

Backing away, Griff opens his mouth to talk trash. Then he sees Bubba raise his fist and decides to keep quiet. I hold the shotgun at him until he finally—after bitching quietly about the paint on his bike—speeds away.

I lower the weapon and look at a bloody Bubba watching me.

"Why are you here?" I ask.

"I missed you."

His answer kills my tough chick boldness. All those tears I couldn't whip up last night arrive in full force.

THE RUNAWAY

Soso's tears ignite a deep rage inside me. I was already pissed when I saw that motherfucker looming over her. Yeah, yeah, I know she scared him off with her shotgun. She's a tough broad. I get all that, but she looked so vulnerable backing away from that asshole.

I knew the second I saw her that they weren't playing. She reminded me of the hookers out at the Rossiya Motel when they're in fear of the Dogs. I hate the look on any woman but seeing Soso that fragile tore up something inside me. Her tears are salt on the wound.

"I should have checked who was at the door before answering," she says after insisting I right my Harley and get it parked next to her truck. Though her tears stop by the time we're inside, the unease in her eyes remains. "I heard the chopper and thought it was you. That was dumb."

"You should be able to answer your damn door without worrying."

"Should doesn't mean I can. I know what he's like, and I know he's freaking out about…" Soso doesn't finish as she slides her shotgun into an umbrella stand. "I need to clean up your eye. You might even need stitches."

"I'm not going to the hospital."

"No need. I know someone who fixes up the guys. No legal paper trail to worry about."

"Think they'll be cool with fixing up one of the Reapers?"

Soso doesn't answer as she guides me to the tiny kitchen table while she applies a wet cloth to my bleeding eyebrow. I rest my hands on her hips, craving her closer.

I look up and hold her gaze. Soso needs to understand that I'm not playing around with her feelings. But saying the words terrifies me. What if I bare my heart to her, and she stomps on it? Will I turn into a psycho like Griff?

"Explain to me why your father doesn't end that guy?"

"The Brotherhood has a policy of staying out of relationship drama."

"That crap wasn't drama."

Soso runs her fingers through my hair and lowers her voice. "I can't prove he was the one who destroyed my garden and got rid of my birds. I have cameras around. Security that my brother put in, but the camera out back got smashed before catching who did it."

"Did Griff know about the security cameras?"

"Of course. When Dad asked if I thought Griff did it, I said sure, but we both know there's no proof."

"He should still pound on him."

"Years ago," she says as her voice dips into nearly a whisper, "a guy and his old lady broke up. It was ugly. He cheated over and over for years. Didn't even hide it either. Then she went to Nashville for a concert and screwed some guy. One of the old ladies ratted her out to her man. Drama blew up. You know how stupid men are, thinking their cheating is normal, but a woman's cheating is an affront to God."

Soso pauses to check my eye and seems relieved by whatever she finds. Once the towel is back against my brow, she continues explaining a situation I will never understand.

"Everyone took sides, and Camden got involved. He tried to make peace, but everything got worse. The guys didn't like how their president was sticking his nose in the relationship. No matter whose side he took, people got mad that he wasn't picking theirs. Camden finally got fed up and said relationship drama wasn't club business unless the cops might get involved."

"What Griff did isn't cheating."

"Yeah, but no one around here calls the cops over property damage."

"He was ready to hurt you."

"I know, but he didn't," she says, holding my irritated gaze with her resigned one. "I guess I could have pushed him to bang me up a little and then dump the problem in my father's lap, but that isn't how I was raised. Mom didn't want me relying on the club or my family's money to fix everything."

"But he's dangerous."

"Don't talk down to me," she growls, stepping back. "I was the one threatening him with a shotgun. I know what he is."

"But you only did that when he came at me."

"Because I thought I had things handled at first. When I realized I didn't, I was afraid to run for the house. Once you got here, I saw my chance."

Wrapping my arm around her waist, I tug her back toward me. I press my face against her stomach and try to calm her annoyance. I grew up with a high-strung mom, so I've seen how quickly that fire can cool with a little affection.

"Seeing you with the shotgun is in my top ten list of sexiest things."

"What's number one?" she asks, waiting for me to mention another woman as if I'm twelve and lack any fucking common sense around the ladies.

"Easy, seeing you come in the truck the first time. The second time was my second favorite sight."

Soso smiles at my answer, and her earlier edginess disappears. "Thank you for saving me."

"And thank you for saving me. I mean, I didn't need the save, but it was still hot and much appreciated."

"This is a handsome face, Bubba," she says, stroking my freshly shaven jaw, "but it won't stay that way if you keep getting pounded."

"I do plenty of pounding too."

"Yeah, but give it a rest for a few days."

Reminded of how close that shithead came to putting his hands on her, I mutter, "I will if Griff stays the fuck away from you."

"And you'll avoid your brother's fists too, right?"

Hearing the real question behind the one she asks, I murmur, "I won't see him for a while."

Soso gets the message. I'm not bailing on Hickory Creek yet. We have time. Eventually, one of us will need to make a painful decision, but that won't be today.

THE BOHEMIAN

I fight my nervous shakes more than once after guiding a bloodied Bubba into my house. The tide shifted too quickly outside. I went from hyper-alert dodging Griff to watching him and Bubba violently tango. Now, everything is quiet.

The urge to call my family feels right, but I want to protect Bubba too, and I'm not sure they'll agree. Dad believes in cutting people loose. Not his people, of course. But Bubba isn't one of the select few he cares about, and I can't imagine that'll change anytime soon.

"Here's the deal, Bubba Davies," I say, and he perks up at the sound of his name. His adoring gaze demands I keep him with me forever. "We have two choices. One is that I call my dad and tell him what happened with Griff. Rather than check the security footage on his phone, he'll show up. Probably bring Keanu. Once he sees Griff's behavior, my beloved father will focus his anger on you because you're nearby and he doesn't like you."

"I'm shocked to hear my charms haven't wowed him yet," Bubba says, wearing a smart-ass grin.

"You're a Johansson, and you're banging his daughter. He can tolerate one but not both."

"What do you think he'll do to Griff?"

"I don't know. How much did you fuck him up?"

"Oh, I fucked him up plenty," Bubba says, and I know he's replaying the fight in his head.

"As much as I loved watching him puke, I don't know if most of his battered face came from Sunday's fight or today's. Either way, my dad will talk to Griff. A fight will probably break out. If Keanu is there, it'll most definitely happen. My brother loves starting shit. Then Griff will behave for a day or two until he remembers how I've enjoyed another dick inside me. Everything will start over, but you'll be back in Conroe by that time."

"Maybe," he says, teasing me with the impossible. "Are you sure your dad can take Griff?"

"Did you just call my dad old?" I ask, lowering my voice to emphasize my disapproval.

"Sure, let's go with that."

"My father might be a middle-aged man whose best days are behind him, but he's also very aware of that fact. That's why at the start of a fight, he always kicks his opponent straight in the nuts. Making a guy's ears ring and his balls squeal provides Daddy with the upper hand," I say, full of pride. "Even if Griff managed to overcome his swollen balls long enough to fuck up my dad, Keanu would end him."

"He's a feisty little guy, huh?"

Rolling my eyes, I toss the cloth in Bubba's face. "Bikers are all the same. You respect Cap because of his size, but he could be a giant, lumbering wussy. He's not, obviously, but he could be. Then you look at Keanu who's less than your weight class and half a foot shorter, and you giggle at his talents. Well, keep snickering, asshole, because he'll fuck you up sideways."

Bubba leans his head back and bursts into laughter. Assuming he's mocking my brother, I plan to close up my pussy for business. I don't care if Bubba helped me out today. No one talks shit about my big bro.

"You're so damn sexy when your bitch meter goes up," he says, reaching for me. "I saw Keanu take down that biker with a karate chop at the bar. It was a sweet fucking move."

Once I realize he's showing my bro respect, I melt against Bubba. "Keanu always protects me. That's why I know if he gets unleashed on Griff, he'll end him. Keanu feels no loyalty to the club. He likes some of the guys, sure. Obviously, he's a huge fan of our dad. He even likes our uncle, who we are contractually obligated to state is less cool than our dad. But in the end, Keanu doesn't give a fuck if he has to kill a few bikers. He works for the Hayes family, not the Brotherhood. He's protected by Hallstead money too. In fact, I'm surprised Keanu doesn't walk around killing people willy-nilly."

Losing his boyish grin, Bubba hisses, "I'd rather be the one who ends Griff."

"Do you really want to kill a man you don't know or is your declaration based on horny bravado?"

"I know he wanted to hurt you. There's nothing else to learn about the fucker."

"Then should I call my dad?"

"Wait, what was the second choice?" he asks, sitting on my tiny kitchen chair, arms wrapped around my waist, and smiling like he's hit the motherload.

"We get naked and blow through the box of condoms I bought last night."

Bubba lifts my shirt, sighing deeply enough to warm my tits with his hot breath. Then he grins up at me again. "I didn't hear anything after naked, but, yeah, I vote for the thing where you're spread out on the bed with your pussy wet and willing. Yes, that."

I've craved his lips on mine since I drove away from Audrey's house. This kind of need isn't like me. I've never been the sexually obsessive type. In fact, I gave up dating in high school after a guy roughed me up at a party, forcing me to accept I wasn't the badass I'd assumed. That wake-up call made me wary of men. I'd opened up to Griff completely, and he made me pay for that decision.

I should be afraid to do the same with Bubba. Some part of me is probably scared. But I want this man so fucking bad that I can't see past him, me, and the box of condoms.

THE RUNAWAY

Soso hypnotizes me with her belly dancing. I watch her rolling hips as she strips out of her clothes. The floral shirt sails onto a plush chair where her dog lounges. Her ratty blue jean shorts fly toward the couch. Her bra whips past me. When her panties fly in my direction, I catch them.

Moving closer while her hips drop and rotate to a silent song, I'm careful to avoid spooking her and ruin her mating dance. Soon, she reclines naked on the couch, knees up with her pussy in full view.

Soso offers me a gift, and I know exactly how to thank her.

My hands rest on her knees as I sink down to the ground. Her pink flesh glistens with arousal before I even touch it. Soso breathes heavily, nipping at her bottom lip. Her nipples are rock-hard.

"I don't know what to taste first."

Then I catch sight of the worry in her deep brown eyes. No one forced her to expose herself completely to a man she's known for less than two days. Soso removes all barriers, stripping totally bare because she knows I'm not any guy. Just like I've known she isn't any woman.

My lips cover Soso's, wanting to reassure her. I'm not that asshole Griff. I'm an asshole, for sure, but never like him.

When our lips part, her gaze only reveals arousal. With her worry gone, she gently strokes my jaw and then my throat before tugging my shirt over my head.

I kiss her again, sucking at her lower lip. I nip at her jaw, lick at her throat, moving lower, wanting to taste and tease my way to the sweet spot waiting between her legs.

My teeth nibble at her teardrop-shaped tits. Nuzzling my face between them, I inhale her sweet, earthy scent. Soso's right hand slides between her legs, hoping to soothe the wet flesh.

I hold her gaze while shaking my head. Replacing her hand with mine, I smile at how her breath catches when my index finger circles her swollen clit.

Her hips flex, wanting more. Sweat breaks out across her body, and her cheeks flush.

Throbbing in my jeans, my dick begs to come out and play with the hot pussy at our disposal.

I keep it locked up. There's time. First, I want to suck on her pale nipples and make Soso come hard enough to forget anyone's ever fucked her before. Then I'll fill her with my cock and make her beg for more.

Soso cries out when I suck her left nipple into my mouth and apply more pressure to her clit. Her hips buck, and her fingers comb through my hair.

I use my free hand to pinch at her left nipple. Her whimpers make my dick hurt. Unable to fit in my fucking jeans any longer, I finally tear open the fly and shove them down to release my cock from its prison.

Soso sees my erection, and that's all she wrote. Crying out my name, she gasps in a way that'll feed my ego for a long fucking time. Soso throws her head back and moans overwhelmed with pleasure.

But I offer her no time to recover.

Lowering myself between her legs, I sigh with approval at the sight of her wet pussy spread for me. My fingers open her wider before my tongue savors her juices.

Breath hitching, Soso wears a dazed expression. I don't know why I find the look so intoxicating, but I'm dying to see her expression after her second orgasm.

"Bubba," she whispers. "I want you inside me."

Face wet from her juices, I lick my lips and shake my head. No way am I done. The feel of my tongue fondling her clit makes her whimper again. I promise my dick to hold on for a little longer. Just until I make our woman come undone one more time without its help.

Soso groans with her orgasm, nearly in pain. Her nails dig into my scalp until she's about to draw blood. Then her hands reach for the couch cushions and fuck them up royally. I swear she throws one of them over my head during her last wild cry of pleasure.

"Hell, Bubba, I need your dick!" she cries, gripping her tits.

I smile up at her from my tasty spot between her legs. "You didn't say please."

Soso opens her mouth, and I sense I'm about to get some attitude. I don't know what happens in her head. If she sees or feels something that turns off the bitch alarm. I only know her irritation disappears, leaving behind a smile.

"Please, fuck me, Nikolas Davies."

Hearing her say my real name seals the deal. I'm marrying this woman. No logic about it. I just know I need to spend the rest of my life with Soso. No one else will ever fucking do.

The way she sighs when I finally fuck her says what words never can. She opened herself up to a stranger, tried not to hope too much about my potential, got her heart set on me anyway, and now she knows she's won the lottery. Yeah, her expression says it all.

I fuck Soso on the couch. It's quick, hard, and a little angry since my dick's been in heat since we left her yesterday.

The second time begins when she slides off the couch and turns around so her ass can tease me back to full-staff. She's come plenty. I ought to be begging her for more, but she's the one in heat. I don't blame her. Everything feels better with her, and I see the same realization on her face when I wrap her in my arms. The woman knows we're the real deal.

Our third round moves to her bed with the elephant looking down at me while she leisurely rides my dick for thirty minutes.

"I can't believe how incredible you make me feel," she whispers, cuddling next to me after we wear ourselves out for now.

"You're welcome," I say, and Soso laughs while pinching my belly.

"I'd be mad for such arrogance, but you earned it."

"I'm staying here tonight," I announce after she's quiet for nearly a minute.

"Okay."

Exhaling with relief, I'd been ready to beg, threaten, and beg again if necessary.

"I brought my crap."

"I saw that."

"Would you have let me stay if I hadn't satisfied you so thoroughly?"

Soso sits up and smiles down at me. "I woke up this morning fully planning on tricking you into hanging out at my house until your vacation was over."

"Trick me how?"

"Well, you saw my belly dancing," she says, smiling slyly. "Both saving me with Griff and fucking me into a state of zen were bonuses I didn't need, but I'm very thankful to have."

My ego fucking explodes under her gaze. I swear I was a little boy when I arrived in Tennessee. Soso's made me a full-fledged man. Not bad for a hippie chick.

"He's jealous," Soso says, picking up Freki and resting him on the bed.

The dog watched us fuck. Like just stared at us the entire time. Though I bet some of his curiosity was from the noises Soso made. She sounds so shocked when shit feels good. No doubt Griff was terrible in bed. He's got the look of a guy with performance issues.

"You don't seem like a little dog kind of woman."

"Freki was a gift from Griff," she says, and I immediately lose my smile. I want that guy erased from existence. The fact that he ever owned a moment of Soso's time pisses me off to no end.

"What kind of man gets a dog for his girlfriend?" I ask despite knowing I'd buy anything for Soso just to earn a smile from her.

"He wanted me to have a normal pet," she says, stroking the dog in her lap. "He claimed birds weren't friendly, but the girls just didn't like him. He was always hinting that they'd be happier at the sanctuary. Then one day, he showed up with a little dog he thought would be a good pet."

"The guy's a control freak."

"Yes, exactly," she says, looking relieved to hear someone else say it. "And I was very aware of how he didn't get me a big dog that might react negatively to his yelling."

"How often did he yell at you?" I growl, sitting up and preparing to hunt down the asshole.

Soso wants to laugh at my anger. She fights against a smile, finally biting her lower lip while stroking my forehead.

"None of that matters because he and I have been over for months."

"It matters to me."

"The irony is Freki was the reason we finally broke up. He bought me this little dog, thinking it was no threat. Then Griff would get pissed when Freki barked at him when we'd argue. Every time, Griff would yell at the dog. That final time, he grabbed Freki as if he was going to throw him. What kind of man would hurt something so small and defenseless?"

"A monster."

No matter how much Soso pretends she's unbothered by her past, I see the darkness in her eyes. She nods at my response, relieved that I understand how she saw Griff that day.

"I should have dumped him long before he tried to hurt Freki. In some way, I was just as bad as Griff. I didn't see him as him. I found excuses for his behavior. When he brought me random gifts that I'd never in a million years buy for myself, I should have wondered why he never picked things I'd like. Instead, I assumed he was just clueless. Men aren't great at gift giving. When he lost his temper and yelled, I should have worried. But he's a biker, and you idiots have tempers," she says, giving me a little smile. "My parents argue. Sometimes loudly. I just kept thinking Griff was like my dad, but I saw qualities that weren't there."

"You have an idealized view of your parents' marriage," I murmur and smile. "I know the feeling."

"I often wondered where Griff got Freki," Soso says, lowering her voice as if sharing a secret. "He wasn't a puppy and was well-groomed. I even questioned if Griff stole him. When I took Freki to the vet for the first time, I was ready to hear he was microchipped, and someone was looking for him. He wasn't, but I've always worried Griff stole Freki from an old lady or one of his side pieces. He gave me a bracelet once that I got the feeling was stolen too. Not from a store but from a person."

Soso sighs, looking almost embarrassed by her confession. "I ignored those feelings. Even when he started pushing me to do things I didn't want to do, I found reasons why he wasn't a bad guy. Then he freaked out on Freki, and I knew he was wrong in the head. It's normal to get frustrated with your girlfriend. I get that. Plus, I can stand up for myself. But picking on a defenseless creature is sick."

Soso trails off and shrugs. "I asked myself why I was staying with him. Why make excuses for a guy when there were plenty of others in the world? Besides, I didn't love him. We'd been together for months. He said he loved me. I couldn't say it back. I wanted to lie just to get him to stop nagging me, but the words hold too much weight. He still claims I said them, but he just heard what he wanted. Then after the crap with Freki, I really looked at Griff and asked myself how I felt. And the answer was 'eh.' I didn't feel much of anything. We were only still together because I'd gotten used to putting up with him at that point."

Soso studies my face and then smiles. "You want to know what I think when I look at you, don't you?"

"No. I'm good," I lie.

Smiling, she rests the dog next to us before crawling closer to me on the bed. "I think I wouldn't have let you close if you hadn't been wasted that first night. I saw a side of you that made me want to see more."

"But you like sober me too, right?"

"I like every version of you," she says and then adds, "So far."

"As compared to Griff?" I ask, needing reassurance. Is she just into bikers? Am I reading too much into her behavior? Is this woman going to tear out my heart and feed it to her tiny dog? I need to know we're on the same page out loud and not just in my head.

Soso cuddles closer and strokes my head. "I like you more in two days than I did with him for six months."

"Six months?" I blurt out without thinking. "How could you endure him for so long?"

"I didn't spend every fucking minute with the guy!" she cries, sitting up and putting space between us. The mood in the room shifts and she asks, "What was the longest relationship you've had?"

"Two weeks."

"That's what we'll manage," she says, her lower lip pushing out into a pout. "But you can visit my bed anytime."

"I'm not leaving you."

Soso narrows her eyes. "What does that mean?"

"I think that's obvious."

"You thought wrong. I'm too wound up over you to see clearly."

"I need you."

"And you plan to stay here?" she asks, giving me a distrustful frown.

"Possibly."

"And do what?"

"Live off your money."

Laughing, Soso erases the space she created between us. Now attached to me, she says, "No, really. It's not like you can join the local club."

"Not unless I want my mother to go on a murder spree."

"Who would she kill?"

Unwilling to think of Soso harmed, I lie, "I don't know."

Nodding, she returns to stroking my head. "Do you have it in you to go straight?"

My smile fades. "Before I was born, my pop had a dark streak. He did cage fighting in college and got a dragon tattoo on his back." Hearing about Pop's ink, Soso presses me forward onto my stomach. I know she wants to investigate the dragon tattoo on my lower back. I got it in honor of my pop, but I wanted mine different enough not to copy him.

"Like this one?" she asks, kisses along my flesh and rousing my dick.

"His is bigger. But he didn't want a life in crime. Growing up, he was poor and got fucked up by his dad. Pop's dream was to be normal. He got his suburban, common man life despite the Johanssons' family business happening around him. Pop became a teacher and is now a principal."

"That's a nice story, Bubba, but that's him. What about what you want?"

I adjust on the bed until we're resting on our sides, facing each other. Soso craves reassurance. That makes sense. I'm an unknown. A complete fucking stranger who owns her heart.

"What if I said I wanted to stay here with you and focus on construction work?"

"I'd be okay with that."

"Are you sure you don't want a biker like your daddy?" I ask as my fingers stroke her scarred shoulder.

"At this point, I think I just want you," she says and covers herself with a blanket as if for protection. "But you don't want to go straight."

"I could."

"You could do a lot of stuff, but we're talking about what will actually happen."

"I want you."

"Let's say you have me," she whispers in a voice stripped of all its strength. She's laying her heart bare and asking me not to fucking stomp on it. "What happens then?"

"I don't know."

Soso exhales deeply and reclines on the bed. "I'd glad you're honest with me rather than promising lies."

"Why do you look upset then?"

"I'm going to miss you," she says, fighting a pout while her eyes threaten tears.

"How, when I expect you to be at my side for-fucking-ever?"

"Let's see if you're still so high on us when you're dressed and we've known each other for at least a week."

I scoot closer until we're sharing the blanket. Soso cups my jaw while her thumbs stroke my swollen lips.

"That night at the bar, I thought of you as a hunky puppy. You sorta bounced around, and I wanted you to be sweet under all your muscles and tats. You're so handsome, and I'm a sucker for hot bikers, but I didn't want you to be like him. I wanted you to be sweet inside too."

"Do you still want me to be sweet?"

"I want you to be you. Whoever that guy is, I want him."

Throwing back the blanket, I scoot down on the bed and lick at her stomach. "A puppy, huh?"

Her worry lingers around the edges despite giggling and squirming under my licking tongue. I know fucking won't fix her fears, but it'll distract from them until I can prove I'm worth whatever pain the future offers us.

THE BOHEMIAN

My dad's dark eyes zero in on my throat hickey as soon as he enters the house. Of course, he doesn't say anything about it. His mind is on Griff.

I kept things simple on the phone. His club brother showed up, threatened to take Freki, and fought with Bubba. I skip the part where I dumped paint on Griff's chopper or how he chased me around the yard for nearly ten minutes. My father will see those details on the surveillance footage.

"What's he doing here?" Dad asks after he and Keanu enter my house.

"He was injured during the fight with Griff, and I offered to heal him."

My father allows a small smile. He sees too much of him in me. Yeah, Daddy was proudly pussy-obsessed back in the day. He might not want his only daughter going cock-crazy, but he can't claim he doesn't understand the urge to try new things.

"What did you dump on the asshole's bike?" Keanu asks, having pulled up the footage on his phone.

"Old paint."

"Should have dumped it on his fucking head," Dad grumbles.

"This isn't acceptable," Keanu says in his cold, killer voice.

"Have you gotten to the part where Bubba comes to my rescue?"

"No, I'm at the part where Griff looks ready to punch you."

Dad grabs the phone, glares at it menacingly, and then decides Bubba is the bad guy.

"Where the fuck were you when this was happening?"

"Stuck in traffic, sir."

"Stop calling me that."

Bubba only smirks at my father's complaint. I'm unshocked to learn that Johanssons refuse to be easily intimidated.

"How long did this go on?" Keanu asks, still watching the video surveillance.

"I didn't check my watch. A few minutes, I guess."

Dad glares hard at Bubba. "You did this."

"I can see how you'd think that, sir."

"Asshole," Dad gripes before grabbing Keanu's phone. "Where's the part where Kentucky saves the day?"

I squeeze in between my father and brother. "Is there a way to scan ahead?"

"How much forward?" Dad growls as Keanu speeds us through almost ten minutes of Griff and me circling the lawn.

"It's coming up."

"Dammit, Num-Num, you can't waste that much of your life. Next time, take the shot rather than hoping some idiot from Kentucky will save you."

"I didn't have my gun."

"Well, that was your mistake right there."

"I thought it was Bubba at the door, and then I was just focused on keeping Griff out of the house and away from Freki."

Dad and Keanu look at the dog who yawns on cue. He's never been impressed by them.

"Here it is."

I smile at the sight of Bubba appearing like a missile strike across the lawn. My gaze finds him, and he looks about as bored as Freki.

"Are we keeping you?" I mutter.

"I'm tired after a strenuous day," he says, wiggling his eyebrows.

Grinning like a fool, I return my gaze to the sight of him and Griff clashing.

"I've seen enough," Dad growls and directs his anger at Bubba. "A lot of men wouldn't put their ride in danger to protect a woman. Even one who looks like Soso. I respect that you did that, but you're still a turd in my book."

"Thank you, sir."

Dad grunts at how Bubba's respectful term keeps coming off as an insult. The men eye one another while I focus on my brother.

Keanu holds my gaze for too long. His black eyes ask if I want Griff dead. Years ago, when I thought I was a badass bitch, I went to a party near Nashville. I was thirteen, but my tits had come in, and the college-aged guys were drooling all over me. It was the first time I felt sexy after spending most of my childhood wanting to be a dude like my dad.

One second, I was dancing around, having a ball. The next, my face was pinned against a wall while some guy yanked up my skirt. I couldn't move. Suddenly powerless, I froze up. I didn't know how to handle myself in this grown-up situation.

Then the guy was gone from behind me. Turning around, I found Keanu standing casually over the wannabe rapist.

"You broke my ribs," the guy whined to my brother. "I'm going to call the fucking cops."

"Good because right now you're a stranger to me," Keanu said patiently, leaning over the asshole. "After the police take the report, I'll have your name, date of birth, and address. With that information, I'll get the rest of your info. You'll never again be able to hide from me."

Keanu didn't growl like our dad would in such a situation. He spoke calmly. His face seemed more bored than anything. But I'd never seen that icy look in his eyes before.

I learned a lot that night. As a woman, I was vulnerable, no matter how much my father trained me. I could never let down my guard, especially around strangers—a lesson I tossed aside to bring home a hunky puppy days ago.

I also learned my brother was a fucking badass with the capability of erasing people. Despite that guy not calling the cops and instead hobbling out of the party, I noticed how my brother swiped his wallet. No reason to do that unless he wanted to pay the guy a visit.

Keanu gives me that same look now, and I'm not sure how to answer.

"Daddy, how much trouble would it be to kill Griff?"

"I'll do it," Bubba says immediately.

My father takes a step toward him and growls, "Stay the fuck away from my club, Johansson."

"What would it take to make it happen?" I ask Dad while stepping between the two men.

"We'd just need to ask your uncle who will want to take a vote. Camden's very into democracy since he watched those documentaries about the Revolution."

"How do you think the club would vote?"

Dad's expression is the only answer he gives. The club won't kill one of their own over a relationship tiff. I return my gaze to Keanu. He doesn't care about club rules, but Griff's death—or suspicious disappearance—would be a hassle. If a tiny-ass fight at Salty Peanuts riled up tensions between the Brotherhood and Hayes family, I can't imagine a scenario where Hickory Creek and Mayo Pony don't battle over a dead patched member.

"If killing him isn't an option," I say, and Keanu looks disappointed, "what should I do?"

"You don't do shit, Num-Num. I'll handle Griff."

"How?"

"Embarrass him in front of the other guys."

"That doesn't seem like a good plan."

Dad rubs my head. "No, see, Griff wants approval from his club. No one's gonna applaud him coming over here acting like a bitch and getting his ass kicked by Kentucky."

"I did kick his ass, sir."

Dad's gaze narrows. "Yeah, until my baby girl had to save your ass with a shotgun. Don't think I didn't notice that part."

"We worked as a team, Daddy," I say, standing next to Bubba.

Dad narrows his eyes more until he looks asleep. "What is this? What's happening here?"

"He's on vacation."

"In her pants," Bubba says because all the sex clearly shorted out his common sense.

What he doesn't expect is for my father to be relieved by the idea that I'm only into Bubba's heavenly looks and tempting body. If he knew how hard I was crushing on this Kentucky boy, Dad would sic Keanu on the interloper.

But he doesn't know. That's why he calmly leaves my house. He focuses on handling Griff. Keanu follows him out the door, likely planning to share with Cap how killing one of the Brotherhood is in their future.

Either way, I wrap my arms around Bubba and decide to make his vacation in Hickory Creek the best thing ever. Even if his eventual return to Conroe will kill a little part of me.

Sharing his grin, I know any suffering will be well worth it.

THE CHAPTER WHERE DAYS TURN INTO A WEEK
THE RUNAWAY

I settle into a domesticated life in the triangle house with Soso. With so little space, we can't avoid each other. *It's fucking perfect.*

I quickly gel with Soso's routine. Every morning, she wakes up and nibbles on berries and granola. *Yep, my heart belongs to a squirrel.* However, Soso isn't one of those people who thinks everyone ought to be like her. In fact, I think she'd be horrified if she was normal. No, she realizes I need much more food to be satisfied. That's why on day one, we go grocery shopping and stock up on as much of my crap as her little fridge can fit.

Afterward, we eat dinner out. Soso doesn't like to cook, and I'm an ace at burning food. Then we stop by a health clinic to get tested.

"I don't mind condoms, but I'd rather not have to mind them, you know?" she says.

We share a smile, relieved to prove our healthy statuses. I don't blame her for worrying. She knows how bikers and club whores go together like peanut butter and jelly. *Or chlamydia and herpes.*

We finish out that evening at the bird sanctuary where Soso introduces me to her first love—Odin. The enormous gray African parrot speaks a lot more than cuss words like Grinch. Odin says her name—well, Soda—and how he loves her. He even sings part of "Cruel Summer" by Bananarama while riding her shoulder as she walks around the enclosure. A few times, he eyeballs me as if I'm moving in on his chick, but there's no violence. Mostly because I don't throw attitude back at him. Soso insists I respect the power of these birds in a way Griff never did.

"They'll fuck you up," she warns more than once.

"Would you still want me if I lost an eye to your boyfriend?" I ask one day as we leave the sanctuary.

"Sure. Would you still want me if I lost an eye?"

"I think I'd want you more."

"Why?" she asks, wearing the sexiest frown.

"Because everything makes me want you more."

Words like those make it difficult for Soso to stay practical. Oh, sure, she tries. Like how she regularly mentions that driving down to visit me in Conroe will be easy. There's much talk of a long-distance relationship.

"I'll visit you. You'll visit me. It'll be fun," she says more than once.

I nod along when she claims long-distance loving is going to be a fucking ball, but I'm full of shit. No way can I tolerate being away from Soso for days at a time. I've never wanted a girlfriend before. In fact, real dating felt like a hassle. I've seen how much work my parents put into their relationship. No woman before Soso inspired me to put in the effort.

But she isn't ready to accept what we both know will happen. Either I'll give up my family and town, or she'll give up hers. Which way that tide turns is what scares her most.

One big step for Soso is taking me out to eat in Hickory Creek rather than hiding in White Horse. People notice us. I catch them staring. Their existence means nothing to me, and I can't tell if they mean anything to her. Soso pretends not to notice. Able to read her body language, I'm not fooled by Soso's cool demeanor. She hates feeling on display.

Her gaze is always searching for trouble, meaning Griff. She gets tense when Harleys ride by. Her safe hometown is no longer so serene.

Conroe doesn't sound like it's running smoothly either. Mom calls a dozen times a day. Butch eventually texts too. Nothing about Sissy or our fight. He just asks when I'm returning. Butch wouldn't contact me if he weren't agitated.

I finally break down and call Mom on Sunday when she claims my uncle Cooper is out to get her.

"Hey, Mom. How are you?" I ask while Soso works in the backyard on her garden.

"Thank the Lord, my boy is safe," she says, faking a vulnerability I'm not buying. "Where are you, baby?"

"In America."

"Did I not love you enough?" she demands, dropping on a dime her soft mommy persona. "Is that why you're fucking with me?"

"You loved me the exact right amount."

"Then why are you pulling this game with me?" Mom asks, sounding brokenhearted now. "Why can't I know where you are?"

I'm certain Audrey has told her pop where I am, meaning Cooper hasn't shared this information with my mom. *Typical Johansson sibling rivalry crap.*

"If you know where I am, you might show up and lecture me."

"Ah, that means you're close enough for me to show up," Mom mutters before hissing the words, "If you're hiding in Conroe, I'm kicking your ass."

Laughing, I can't deny missing her bitchiness. "I'm not in Kentucky."

"When are you coming home?"

"Soon."

"Your brother is very sorry he hurt your heart."

"Yeah, and I'm sure he used those exact words too."

"He's been seduced by the Mullen hussy."

"Sissy doesn't know how to seduce anyone," I say, feeling like my time with Butch's girl was a million years ago.

"Don't be naïve."

"You aren't mean to Sissy, are you?"

"Of course not. I'm a fucking saint."

"Good. Butch needs someone who can put up with his shit."

"He's a saint too."

Before I can push the subject, Soso asks if she can turn on her New Age music. Mom's mommy-senses kick into gear.

"Who's your hussy?"

"A goddess."

"A woman from Conroe?"

"I'm not in Conroe, remember?"

"Maybe you had a whore here and you two ran off."

"But I was dating Sissy before I left."

"Well, maybe you're a whore too. So many fucking whores," Mom grumbles.

"She's someone I met here."

"Where?"

"In the place I am."

"Where?"

"That's not going to work."

"I miss you, honey," Mom says tenderly.

"That's not going to work either."

"Who's the hussy?"

"I'll tell you when I get back to town."

"And when will that be?"

"Soon."

"Is this whore keeping you captive? Signal me if you need saving."

"How would you save me if you don't know where I am?"

"I'll find you, Nikolas Davies. My uterus will locate you and draw me to your location."

Despite knowing Mom isn't kidding, her words still make me laugh. "I wanted you to know I'm safe, and I'll be home soon."

"I want you home now."

"I need a little more time."

"Why? Butch is sorry. He told me this morning," she says and adds, "While he was crying."

"Yeah, you didn't really sell that lie."

"He just isn't a crier," she says, sighing. "Buzz cried, though. He misses you so much."

"That I believe."

"We all miss you."

"I'll be home soon."

"Alone?"

"No."

"Ugh, you're all whores. It's this family. Pop and Mom were great, but then it all went to shit with your uncles. I'm not a huge fan of your aunt right now either. She's trying to make me fat."

"I love you."

Mom sighs again, and I feel her anger deflate. "Come home, baby. Even if you have to bring a skank with you, I just miss my boy."

"Soon. I promise."

Hanging up with Mom, I'm torn. Conroe needs me back, but I can't take Soso from her home yet. She isn't ready to willingly leave with me, and forcing her to go isn't an option. Not while her family still thinks I'm a fling.

There's too much hanging in the air, but something will have to give soon.

THE BOHEMIAN

Every morning, I wake up terrified today is when Bubba will leave Hickory Creek. Then I roll over to find him watching me—the guy runs on so little sleep—and he smiles in a way that makes the fear bearable.

Right this very second, we're happy. Nothing else matters. Tomorrow might suck. The next day might break my heart, but for this minute—hour, day, week—we're happy.

Sharing a space with Bubba is so different from how life was with Griff. My ex never stayed over for more than a night, but we were always on each other's nerves. Griff seemed restless, bored maybe, but when I tried to pull away and give him space, he'd hold me tighter. He was at his most adoring when I had one foot out the door.

With Bubba, I see how relaxed life should be. Not that we don't get on each other's nerves, of course. It's all so new. The house is small. And there's no privacy. But when we snap at each other, the tension quickly shifts into either sex or laughter. His angry face cracks me up, and my pissed expression makes him super horny.

Best of all, when the tension is over, it's just gone. Nothing hangs in the air. The oppressive, unspoken strain that clung to Griff and me doesn't exist in my relationship with Bubba.

But my ex-boyfriend isn't gone from my life. Dad talked to him, man-to-man. He also threatened to show the surveillance video to the rest of the club to embarrass him. Griff agreed to stay away from me.

Yet I'm not particularly surprised to spot him climbing out of a truck parked in front of my house. Out of habit, I freeze at the sight of him. The fear of running into him often lingers in the back of my mind. Now he's back at my house.

Behind me, Bubba warms a TV dinner to hold off starvation until dinner. We spent the afternoon working in the backyard, followed by garden sex, and then the most awkward shower foreplay imaginable—my bathtub is NOT built for two—and finally a quickie in bed to finish off what we started under the water.

Hearing the truck park outside, Bubba glances up, but I don't react to his silent question. Instead, I peek out from the curtains to find Griff carrying something behind him as he walks to the porch.

"My mom texted to say worrying over me has given her malaria," Bubba says, snickering. "I've gone ahead and sent her 'get well' flowers."

I don't know what to do. Do I sic Bubba on Griff? Or not answer the door he's about to knock on? Perhaps open it while pointing my gun?

Then before I can decide, I hear the distinctive song of my girls.

Heart pounding, I look back outside and spot a small birdcage behind Griff's back. I take a deep breath and demand I remain calm.

I can't go off half-cocked and get my birds killed. No ego right now. I need to keep my cool. Griff isn't a stranger. I know how to talk to him. My anger can stuff it until I get my birds to safety.

Reaching for Bubba, I force him to look me in the eyes. "Remember when I told you to back away from Grinch, and you obeyed me without asking a million questions?"

"Sure," he mutters, narrowing his gaze and focusing on the knock on the door.

"This is the same situation, Nikolas Davies. You must trust me. Obey me too. Mainly stay the fuck in here while I deal with Griff."

"No—"

I snap my fingers at Bubba and point at the ground. "Stay."

"I'm not your fucking dog."

"Prove you're smarter than Freki who refuses to stay when I tell him."

Bubba grits his teeth and shakes his head and maybe stomps his feet. Ignoring his momentary irritation, I focus on my long-term goal. Finally, I open the door just enough to slide through without revealing who else is inside.

Two days ago, Bubba moved his Harley to the backyard after I got paranoid about someone fucking with it. I'd guess that's why Griff feels it's safe to stop by. He believes I'm alone. I want him to keep thinking that.

Griff holds the birdcage behind him as he stands straighter at the sight of me.

"What's up?" I ask, trying not to sound too friendly or particularly bitchy.

"I wanted to talk to you."

My gaze remains on his still bruised face rather than focusing on the birdcage. I know it's there. He knows I know. Yet we dance around the obvious.

"About what?" I ask.

"I know I fucked up things between us. I should have listened more. Been a better man for you. I didn't show you how much you mean to me. How much I love you."

A worried lump sits at the back of my throat. I'm so sick of talking about us. If he didn't have my birds, I'd flip him off and run back inside.

But he does have them.

Bjork and Ula chatter to each other in the cage. The sound is like magic. I'd accepted they were dead, gone forever. Now I have them within reach, but Griff is the kind of man who'd bring them here only to turn around and kill them as revenge.

Icy calm, I say, "We both made mistakes."

Griff almost smiles at my answer. He's convinced if I just listen that he can talk me into loving him again. During our time together, I did a lot of stuff I didn't want to do because he kept talking, nagging, bitching, whining, whatever it took to wear me down.

Now, he sees an opening to do it again.

"I was never going to hurt Freki."

"I think I knew that," I say and then add since I sound too soft to be believable, "But you scared me that day."

"I know. I got jealous. Wouldn't you be jealous if I was with someone else?"

Without a doubt, Griff has fucked plenty of women since we broke up. I always assumed he had a few on the side when we were dating too. No way was I enough for him.

But I only nod because I want my birds back. That's how Griff always won. Wanting to sleep, I'd agree to sex to shut him up. If I wanted to go somewhere, I relented to whatever stupid thing he wanted. I backed down over and over.

Until one day, I just didn't. I'm sure for Griff—whose world revolves around himself—that my change in behavior must have come as quite a shock. In his mind, I was irrational. He probably convinced plenty of the club guys and their old ladies of the same thing. I didn't know what I was missing. He just needed another chance. I was too young to know what I gave up. *Blah, blah, blah.*

Now I stand in front of him, backing down to his will again. The tension around his jaw and shoulders ease. He even smiles.

"I wanted to do something for you to show I was sorry."

I swallow hard, begging Bubba not to come outside just yet. I can feel him watching us from behind the curtains, or maybe he's spying on the security camera. I catch Griff looking at the window more than once. *Please, Bubba, behave...*

"I asked around to see if anyone had found any birds a few months back. See, I thought that since they were domesticated that someone might have found them and taken them in as pets."

"That makes sense," I lie, wondering where the fuck my birds have been.

"This lady got back to me about two birds she found in her yard."

I could tear apart his stupid-ass story so quickly, but my ego is on sleep mode. I just want my girls back safe and sound. They're gurgling and chirping behind him. They're within reach.

"Those are my birds?" I ask like an idiot. "I mean, Bjork and Ula? I thought maybe you brought me new ones, but those are my actual girls?"

Griff sees my reaction and smiles in that way I used to find endearing. He can be so handsome and likable when he wants. Right now, he really, really hopes to charm the hell out of me. That way, I'll dump Kentucky and fuck him again. In his mind, my pussy is within reach.

"Can I see them?" I ask in a tender voice I'm not faking.

The reality of my girls being alive hits me hard, and tears well up in my eyes. Griff's loving my reaction. He probably enjoyed the tears I shed when they went missing too. The guy's a dick, but right now, I will kiss his whiny ass to get my birds safely into the house.

Gesturing for me to come closer to them, Griff basks in my tears and smiles. When I say hello to the girls, and they hear their names, they dance around. I instantly descend into laughing sobs. I dreamed they were alive and would show up at the back porch. I couldn't understand why they'd leave. That's why I had to accept they were dead.

And now they're singing to me!

"The lady took good care of them," Griff says, stroking my head as I kneel down. "They look healthy, don't they?"

"They're beautiful."

My problem is how do I get them into the house without him freaking out? Birds can't handle stress, and I have no idea where they've been. While they're singing now, Griff could easily fuck up their cage before I have a chance to protect them.

Remaining calm, I stand up and stare into his blue eyes. I pretend I'm basking in the beauty of my hunky puppy. My heartbeat calms, and I wear a relaxed smile.

"You can't know how much this means to me," I whisper, wiping my wet cheeks. "There are no words."

Griff reaches for my face, but I pretend to notice something behind him. "Is that a hawk?"

"What?" he asks, frowning in the direction I pretend to see the threat.

"There's a nest around here. Let me stick the birds inside to be safe," I say, brushing my hand against his.

Griff is so accustomed to getting his way with women that he doesn't even consider that I'm playing him. I'm sure Bubba suffers from the same blindness. Gorgeous men—especially dangerous ones—lose sight of other people.

I don't even look into the house when I shuffle the birds to safety. Watching Griff, I pretend I can't take my eyes off him. It works, and I shut the door behind me.

Now what?

"You did a good thing today, Griff," I say as his hand again reaches for me.

"I just need another chance to make you happy."

"Let's get together for coffee tomorrow and talk," I say, needing him to leave.

His jaw clenches while his fingers dig into my loose hair. "Why can't we have coffee now?"

I realize this situation is about to get messy since there's no way I can invite Griff into the house, and there's no way Bubba will let me leave with the douchebag.

Before I can panic, the door opens, and Griff steps back, ready for a fight.

"Cool move with the birds, dude," Bubba says, walking onto the porch.

I notice two things. One, there's a pistol shoved into the front of Bubba's jeans, opening up the possibility of a mishap that'll cause him to lose a testicle. Two, he took off his shirt before exiting the house.

Griff's gaze is so locked on his competition that he takes a minute to realize he's lost his bargaining chip now that the birds are inside. Once he accepts that he's been duped, I see his expression shift from anger to something uglier.

"Thank you for finding them, Griff," I say with as much heartfelt emotion as I can fake. "It means so much."

"Sure, it does, bitch."

Hearing that word directed at me, Bubba makes a move for Griff. I step between them and whisper to my hunky puppy, "Let's go inside."

My current man glares over my head at my former man. Both want a third matchup while my goal is to keep everyone in one piece. *Bubba's poor face has been battered enough.*

"I'll be sure to let my dad know how you found the girls," I tell Griff despite him being well past buying my bullshit.

"You deserve each other," he hisses and storms off to his truck.

Bubba wraps his arms around me and sighs. "He isn't wrong. My mom always told me I was a superstar and look at who I ended up with."

"You and your fucking mom," I grumble, pushing him into the house where he can stop showing off.

I close the door, lock it, and exhale unsteadily. Freki sits next to the cage, smelling the birds who talk to each other. I'm still so afraid something bad will happen that I can barely catch my breath.

Then seeing Bubba standing there, I burst into laughter. "You took off your fucking shirt? What's wrong with you?"

"If you've got it, flaunt it, babe," he says, lifting his arms and proudly spinning around.

"Did your mom tell you that?"

"I know you worry she won't like you but don't stress, Soso," he says, kissing my head. "She doesn't like any of the women I bang."

Poking him in the ribs, I ignore his laughter. "I fucked nineteen men."

Bubba's amusement ends immediately. "I'll need their names and addresses."

"For what?" I ask, kneeling down to check my birds.

"I'm making a list. Griff's on the top, but those other guys are on it too."

"Might have been closer to thirty, now that I think about it."

"Why are you trying to make me cry?" he asks, sitting down next to the cage and looking at my birds.

Smiling, I stroke his jaw. "It might have been less than nineteen."

"Better."

"How many women were you with again? I forget the number."

"Only the one before you. I think she taught me well, but I don't remember her name."

"I like that answer. Griff might have been my only other lover, but he didn't teach me shit."

Enjoying my response, Bubba smiles like a happy kid. Then he gestures to the cage and asks, "Want to introduce me to your girls?" His kind gesture sends me immediately into tears. Of course, to a man, my behavior is insane, and he assumes the worst. "They're not messed up, are they?"

"It's not that," I mumble, overwhelmed by the realization that I'll follow this man anywhere. How can I not? Bubba obeyed me when I told him to remain in the house. I know it had to kill him, but he trusted me enough to let things play out.

"You're going to break my heart," I whisper. "I thought I could fuck you and forget you, but you're so you. How can I not love Bubba Davies?"

"I love you too, Num-Num. There's no reason to cry."

"What about when you leave?"

"I'm taking you with me."

"It's been less than two weeks," I whisper, struggling with the logical part of my brain. "That's shorter than your longest relationship."

Bubba's knuckles stroke my cheek. "Does this feel like anything you've ever known?"

"No, but I'm twenty-one, and you're twenty-two. We're too young to know better."

"You know that's not true."

"I'm afraid to leave my home."

"I know, but I have to have you," he says with complete sincerity. "There's no one else."

"But you also want Conroe."

Bubba looks pained when he says, "I can't be a working stiff like my pop."

"I know," I mumble, now sitting between his legs and resting my head against his hard chest. "There's no way I get to have everything. It's either Bubba or Hickory Creek.

"The winner is most definitely Bubba. Now that we've settled that, can you tell me their names again?" he asks, watching the girls in the cage.

"Bjork and Ula."

Bubba strokes my hair while studying the orange-yellow-and-white-feathered birds chattering at us. "They're smaller than Odin."

"He's an African parrot while they're Caique parrots. My dad wasn't okay with me adopting them until he realized they'd be less than a foot long and weigh less than a pound. He figured they couldn't hurt me like Odin did."

"You do what your father wants," he says, absentmindedly stroking the scar on my shoulder.

"About eighty percent of the time."

"And when he says to stay in Hickory Creek?"

Bubba's tone suddenly lacks his earlier boldness. Comforting him like he did me, I nuzzle his jaw. "My response will belong to the twenty percent."

He lifts my chin, and our gazes meet. "If you come with me to Conroe, I'll give you anything. Any weirdly shaped house you want, I'll buy or build for you. If you want a bird sanctuary in our backyard, it'll happen. I don't care what goofy names you give our kids or if you force me to watch you walk around the house naked all the time. I swear I'll be your slave if you give me this one thing."

My kiss reassures us both. I even find myself grinning at how much he wants me to give into my nudist leanings. Feeling raw after Griff, I hadn't been comfortable enough to be naked around the house. Now, I have my birds back and Bubba at my side.

After I check them over, Ula and Bjork get reacquainted with the house. Not knowing where they've been—their toys smell of cigarettes and the newspaper on the bottom of the cage is from Nashville—I don't rush them to do anything besides settle back into their home.

An hour later, I put on Loreena McKennitt's "The Mystic's Dream" and dress in my belly dancing costume. Before Bubba can devour me, I show off more of the moves I learned years ago in classes with my mom and aunts. Halfway through the song, the beat increases, and the birds take flight. They sail across the house, enjoying the high ceiling. Falling into their old habits, they rejoice at being home.

Soon, they'll have a new one. I doubt moving will be any easier for them than it is for me, but Bubba Davies—in all his shirtless glory—is worth any price.

THE RUNAWAY

Birds aren't my ideal pet. I never found them particularly interesting, despite spending time at the sanctuary. Odin makes me nervous because he clearly adores Soso, yet fucked up her shoulder when she was barely a teen.

However, after spending two days with Ula and Bjork, I'm pretty hooked on the girls. Ula is hilarious, always dancing around and being a crackup. Bjork enjoys cuddling and whistles whenever I speak to her.

Even if I didn't fall for the feathered flirts, Soso's smiles when with her birds would be enough for me to love them. In fact, their return makes her choice to move easier. Something just clicks inside Soso, and she's now willing to suffer a little pain to enjoy a bigger payoff. Hell, that asshole Griff did me a real solid. I'd thank him except he's also the piece of shit that hurt Soso in the first place. *The fucker can rot.*

Soso decides if she's moving to Conroe that I need to give her the details about my club and the town. No more dancing around the Dogs or how things work. One afternoon, we sit in the back booth of a nearly empty Hickory Creek restaurant, and I spell out the situation to ensure she can "have my back."

"If you're my man, I need to know your life," she explains. "I don't care if that's how it's done or not with the Reapers. I've got to be able to help you. When you're stressed, I can't wonder why. That's not going to work. You need a safe person to dump your shit on, and I'm going to be that person."

Without a doubt, loving Soso is the most natural thing I've ever done.

I tell her about the seven members of the Midnight Dogs Motorcycle Club. I explain how Vlad was their president and now Conroe's VP. His cousin, Lex, handles the prostitutes because he's a violent pig who wants power over vulnerable women. There's psycho Vigo who is one bad day from going on a shooting spree. The other guys hide behind Vlad and Lex. They barely even acknowledge I'm the president.

"Because I'm their leader in name only," I admit.

"That's going to change," she says immediately. I smile at how she doesn't even swallow before blurting out that reassurance. Soso refuses to let me feel like a failure.

"First off," she says in a low voice after I finish laying out the power structure in Conroe and the Reapers overall. I know it's a lot of names to learn, but she doesn't miss a beat. "You need to kill the Dogs. I know killing isn't easy. Why do you think I haven't just asked my brother to off Griff? I pretend I'm choosing rational over emotional as a way to prevent trouble for the club and the Hayes family. The reality is I can't be responsible for his death. He was a part of my life even before we dated. Having him killed is more than I can handle, so I do get that whacking seven guys isn't an easy suggestion."

I snort and mumble, "Whack."

"I do a brilliant Joe Pesci impression, but that can wait," Soso says, sharing my smile. "The point is those Dogs people will never be safe. They don't respect you. Nothing's going to change that. You can return to Conroe and act like the biggest badass, and they'll still see you as a kid. In fact, they'll be more dangerous if you actually intimidate them. That Vlad guy wants to be in charge. He can't do that if you're a badass. I think he's only behaved this long because he figures you're a child he can manipulate. Once he knows differently, he'll stab you in the back."

"But killing me just ends with him dead."

"I don't think a guy like Vlad thinks that far ahead. I'm sure he believes he's a wise motherfucker playing you all. From what you've said, Conroe wasn't much of a crime hub before the Reapers stepped in. I bet there are tons of solo dealers and hookers running around that ought to be under your power umbrella. The Dogs weren't smart or organized enough to expand their meager business. They started small and stayed that way. Because it's not business to them. It's about their egos. They want money to pay for shit and women to fuck. Everything else is beyond their tiny brains."

"Every time I think you can't make my dick any harder, you say or do something to prove me wrong."

Soso winks at me. "When you go back, you can't start wagging your dick around. I know you have it in you to be in charge and make men respect you. Hell, I bet you can even get your mom to treat you like a grownup."

"Did you just call me a mama's boy and her a bitch?"

Grinning, Soso refuses to take my bait. "I suggest you go back and seem weak until you can get the drop on Vlad and his men. Make peace with Butch first. Get things in order. Right now, Vlad's probably wondering where you went and what's up. If you come back like you're on the warpath, he might lash out and get lucky killing one of your people. Instead, let him believe his lies about you until you get your people in line. Butch, your uncle Jace, your nudist cousin Jack, and that old guy on steroids. They're your core club. The Dogs are just dead weight. Once you kill them, you can build a bigger, stronger club. Those new guys will answer to you. Not your mom or Cooper."

"I've never killed a man."

Soso's gaze reveals no disappointment. "I figured. Your family is like the mob with special rules for family and different ones for outsiders. You never had to prove your worth or toughness like an average guy, but that doesn't mean you have no worth or toughness. I know you can run your club. You sure have the arrogance for it."

Snickering, I lean over and kiss her head. "Do you think I should lay a trap for Vlad?"

"If possible. His guys outnumber your guys. But he underestimates you. That allows your guys a chance to surprise his guys. See, I think you should use your weaknesses to your advantage. Like my dad knew people didn't think he was particularly loyal to management. This was back before he was VP. Dad came off as a drunk with no discipline. When he decided to cozy up with an asshole cousin—" Soso pauses to sigh. "Okay, I need to step back and explain. My great-uncle created and ditched bastard kids all over the place. But when this one son showed up and wanted to be part of the club, Dad didn't trust him. The guy was on his best behavior with everyone else. He knew they were watching him. But because Dad had a rep of not giving a crap, he was able to get close to his cousin. He used the weaknesses people saw in him. That's what you need to do until the Dogs are gone."

"After eating shit for years in Conroe, I'll finally be doing it for a goal besides obeying my mom and uncles."

"Bubba, you don't have to be your uncles or your grandfather," she says, cradling my hand in both of hers. "I get how you look up to them. But if you spend all your time wanting to recreate their greatest hits, you'll never appreciate your own."

"That's uplifting."

"I read a lot of self-help books when I was younger."

Wrapping an arm around her, I tug her close. "I'm a different man with you at my side."

Soso's smile reassures me that she knows the next few months—hell, maybe years—could be bumpy. With my family, her family, my club in disarray, needing to prove myself, leaving behind her hometown—there's a lot of shit that can go wrong.

But we're in this together, and I'm ready to stop running.

THE CHAPTER WHERE CONROE MAKES A COMEBACK
THE BOHEMIAN

It's wild how quickly things can change. I wake up with plans to take Bubba to my parents' house for dinner. Last night, I called to tell them I was moving to Conroe with Bubba. I assumed Mom would be supportive while Dad would demand I stay. I got their responses backward.

"It's too soon," Mom complained.

Dad added quickly. "Bubba's smart to nail shit down quick."

It makes sense for them to feel the way they do. Mom and I spend a lot of time together. Her closest friends are all family—her mom and sisters, Layla, me—and she isn't comfortable with loss. Dad, on the other hand, knows what happens when a man doesn't stake his claim soon enough. That's why Keanu has a different father. Dad didn't nail shit down fast enough.

Tonight offers an official opportunity for the rest of my family to meet Bubba. In a few days, we'll head to Conroe with a suitcase of my clothes and a ton of pet-related boxes. Bubba says his family's house will provide plenty of space for the birds to stretch out.

"What if your mom doesn't want me in her house?" I ask as we're cuddling in bed.

"She won't, but Pop will overrule her. He's going to get a kick out of the birds."

Bubba still doesn't seem in a hurry to return to Conroe. It'll happen, but he isn't chomping at the bit to go. He's gotten accustomed to the weird angles of the ceiling in my house. He enjoys working in my yard. He's always flirting with Bjork and laughing at Ula's antics. Life in Hickory Creek is fun, but it'll never be his home, and his vacation is nearly over.

But I don't expect it to end so suddenly and with such a shock.

Bubba gets dozens of texts from his mom a day. I think nothing of his phone chiming every thirty minutes, especially after the rest of his family get into the action with requests for him to come home.

"My brother's been shot," Bubba says, jumping to his feet so fast that Bjork nearly slides off his lap to the ground.

Despite wearing a look of pure panic, he somehow manages to catch her mid-fall. I grab his phone and read the text from his cousin Jack.

"Butch shot by now dead Dog. Bro on way to hospital. Not clear how bad hurt. Ditch the pussy and get your ass back here."

"Put the girls in their cage, Bubba. I'll grab my suitcase, and we'll take my truck."

"We're going to leave them?"

"There's no time to prepare them, and we can't leave them in the truck when we go to the hospital. I'll ask Layla to housesit until we can return to get Freki and the birds. Right now, we need to focus on getting you to your family."

Bubba nods, but he already imagines Butch dead. The brothers never made their peace, and he believes they never will.

I hurry to the partially packed suitcase in my room. Tossing a few weapons into the bag, I return to the kitchen where Bubba stares at his phone. He's messaging someone while I nudge him out the door. His mind is too focused on learning details about the shooting for him to drive safely.

Taking charge calms me. I call Layla to ask for her to stay at my place until I get back. She quickly agrees and then suggests we get one of the local patrol guys to escort my truck to the Kentucky border.

"That ought to save you some time," she says.

Dad gets in touch with someone, and we end up with a Hickory Creek Township officer escorting us all the way to the Tennessee/Kentucky border. With the help of my family's connections, we arrive in less than two hours.

Bubba doesn't speak much during the drive. His cousin says Conroe is on lockdown for those who matter. His father says Butch is in surgery. His uncle Jace says Vlad wants a meeting to explain what happened. Bubba's green-eyed gaze rages at the thought of the Dogs explaining away an attack on his brother.

"My cousin Lily is in labor. That means her pop and brother are likely in Conroe or at least on their way."

"Reinforcements are good."

Bubba frowns darker. He doesn't want anyone helping him get revenge. His anger makes sense. He's itching to take charge, kill his enemies, and be a real leader.

"Remember to play to Vlad's view of you," I say when we're twenty minutes out from the hospital. "He thinks he's got you pegged. Let him think those lies until you're ready to gut the fucker."

I worry my words might come off as condescending to an already agitated Bubba. Instead, he gives me a smile. Even out for blood, Bubba remains in control of his emotions. Just like when he stayed in the house while I talked to Griff about the birds. Bubba knows when to play it cool and when to fuck everything up.

Only as we pass through the hospital doors does it really hit me that I'm about to meet his family. For the last few days, I had everything planned out. Nothing is going like I expected, but I still expect to compliment his mom's appearance if she gives me the stink eye. Women love praise, especially about their hair. I'm good to go there, but today isn't about me or my feelings. It's about keeping Bubba sane in case his brother doesn't survive, and they never mend what their egos fucked up.

THE RUNAWAY

When I was little, Mom always had me hold my brothers' hands during trips out. She figured if we got separated from her or Pop that we'd be safer together. I took my job as big brother very serious back then. Butch and Buzz were my responsibility.

But over time, we got stuck in our personas. I was the responsible firstborn. Buzz was the carefree joker. Butch was the silent grump. The walls we created on our way to manhood ended up separating us. Somehow, we lived in the same house and spent endless hours together yet grew apart. Now, I might never be able to fix shit with Butch.

The first part of the drive is manageable. I'm busy texting people, finding out how the situation went so wrong. Then things get quiet on Conroe's end as everyone settles into waiting mode.

Butch is in surgery. Gut wound, lost a good amount of blood, should recover. Nothing definite. Only vague hopes.

Then there are the Dogs. Vlad texts to say he's getting to the bottom of what happened with Vigo. Calls his longtime friend "nuts" and claims the asshole went "rogue." Sounds possible. Vigo's attacked people before over the smallest offenses. He's clearly wired wrong, but I don't buy it. Even if I did, Vigo was Vlad's guy, and he promised years ago that he could handle his people.

"I'm a man of my word," he told me many times in his Ukrainian purr.

Vigo might be dead, but someone still needs to pay for the bullet in Butch's gut. Today might be the day when all the Dogs go down.

They'll be expecting that, though. Can't imagine we face off against them without at least one of our people getting fucked too.

Cooper, Farah, and Colton are in Conroe. The men might want to help with the situation. Knowing Mom, she'll keep them on the outside. Conroe business is our business, she likes to say.

My mind races for the first hour of the drive. We make excellent time with the cop escorting us, lights flashing, siren blaring.

Adrenaline keeps me calm. I'm going to fuck up people. Conroe will run red with blood. All great shit in my head.

Then we lose our escort and slow down, and I suddenly see Butch with a bullet in his gut. My brother can't handle crowded, loud places with everyone focused on him. If he's conscious, he's in hell.

I believe he'll die. In my heart, he's already gone. Confidence sagging, I think about how I made this happen. All my doubts return. I was supposed to protect Butch and Buzz. Now, one's getting his insides fixed while the other is locked down at home.

Soso brings me out of the madness in my head. First, she talks about small things like how the birds will need a special vet. "We'll drive them to Hickory Creek a few times a year to be checked out."

I only nod. There's nothing to say. Her voice acts as a salve, though.

And she keeps talking. Little things at first, like wondering if Conroe has a good Thai restaurant.

Soso mentions we should change our clubhouse's name. "Seriously, who the fuck is Morty?" she asks, shaking her head. "You need to have a name that'll remind everyone who runs it."

"Mom thought we should try to blend in."

"Back in Ellsberg, did your family blend in?"

"Never."

"Then there's your answer. People in Conroe need to remember who runs things behind the scenes. That's how it works in Hickory Creek. The Brotherhood ride around town, loud and proud, constantly making a racket. Never let people forget your family and club mean power."

Soso's right about changing the bar's name. I don't even know if there was ever a Morty in Conroe. Why is his name on the Reapers' bar? Yeah, that'll be an easy change.

Thirty minutes away from Conroe, Soso pulls me out of my head again. This time, by talking about where we'll live.

"I don't need a weird home to be happy," she says, gaze on the road, solely focused on getting us to the hospital. "I know after seeing the A-frame house that you might think I need a wacky place, but I just want somewhere with a little privacy. That'll be important because the birds can get loud. Well, you know that," she says, smiling at me and reaching for my hand. "Also, a house with high ceilings would be best. The birds need space to fly, and you can't be banging your head all the time. I don't really care about anything else. One story, two stories, old, new. None of that matters. I don't even care if we have a decent kitchen since I don't want to cook."

Smiling, I suggest, "We can learn to cook together."

"Yeah, after your brother is home from the hospital, and we've found our own place, you and I can practice cooking," she says and then adds quietly, "Preferably while naked."

Soso is fucking everything. I couldn't have asked for anyone better. Even her food choices—oatmeal is nasty—make me love her more. This incredible woman sees greatness in me even when I don't.

Her devotion deserves a reward, and I promise I'll remain at my best. No more doubts. I've got this shit in the bag. And when it's done, I'll have the sexiest woman in the world at my side.

Then as if she hasn't been perfect enough, Soso grabs my hand before we enter the hospital. "Whatever you need to do, just do it. Don't worry if you have to leave me behind to get it done. I can entertain myself. I'm not nervous about meeting people or being on my own. This is a triage situation. I'm at the bottom of the list of concerns right now, and I'm okay with that."

"Remind me to thank Keanu for getting me plastered that night," I say, kissing her forehead before we hurry to the waiting room where I find my parents along with Sissy and her five-year-old son, Hart.

"My boy came home!" Mom cries dramatically and throws her arms around me.

I admit her hug feels good. My pop offers a tight one too. Hickory Creek and Soso's life consumed me so completely that I feel oddly disconnected from my family. They're not strangers, but I feel out of place.

Mom's relieved smile disappears as soon as she notices Soso behind me. "You brought a hoochie on a date to your brother's deathbed?"

Her words instantly crush me under a million regrets about my relationship with Butch. "He's dying?"

Pop's expression immediately calms me, and I realize Mom's fucking with me. "No, he'll be fine," my father says.

"For fuck's sake, Mom," I mutter. "You scared the shit out of me."

"Good. I'm angry with you," she says without a hint of regret. "That's your punishment. Now, hug me again."

Mom embraces me while shooting daggers at Soso who only smiles.

"I don't like her," Mom whines. "She's too happy."

Feeling on the spot, I ask Soso, "Didn't I tell you?"

"You forgot to mention her great hair," she says, hitting my mom with a compliment before adding, "Or how much you look like your father."

Mom does love praise. She strokes her blonde hair and then sighs. "Fine, I'm Bailey. I assume you're the Tennessee hoochie he's been banging."

"Soso Rutgers, and yes, we've been banging quite often, ma'am."

I do love how she chooses to call my mom "ma'am" in the same smart-ass way that I always refer to her father as "sir." However, I get defensive about my mother talking shit about the woman who owns my heart.

That's why I blurt out, "We're in love and getting married." Sliding my arm around her shoulders, I ignore the part where I never actually proposed to Soso. I mean, we're planning a life together. Of course, we're getting married.

Soso's dark eyes cling to the happy determination she's been rolling with since we arrived. No longer feeling as defensive, I sigh. "But right now, let's focus on Butch and business."

After telling Mom how I've got shit handled, I'm forced to leave Soso with my family in the waiting room. She promises she'll be fine, and I swear the same thing.

Downstairs, Jack and Roid Ron wait for me in the parking lot.

"About fucking time," my cousin says, looking and sounding like a younger version of his blond dad.

"Where's everyone?"

"Right here at the hospital. Jace is inside, talking to Cooper."

"Vlad says he wants to meet to discuss what happened," I mutter, thinking of my uncles plotting upstairs. "We need a spot where we don't need to worry about locals."

Roid Ron—a transplant from Ellsberg and someone I've always assumed shares our every conversation with Cooper—looks around the quiet lot. "The park with all the broken equipment is empty. Only teenagers hang out there on the weekends to drink, smoke weed, and fuck. It'll be abandoned on a weekday, and there aren't any neighbors nearby. If we need to get messy, no one will see or hear shit."

"We'll set up a meet there with Vlad. I'll have him bring the remaining Dogs. As insurance, Jace can find a spot with his rifle."

"What about Cooper and Colton inside?" Jack asks.

"They're here for Lily. The shit with Vlad is Conroe club business."

My cousin's frown turns ugly. "Well, Cooper's the one who made a deal with Vlad and the Dogs."

"If he comes with us, he'll take over and then our balls might as well go back with him to Ellsberg," I snap at Jack. "Or we can handle this ourselves tonight."

"And if he hits us with an ambush?"

"Then we die, and he dies, and someone else runs Conroe. Or would you rather Cooper take the bullet while we hide behind him?"

These guys are in the same boat as me. Roid Ron burned all his bridges back in Ellsberg—he fucks anything that moves, and his roid-induced fits pissed off everyone. Jack lives in the shadow of his father—Ellsberg's VP. We're the misfits. Only my uncle Jace didn't end up in Conroe with something to prove. His wife—Sawyer Johansson—wanted to work with my mom and get away from Ellsberg. Jace is here because he's pussy-whipped, but he's still the toughest guy in our chapter.

"Set up the meet, and I'll grab every weapon I can," Jack says.

I message Jace, telling him to grab his rifle and where to meet us. Vlad agrees to round up his guys for a face-to-face at the park.

Logically, I know the man doesn't want to die. Killing me would be an instant death sentence since every other chapter would descend on this town and destroy the Dogs. There's no scenario where he kills me and wins.

But he sent Vigo after Butch. I feel it in my gut, even if I'm having trouble with the logic behind his move.

"Butch moved into Sissy's house," Jack says after we arrive at the park minutes before dusk. "Her pastel fucking house."

"Then you know he loves her."

My cousin nods. Age-wise, he's between Butch and me. Maturity-wise, he's a fucking kid. A violent, temperamental giant, but a child nonetheless. Being spoiled has its disadvantages.

I should know.

Jace messages me to say he's in position. Ron stands near the old swing set, now just dangling chains. I'm not nervous. I should be, but I got word that Butch is out of surgery and looks good. I imagine Sissy's relieved. Her kids too. I can't picture how Butch is with any of them. I've never seen him capable of relaxing around noise and needy people. For Sissy, he must have found a way.

I expect the Dogs to arrive on their bikes, but they rumble up in an ancient SUV. My assumption is they plan to use its size to block Jace from the woods. Did they scope this place out already? I don't reach for my gun when the SUV roars past us and to the left. The rear faces Jack, Ron, and me.

Vlad steps out of the front passenger door. Andrei is driving. Pavel appears from behind the driver's seat. Diak emerges from the back, passenger seat. Finally, Tolya scoots out from his spot between the last two men. With Vigo dead, there should be six Dogs left.

"Where's Lex?" I ask Vlad as he approaches.

The Ukrainian's long, dark hair is tied into a braid, and his head is covered in a black beanie. He's wearing his Reapers vest and carrying a pistol in his front pocket with the handle very clearly sticking out. He's older than my pop, but still impressively burly for a man who's spent the last decade doing little more than eating, drinking, and fucking.

"Your brother is good, yes?" Vlad asks me while gesturing for Tolya to open the back door.

"He'll be fine," I mutter and prepare to ask about his cousin again. Then Diak and Pavel yank a bound-and-bleeding Lex from the SUV and drop him on the ground. "What's this?"

"He sent Vigo."

Lex can't say differently since his jaw looks broken. I doubt he's got a single tooth left in his fat head. He stares at his cousin with begging blue eyes.

"Why?" I ask, certain this is a trick.

"Lex wanted revenge for Butch firing him from a worksite."

The man on the ground moans as if to speak, but Tolya shuts him up with a boot on his shattered jaw.

This isn't what I expected, but I remain calm. They might be pulling a ruse to get us to lower our guards. Perhaps, they worry Cooper and Colton are hiding nearby.

I'm not sure what they want to happen next. I only know I'm the one Vlad wants to impress.

"You've always been loyal, Vlad, but I have trouble believing your cousin would have made such a big fucking move without your approval."

"I've carried him all my life, and this is what he does to me," he says, spitting on Lex.

Vlad doesn't answer why Lex would screw over the Dogs by shooting Butch. If I had to crawl into the heads of these men, I'd guess they thought Vigo would kill Butch and get away clean. No one would know it was them. Or at least be able to prove it. My brother fucked up Vigo, though, ruining their Plan A.

What I'm looking at now is Plan B.

"I understand he's family, but this shit can't stand," I tell Vlad.

Without missing a fucking beat, he pulls his weapon and fires down into his cousin's face. I feel Jack adjust behind me. Ron might be nervous too. None of us expected Vlad to kill his family. Hell, why not fuck up one of the lesser guys?

I hear Soso's voice in my head, explaining that Vlad wants to live and he didn't know if Butch would survive. Killing a Dog that I've barely spoken to wouldn't be enough to make peace. He had to sacrifice someone important in case my brother died. Now he's proven his loyalty.

I remember Soso's advice about these men. They aren't worried about me. They fear my uncles and the sheer numbers in the Reapers club. If I want to take them down later with Butch's help, I have the opportunity to walk this back. Vlad thinks I'm dumb enough to trust him. I decide to play into that misconception.

"Talk about fucking loyalty!" I announce, smiling and clapping my hands. "Did you see that shit, Jack?"

"Yeah, I saw it."

Waving off Jack's grumpy cat routine, I smile at Vlad. "I was just saying to my cousin how I didn't think you'd betray the club. My uncle said you were solid. That's why he made you VP. No, fuck, this," I say, pointing at Lex, "is why he made you VP."

Vlad mimics my smile. The Dogs relax behind him. Their hands no longer linger near hidden weapons. Their leader's plan worked. No one else has to die. They can go back to the way it was. Well, until they get another shot to take over.

I've accepted their payment to make peace and stay alive. Their Plan B was a success!

And I'll let them believe this lie until Butch is ready to help me ruin them all.

THE BOHEMIAN

Waiting for a man to come home from club business isn't new to me. Even as a kid, I understood when Dad's work got dangerous. The vibe in the house changed. Brotherhood guys talked outside rather than coming into the house. Dad's body language shifted too. Not enough for most people to notice, but I was obsessed with him as a kid. I imitated his walk and talk. Mom used to follow me around with her phone, recording my "Dayton swagger."

Then he'd be gone. Sometimes for days, doing things I never got to know about. For hours, I'd sit at the front windows of our house, waiting for his return. Keanu coped by staring at his aquarium, but no amount of colorful fish could settle me down.

That's how I got into meditating. Mom insisted I learn after she caught me tugging out my hair while worrying if I'd ever see my daddy again.

Now I'm waiting on Bubba. He's somewhere in this town I don't know, with people I've never met, and doing things that might get him killed.

Meditating as I sit in the waiting room, I only speak when spoken to. The Johansson family keeps its distance. Butch's woman, Sissy, is lost in her head. Her eight-year-old daughter, Haydee, though, talks to me about cats. Mostly, she wants me to adopt one that she'll take care of for free. I suggest she get one for her house, and she decides my idea is better.

Then I'm alone in my head again.

Mom texts to say she and Dad will visit Conroe this weekend to check out my living arrangements. They'll also transport Freki, Ula, and Bjork along with anything else I need.

Home feels far away, and I'm a little too aware of how it'll never really be mine again. But I don't let myself fall into the dumps. Finding a happy place in my head, I remain there as the hours drag on. Activity happens in the background, but I emotionally separate myself from the stress.

Butch is out of surgery. The family visits him. Cooper and Colton Johansson show up and then leave. I keep my mouth shut and my head down. Bubba will eventually return.

Until then, I hide in my head where I fly with my birds. My hunky puppy lives in my happy place too. Always shirtless and smiling. I erase the bruises and cuts from his face. He's safe here with me.

"Rutgers," Bailey says after more time has passed and the sun's set. Sissy is no longer in the waiting room. Her kids sit with Nick, watching a video. Now Mama Bear Johansson changes seats and plops down next to mine. "How do I know that name?"

"It's a common name, ma'am."

"Don't call me that."

"What would you like for me to call you?"

"Bailey. No, Bubba's mother."

"Well, Bubba's mother, I'm sorry we had to meet under these circumstances, but I won't pretend to fear you just because your boy's been shot."

"Rude."

"That means a lot from a woman who called me a hoochie before knowing my name."

I suspect Bailey isn't accustomed to people pushing back against her bad attitude. My grandmother is the same way. Long before I was born, the Hallstead women branded fear in people's hearts until no one dared to cross them. Then over time, their asses were kissed so much that they forgot what saliva-free butt cheeks felt like.

Though no one avoids me out of fear, I'm very comfortable at the top of the power food chain.

"So, Bubba was in White Horse with Audrey."

"At first. Then he was in Hickory Creek Township with me."

Her expression freezes while her brain likely scans old information for why my hometown and last name matter.

"Which twin is your father?"

"The good-looking one," I say, giving Keanu's and my standard response to that question. Deciding Bailey's dealt with enough stress for the day, I add, "Dayton."

"He's the slutty one, right?"

"Probably. Like I said, he's the good-looking one."

"I never liked your father. Handsy, rude, a little dumb."

Okay, I can't go full vengeful wrath on this woman since her son just got out of surgery. But no one talks trash about my family and gets away free.

"When I texted Dad to let him know what was going on, he asked if you still had your fake boobs. Unable to tell with the shirt you're wearing, I figured it was best to ask."

"Bitch," she hisses.

"She had them taken out years ago," Nick says without looking at us. "It was an anniversary gift to me."

"That's sweet," I say.

Nick is definitely where Bubba inherited his softer side from, and the physical resemblance is striking. I ignore Bailey for a few minutes while watching her husband entertain Sissy's kids.

"Are you finished thinking about my boobs?" Bailey asks, leaning over to get my attention again.

"I was thinking about your son actually," I lie, having been very much wondering how big they might have been during her plastic phase. "Bubba's something special."

Bailey frowns, thinking I'm playing her. "Why did Bubba say he was away from Conroe?"

"He fought with his brother and needed space to think."

"They fought over Sissy," Bailey whispers so the kids won't hear.

"I know."

"Does that make you jealous?"

"Of course not."

"Why?"

"Bubba loves me."

"He met you on this trip, correct?"

"Our first sexual experience was in my truck last week," I announce in my perkiest voice.

Bailey sighs dramatically. "I'm not talking to you anymore."

Smiling triumphantly, I lift my tablet as if I'm reading. Bailey realizes she's losing and leans over again.

"I will kill you if you fuck with my boy's heart."

"Then, my family will kill you. Then your family will kill someone in my family to avenge you. It could go on for quite a long time. Though I suspect there are more Johanssons than Rutgers. We'll likely need to call in outside help."

"Saint is ours," Bailey blurts out immediately.

"Fine, but we get the Arizona Moving Company. Also, my uncle Lawman will most definitely kill for us. Come to think of it, this war could become very messy. As such, I choose to avoid breaking your boy's heart. You know, to avoid wiping out the Johansson and Rutgers bloodlines."

"That's right," Bailey grumbles. Despite her frown, I suspect she likes playing with someone who can fight back. I can't imagine the lopsided battle she has with Sissy.

"You can have a peanut," Bailey offers, handing me one from the snack bag in her lap.

Nick chuckles nearby. Maybe it's the movie, but I think he's always listening. Bailey frowns at her husband, making me believe she suspects the same thing.

I take the peanut and pop it in my mouth despite hating all that salty crap covering it. Peace offerings are sometimes gross. Like the time my father wrote "I'm sorry" in honey on his stomach for Mom. I had no clue what his plan was with that. The words were upside down, and everything attached itself to the honey. Of course, a shower was necessary to clean him up, and my parents swear Dad "rocks wet." In the end, the thought is what counts.

"Can you really call in the Arizona Moving Company?" Bailey asks.

"Of course. I'm sure you could too. Not against us, but for other business. But you have the Ramsey Security team on your payroll. Why do you need more assassins?"

Bailey shrugs. "Never say never."

"Do you think Bubba will be back soon?" I ask since that's the only question that really matters to me.

"Am I boring you?"

"I'm worried he isn't in the right mind to handle those Dogs."

"The Russians can't win against my boys. Look how one tried today, and Butch fucked him up."

"I thought they were Ukrainian."

"Don't start with me, Soso," Bailey sighs. "What kind of name is that?"

"Calypso is my full name."

"I'm calling you that."

"Go for it, but I'm not a dog, and I won't respond."

Nick chuckles again, causing Bailey to glare at him. When he doesn't react to her frowning stare, she finally relents and smiles. "Did you know Bubba's named after his pop? Nick didn't want that, but I put my foot down. It's a handsome name, but I started calling my baby Bubba and couldn't stop."

"He said I could pick our kids' names."

Bailey's smile is gone in an instant. "It'll be Sunshine or Peacenik, won't it?"

"I'm not a hippie."

Bailey adjusts in her seat, not believing me. "I know what I see. The flowery skirt, those sandals, the bag of granola. If it eats like a duck, the fucking thing's a duck."

"Look, Bubba's mom, you and I won't see eye to eye on many things. That's fine, but we'll need to get used to each other for Bubba's sake. You're his beloved mommy, but I'm the woman who owns his heart. He's mine. I love him. Deal with it, lady."

Bailey gasps, and I catch Nick fighting laughter. They're an odd couple. My parents are similar. Salty and sweet is how my dad describes him and Mom.

Bailey prepares to give me grief over calling her "lady" since she's looking to give me grief over something just to pass the time. Before her bitchiness is unleashed, her firstborn enters the room.

Just like when my dad returned from his work trips, I'm flooded with relief at the sight of Bubba. Until now, I'd fought the urge to imagine him facing off with the Dogs. I couldn't picture the people with him, where they were at, or what his plan might be. I remained in my happy place, detached from real world worries. Even Bailey couldn't force me to submit to my fears.

Bubba's appearance—no obvious injuries, a relatively relaxed look on his sexy face, and that smile when his gaze finds me—are all the proof I need to be sure my hunky puppy is in charge.

Whatever happens next will be a breeze.

THE RUNAWAY

Vlad doesn't lie well. I don't know if he hasn't been human for so long that he can't remember how they behave, but he ought to show at least some sadness or grief over murdering his cousin. Raised together, these men were lifelong friends. They fucked women together. *A lot.* If you can pick another man's dick out of a lineup, you've reached a whole new level of friendship.

I don't expect Vlad to burst into tears at the sight of his dead cousin. He's the one who pulled the trigger. But he claims he didn't know anything until a few hours ago. Shouldn't he at least pretend to be shocked by the sudden violent turn of events that led to his cousin's death?

Vlad doesn't seem like a sociopath. I've seen him show plenty of emotions from joy at a new virginal club bunny to rage at his pizza missing its sausage. The guy doesn't react tonight because he always knew his plan with Vigo might go sideways, and this was his contingency plan.

And he doesn't waste time pretending to care since he figures I'm too stupid to notice anyhow. His arrogance is the reason I insist my guys dispose of Lex's body. Vlad wants to do it, of course.

"He was your cousin," I say, faking sympathy. "Killing him couldn't have been easy. Let us handle shit for you."

Vlad thinks to push the subject, but I turn away and tell Jack to use the plastic we brought along to wrap up Lex's body.

I want Vlad and his men to know we came here tonight, planning to kill someone. My goal is for them to behave long enough for Butch to get healthy and help me end these shitheads.

When Jack whips out the plastic, I hope each Dog imagines himself rolled into it. Let them worry while my brother regains his strength. Then we'll wrap them in plastic for real.

Vlad and his men leave while Jace brings around the truck we planned to fill with dead Dogs. My uncle says nothing about Lex's death. He'll no doubt be Chatty Fucking Cathy when he sees Cooper, though.

I can't worry about their judgments tonight. Butch nearly died, and Soso is alone in a new place.

The hospital is eerie after dark. In the maternity ward of the small hospital, my cousin Lily and her newborn son rest. In intensive care, Butch recovers. I don't know how bad off he is yet. Mom and Pop keep their info vague. I only know he's out of surgery and Sissy is with him.

I find her kids with Pop on one end of the waiting room while Mom glares at Soso on the other side. My mom sees me and hurries for a hug. She whispers about Vlad. I whisper my response about Lex. She looks surprised. I know she wants more details, but there's time for that later.

"Has Soso eaten?"

"I gave her a peanut."

"That she did," Soso says, standing behind Mom.

My arms can't get around her fast enough. Soso's scent brings me back to the triangle house and our evenings together. We rarely watched TV—her set is hidden in a hutch—but instead talked. I feel like I know her better than I know anyone despite us being strangers two weeks ago.

"Do you want to see Butch?" Mom asks, bothered by my need for Soso. I see the disconnect in her expression. She doesn't understand how I can be this attached to someone I just met. One day, when shit settles down, I'll fill in mom on the details. Tonight, though, I have two concerns—my brother and the woman I love.

Butch looks so small in the hospital bed, covered with white blankets and hooked up to machines. I haven't seen him this fragile since we were kids.

Sissy stands on the other side of the bed, lost in her thoughts. She says Butch woke up earlier, though he doesn't react to my presence.

I need him to know I'm here, and things are handled. He'll worry once he's awake. Butch is always stressing about something, and now he has a family to concern himself with. I need to make him understand they're safe, and I won't run away again.

Before I leave his room, Butch does wake, and I try to find the right words to express how things went down with Vlad and how I'm back for good. I don't know if he understands. The drugs likely turn my words into gibberish. I hope he at least understands that all the negative crap between us is over. At least for me, it is.

Soso looks tired when I return to the waiting room. She's been nibbling on granola for hours, and she must be bored. But she still wears a smile for me when I return to her.

"We're heading home with the kids," Pop says, picking up Hart. "Want to follow us back?"

Wrapping Soso in my arms, I ask, "Do you want to get something to eat before we drive to my parents' house?"

Her dark eyes study my face. "I want to meet Buzz."

Nodding, I get what she's doing. Soso might want to be alone for a while, but she knows we're in the midst of family drama. My mom requires reassurance. Pop needs Mom to settle down. Buzz is likely being extra kooky at home to overcompensate for his worries about Butch. Sissy's kids need everyone to chill because they're sponges and soak up the moods around them.

Soso and I leave the hospital, following Mom, Pop, and the kids. I notice a familiar SUV in the parking lot, meaning Cooper, Farah, or both are still with Lily and their newest grandbaby.

I slide into the driver's seat of the truck and exhale loudly. "I feel like I should say something profound."

"I'm not going to name our babies Sunshine or Peacenik."

"Wouldn't care if you did," I say, starting the truck.

"Really?"

"Baby, you are Calypso, and no one calls you that. I'm Nikolas, and no one calls me that. You can name our kid Peacenik, and we'll end up calling him Jellybean or Brass Knuckles."

Soso scoots over and rests her face against my chest. "I know we're supposed to follow them home, but wanna make out a little instead?"

"I've had a shit day," I grumble. "My brother almost died. I had to face those Dogs knowing they were lying to me. I watched a man get his face blown off. Once we get to my house, Mom will want to talk to me alone and go over everything that happened."

Soso watches me, knowing my grumpy routine is for show. Man, this woman knows me down to my core. "So, yes, then?"

Kissing her feels like freedom. Earlier, I started worrying that I might fall back into bad habits now that I'm home. Tense about my mother and uncles pushing me around. Agitated over leaving my brother vulnerable.

With Soso, though, I'm the man I need to be. And with Soso, that's who I'll remain.

THE CHAPTER WHERE BOURBON SAVES THE DAY
THE BOHEMIAN

My first few days in Conroe teach me that I'm not nearly as zen as I believe. I'm instantly homesick when I wake up at Bubba's house. I feel far away from my family, friends, and pets. I miss my house even if this one is larger and swankier. Everything feels too different from the scents to the way the birds sing outside.

I want to go home.

But I don't tell Bubba this because he's dealing with too much, and I'm not a child. I knew moving here would be difficult. I just figured I'd have some of my security blankets with me—mainly Freki, Ula, and Bjork.

For the next few days, I only focus on Bubba rather than engage with his family. I get to know them on a surface level, of course. Bailey gives me grief. Nick is kind. Buzz cracks me up. His kid eats my last homemade beef jerky, but I'm too self-conscious in this big house to make more.

That's the weirdest part. My parents have more money than Bailey's. In theory anyway, but the Davies' house is huge. There are four sections—one for the parents and another one each for the boys—that meet up in the middle with a kitchen and family room. There's also an indoor pool and a massive basement with a pool table and play area.

I always knew my family lived modestly, but this fact smacks me in the face now. Feeling out of sorts, I follow Bubba around like a dog.

"My hunky puppy," he teases when I keep asking to go with him.

If the Davies' house is vast and decadent compared to my parents', then Conroe is the flipside of Hickory Creek. There's nothing to do in the town. I promise myself I'll be so busy with my new home and Bubba—along with Freki and the birds—that I won't have time to miss the proximity to a big city. Hickory Creek Township has Nashville. Conroe's closest big town is Bowling Green. Ugh.

But Conroe also has Bubba, and he's the reason I breathe now. However, I can't help giggling like a maniac when my family arrives that weekend.

Mom waves from the passenger window as Keanu pulls the SUV into the driveway. Then I hear the booming sound of the Dropkick Murphys along with the rumble of a chopper. Dad rolls up the road, making as much noise as possible. He even pulls on the throttle dramatically before finally turning off the engine.

"The man loves making a scene," I proudly tell Bubba.

Behind us, Bailey and Nick exit the house to investigate the racket my father makes. Dad walks to the SUV to open the passenger door for Mom, who throws her arms around his neck and plants a kiss on his lips. She very much approves of his display of dominance. In fact, I swear they're ready to go at it against the SUV.

Before they can rip off each other's clothes and give us all a show, Bailey loudly clears her throat.

Dad pops his lips free from Mom's and smirks at Bubba's mom.

"Rutgers," she mutters.

"Johansson. Glad to hear you got your rack reduced. I'm a fan of au naturel," Dad says, wrapping an arm around Mom's shoulders.

Nick mimics Dad's move by sliding his arm around Bailey. I suspect his gesture has more to do with keeping his woman calm, though.

Bubba does the intros while I walk around to the back of the SUV where Keanu holds Freki and checks on the birds under their covered cage.

"They slept the entire way," he says.

"Thank you."

Hearing the emotion in my voice, Keanu hands me the dog and hugs me against him.

"I'm going to miss seeing you all the time."

"I'm scared," I admit. "I'm not sure I can handle all this new stuff."

Keanu hugs me tighter. "You're strong enough to handle anything, Soso. Just think of all the fun crap you and Kentucky can do together. A new house that belongs to you both. Also, your new friends won't know all our stories. You'll seem exciting to them."

Smiling, I wish my family could move to Conroe with me. The idea is dumb, but they're the one part of Hickory Creek I can never replicate here.

"You okay?" Bubba asks.

Keanu steps back, knowing the drill. A woman needs her man. He goes through it with Cap and Audrey a lot. No doubt Keanu needs his woman right now too.

"Lotte will be home by the end of summer," I say, and Keanu nods. He knows she's coming back. I just think he worries she'll need her family like I need mine, and hers aren't a few hours away.

We carry the birdcage and Freki to where my parents stare at Bubba's. I can't figure out what they've been discussing, but Bailey asks, "Are you hippies too?"

"I'm a home care technician," Mom announces, "and he kills people."

"Not a lot of people," Dad says. "And not every day."

"Lots of people kill people," Bailey grumbles like only a Johansson can. "It's not a big thing and nothing to brag about."

"I wasn't bragging."

"My father killed more people than you have."

"My father fucked more ho-bags than you have."

Bailey blinks a few times, unsure how to respond. "I cooked dinner."

"We planned to eat out."

"We could eat here," Mom says helpfully.

"I made spoonbread."

Mom's smile disappears. "Or not."

"Bread for dinner?" Dad asks.

"It's a Kentucky delicacy."

"Is it nasty, Harmony?" Dad asks my mom as if she has access to all the knowledge in the world.

"It's a cornmeal custard."

"So, yes, then."

"I made it for you specifically," Bailey says as her frown grows darker.

"As punishment for Bubba finding his answers in Tennessee rather than in this particular state?"

"Your daughter trapped him."

"Yeah, she'll do that," Dad says and walks past Bailey and Nick. Standing on the porch with Mom, he asks, "Can I have booze with that bread thing?"

"Oh, you want it now?" Bailey asks, shooting him bitchy frowns that he refuses to acknowledge.

Dad peers through the screen into the house. "Are you reneging on the offer?"

"I'm not doing anything."

"I'm sorry you're flustered by new things," Mom tells Bailey. "Many of my clients have the same problem."

"Are you calling me defective?"

Oh, shit. Mom loses her smile. "Are you calling my clients defective?"

Bailey realizes she's crossed a line and mumbles, "I'm not saying anything about anything."

Sensing my family and Bubba's have hit an impasse, I lift my dog up and smile. "This is Freki."

"Is that the kind of thing you'll name my grandchildren? Bailey asks.

Dad smirks. "You should be aware that Soso might be part Sasquatch. A weird name ought to be the least of your concerns."

"I don't even know what's happening anymore," an exasperated Bailey tells her husband.

"You won the argument, and now we're going inside to eat that thing you made."

"Spoonbread is a real thing, Nick."

"I know. You tried something new, and I'm sure it's delicious," he says before adding in a quieter voice, "If not, we'll order pizza."

"I don't want to throw away food."

"Buzz will eat it."

Bailey smiles. "My littlest boy will eat anything."

"I'll eat some too," Bubba says, but Bailey waves off his comment.

"Don't suck up."

Bubba gives me a hilarious pout, and I hand him the dog. "She's right. You should stop caring about her approval."

Bailey instantly changes courses and reaches for Bubba. "You can have it all, baby."

Bubba gives me a wink, loving how I play with his mom. Bailey might run roughshod over these men, but she's pretty easy to manipulate.

My mother enters the house and compliments its size and girth before saying, "I thought someone mentioned alcohol. I strongly believe the only way we'll ever learn to like each other is through a great deal of booze."

"That's the secret to the semi-friendship between Cooper and Hayes," Keanu says, glancing around the house's decor. "You people really like brown."

"It's masculine," Bailey mutters.

"No, I'm masculine," Dad says. "This is just brown."

Bailey realizes she's hitting a wall with my father, so she focuses on my brother. "You're Cap's little friend."

Keanu glances at me and says in Korean, "I'm very sorry, little one, but your future mother-in-law is likely evil."

"Your pity is greatly appreciated, beloved brother."

Bailey puffs out her chest, ready to give us shit, but then seems to remember her brother's name was mentioned. "Wait, do you have any gossip about Cooper and Hayes?"

"Get me drunk, and I'll spill," Keanu says, wearing a smirk. "Trust that nothing happens in the Hayes family that I don't hear about. I mean nothing. I even know the women's menstrual cycles."

"Does Hayes know you know?"

"I don't think he cares. Angus assumes everyone is obsessed with him."

"Cooper is the same way."

"I have an obnoxious brother too," Dayton tells Bailey. "You've met him. Now that we have all this amazing fucking stuff in common, let's get drunk."

"This way," Nick gestures toward the butler's pantry.

"Camden was always my least favorite twin," Bailey tells Dad, and I get the feeling those two will bond over their shared irritation with their families' golden children.

Bubba doesn't head inside with the others. Instead, he wants to let Freki run around after his car ride. I smile at how quickly he adopted my dog and birds into his life.

This hunk is the one. I don't care how young we are or how fast things have moved, Bubba Davies is the only man for me.

THE RUNAWAY

Soso and I decide to hold off telling my mother that we've picked a house. We found it on our first full day in Conroe after I visited Butch in the hospital and made an appearance at Morty's Pub.

Weeks ago, I worked on this rental house after we bought it dirt cheap in an estate sale. New electrical and plumbing. Most of the drywall was replaced, too. We refinished the wood floors and installed new glass in the bay window out front. Since ranch-style homes aren't my taste, I never once considered living here during my time fixing up the place.

But I see it in a different light when I visit with Soso. I'm less focused on the style and more on the seclusion. We're not far from where my cousin Scarlet and her wife Phoebe live with their five kids. They have a farm while this property sits on just over an acre. It's private enough with a distant neighbor on the west side and open land on the east. Across the road is a town park, and behind us is farmland. Ula and Bjork can scream day and night without anyone giving us trouble over the noise.

Despite being basic, boxy, and beige, the ranch offers four bedrooms. That's plenty of space for her family's visits and our future kids. We won't have to move again for years. I sense Soso requires stability. She only seemed laid-back in Hickory Creek because she was in her element. I plan to help her regain that calm in her new home.

We walk into the backyard and study the patio. "The flat land is perfect for an enclosed area for the birds. I'll add heat and air to keep them comfortable."

Soso nearly tackles me when I talk about building a fancy atrium for the girls. She does push me into the house and rip open the button on my jeans.

"We have security in the house. No need to get this on video," I say, turning off the cameras. "Now, where were we?"

We christened our home that day with a quickie against the kitchen counters. Next week, we'll move in.

But again, we don't share this information with my mom, who remains extremely edgy after the wild last few weeks. The woman doesn't need another reason to lose her shit.

Especially not with Dayton, Harmony, and Keanu visiting.

Mom's spoonbread is a big nope, but our Kentucky bourbon saves the crappy dinner. I leave my parents and Soso's in the kitchen where they enjoy their booze and wait for the pizza delivery.

"Cooper's very insecure," I hear Mom telling Dayton.

"I sensed that."

Changing moods immediately, Mom growls at him, "Don't talk shit about my brother."

"Because he's insecure and might cry?"

"Yeah," she says, laughing now.

Mom might have downed too many shots of bourbon too fucking fast, but at least, she's having fun.

Soso and I use the quiet to carry in her belongings and organize them in my large bedroom. Important crap goes on one side, stuff that can wait for the move rests on the other. Freki follows us around, relieved to be out of the car.

Soon, Soso uncovers the birdcage to wake Ula and Bjork. I've missed my pretty girls. Later, they can explore. For now, they'll need to stay secure in the cage.

"Frenchie might try to eat them," I mutter, imagining the horrifying scenario.

"To decrease their stress level, leaving them in the birdcage is the safest move. They've gone from a stranger's house back to their house and now a few hours in the car. It'll be good to keep them quiet and isolated from others until we have a stable location."

"You're going to be a great mom one day."

"And you'll be an indulgent father," she says, and her gaze holds mine.

"I was spoiled as a kid. I know no other way."

"I was spoiled too, but my mom knew when to crack the whip."

Harmony proves her protective nature when she corners us in the kitchen after the pizzas arrive.

"I researched this area, and it's full of caves. Very treacherous," Harmony says, slurring her words. "You could have trolls, baby."

"Better than crabs," Buzz whispers, causing Soso and me to snicker.

"I'm serious!" Harmony yells and then covers her mouth. "Bourbon makes me loud and belligerent. I prefer tequila."

"I'll be careful," Soso promises her mom.

"Carry two forms of weapons at all times. These aren't friendly trolls. They'll eat you."

Harmony's face clenches, and tears begin to flow. "My baby," she whimpers, and Soso hugs her. They comfort each other for a few minutes until Dayton steps in and takes his wife's hand.

"We need a few minutes in our room," he says, heading down the wrong hall for their guest room.

Soso doesn't correct him because she doesn't know the house yet either. Buzz plays bellhop and guides our guests to a quiet place where Dayton can—I assume—fuck away his woman's tears.

"I'm a Tennessee girl, and my heart can't really let that go," Soso mumbles, looking ready to cry. She doesn't, of course. My parents are watching her, and she doesn't show weakness around strangers.

I suddenly realize Keanu disappeared after he claimed his booze and finished gossiping about Hayes' love of K-pop and Pong.

"I'm going downstairs to hang out with the kids," Buzz says, returning to the kitchen to swipe two pizza boxes and a bottle of soda. "Gram snuck in when no one was looking and is playing pool with Soso's brother."

Suddenly, the kitchen is empty except for my parents, Soso, and me.

"Your father is good people," Mom announces.

"My father?" I ask, looking at Pop.

"No, hers. He was always the better twin."

"Damn straight," Soso says and reaches for the bourbon. "No, I'm a bad drunk."

"Please," I beg, "let me see what that looks like."

Grinning, Soso shakes her head. "Not when my mom's already crying, and Dad hasn't given his speech yet."

"What speech?"

"The 'people today aren't as good as they were in the old days' speech."

"He isn't wrong," Mom says. "People were better back in the old days."

Pop nods in a way that makes me think the bourbon's doing the trick. "The music was better too."

Mom snaps her fingers. "We need music. That's what we're missing."

Soso studies me with her dark brown eyes, and I think about us moving into our own place. I feel like we've been waiting forever despite not even knowing her name two weeks ago.

"Time is a myth," she said while stoned one night at the triangle house. "Reality is… Um, something, something."

My woman's quite profound when on mind-altering substances.

"I thought you were going to put on Skynyrd," Pop grumbles when Meat Loaf blasts from the speakers in the living room. "What about 'Free Bird?'"

"That's our song!" Mom yells since she loses volume control when drunk. "Only we can listen to it."

Soso smiles at me. "You have nothing to be embarrassed about," she teases. "My parents are down the hall fucking."

"I'm shocked my parents aren't fucking too just so Mom can prove her relationship is as hot as your parents' relationship. She's very competitive."

"Not that fucking doesn't sound fun, but I want to go to your room and play with the birds."

Leaning down, I nuzzle my nose against hers. "I miss our time at your house."

"Now, we'll have a house of our own," she says, gripping my shirt. "I'll wake up every morning to this face."

We can't rip each other's clothes off, but our kiss gets intense before Mom knocks over one of Denny's toys and the thing starts squawking a kiddie song.

"I drank too much," she tells Pop, who wraps her in his arms in a way that makes me think I might need to leave the room.

"Why is everyone so horny?" Keanu asks, suddenly behind us.

"Bourbon."

"But I drank a ton of that swill, and I'm not horny at all."

Soso cups Keanu's face and smiles softly. "You were downstairs with a bunch of kids, so, you know, good on you for not sporting a boner, bro."

Keanu smiles at his sister, and I'm struck by guilt at knowing I'm taking her away from the people she loves.

There's no other option, though. I left Conroe for less than two weeks, and Butch got shot, Buzz decided to grow a goatee, and Mom claims she's aged ten years. My people need me.

"I know," Soso says when I just watch her.

I'm not sure if she really does know, but I appreciate her comfort.

A few minutes later, Keanu, Soso, and I sit on the front porch while Frenchie and Freki create a wary truce once the little guy learns his place.

"Your dog is bullying my dog," Soso says with her mouth full of pizza.

Keanu shakes his head. "Naw, they're just falling in love."

"They're both boys."

"Love doesn't see dong. It's all about the hearts, Num-Num."

Soso leans her head on his shoulder while taking my hand. We remain quiet until Mom starts screaming in the house. Running inside, we realize she's singing, and our ears would have been better off if we stayed outside.

"Meat Loaf," Dayton announces while entering the room with a now-calm Harmony. "Nice, Johansson."

Mom stops squawking long enough to bow before losing her balance and ending up in Pop's lap. I sense this location was her goal all along.

"I'm very nervous that we'll end up witnessing the public fucking of at least one set of our parents tonight," I mutter.

Keanu cocks an eyebrow. "Now you understand how I feel whenever I'm around the Hayes family and booze."

"You," Dayton says, pointing at me.

"Good luck," Keanu teases as his father struts drunkenly over to me.

"I've been thinking about you and my baby girl. Been thinking real hard."

I fight laughter at how his face scrunches up at the mention of "thinking real hard" as if his brain seizes at the suggestion.

"I'm sure you have been, sir."

"You didn't impress me when we met."

"My lack of a shirt seemed to have bothered you."

"Probably, but I've been thinking. Thinking real hard."

Harmony nods nearby as if she and her hubby were thinking real hard together.

"Not a lot of men are worthy of my baby girl. I only have one, you know? She's something special."

"Thanks, Daddy," Soso says as he hugs her.

"I can't have her marrying a schmuck. I remember hearing a while back that Cooper's oldest daughter was marrying a dentist and I thought he'd done a bad job as a father. That's a low bar for a woman. At least, marry an orthodontist and get the big money."

"That's a fine story, sir."

"I didn't want you to be the one, but then Harmony pointed out how the Johanssons rival the Rutgers on generational cool. That's why I've decided you are worthy. Not because I know shit about you but solely based on your last name. You'll need to earn my respect, but you've got my blessing. Unless my daughter changes her mind, and then I'm kicking your ass."

Laughing, Soso hugs her father again.

"Thank you, sir."

Mom comes over and hugs me. "Dayton, you got a good one here. He's very responsible. Always cleans his room and brushes his teeth."

Soso winks at me as my mother decides to finger-comb my hair. Pop meanwhile starts laughing and nearly passes out from it when Mom decides to use spit to clean pizza sauce from my lips.

"He's just so handsome," Mom says, nearly ready to turn mama cat on me.

"I can't see it," Dayton announces, eyeing me. "But I prefer blondes."

Harmony nods at this comment, but she's so wasted she forgets to stop bouncing her head until Keanu helps steady it.

This is what the rest of the night is like.

Mom alternates between wild displays of bravado—singing, dancing, wanting to have arm-wrestling contests—and bragging about how she gave birth to three manly sons. Finally, she cries over Butch and sings a song that starts with "Danny Boy" and ends with "Tuesday's Gone."

Pop constantly laughs, finding her hilarious when he's not subtly feeling her up. Dayton and Harmony wander around the living room, talking about how they sometimes braid each other's hair. Keanu gets embarrassed and goes downstairs, but then decides he might miss something and returns to the family room. Twice, Buzz walks upstairs, sees the drunken mess, and realizes he's better off with the kids and Gram.

Soso and I sit in a chair and watch our parents work through their feelings regarding the recent changes. At one point, her dad and mine decide they need to fight because Pop was once a cage fighter and Dayton claims he's gone soft. Keanu and I break that up.

Then Harmony challenges my mother to a wrestling match in retaliation for Mom claiming her sister Sawyer is better than both of Harmony's sisters. Soso pries the women apart.

Finally, they settle down and play Dolly Parton's "I Will Always Love You" on repeat.

By the time everyone retires to bed, our parents have come to a few understandings:

1) Soso and I are the real deal, and we'll make fantastic grandbabies for them.

2) Bailey is the best Johansson of her generation while Dayton is the best Rutgers of his generation.

3) Angus Hayes is too tall.

4) Spoonbread is gross while pizza is perfection.

5) And bourbon is mandatory at future visits.

THE CHAPTER WHERE CONROE GETS A MAKEOVER
THE BOHEMIAN

As soon as my parents leave Conroe, I scramble to keep myself busy and distracted from my homesickness. Helping Sissy and Lily is the easiest solution. Not long after Lily and her newborn Byron arrive home, Butch is discharged. Sissy is overloaded with stress, so I help as much as I can. Of course, I don't know anything about babies or gunshot wounds. I'm also a bad cook, but I do learn a few recipes for liquid meals.

Sissy is easy to be around. The blonde blurts out whatever's in her head. There's nothing fake about her. Everything I see is the real Sissy.

Lily is more like me. We grew up with the understanding that people were watching and expecting certain things from us. We're reserved around strangers. I see how Lily smiles differently when she doesn't know I'm around and thinks it's just her and Sissy. They have a long-time bond. I'd easily feel left out if not for Sissy's infectious friendliness.

A week after I arrive in Conroe, Bubba and I move into our house. We use the bed and dresser from his room at his parents' place, but we'll need to buy everything else.

That means, Bubba—a man I've known for only a few weeks—and I need to furnish a 2000 square foot house. Instead, of proving we rushed into our relationship, shopping together is more evidence that we're perfect together.

Bubba and I don't initially agree on anything. He likes dark leather and sharp lines. I like nonconformity and lots of color. We ought to drive each other crazy while filling our house.

Our first battle involves furniture. He wants a large leather couch. I prefer furniture to be colorful and lower to the ground—for Freki. I'm not blind, though. I watched how this large man was forced to crawl off my couch back in

Tennessee. After a long day of physical labor, the last thing Bubba needs is to struggle with a piece of furniture.

We compromise. He buys a massive, masculine couch that I cover with a colorful afghan I've had forever. Plus, Freki enjoys his new ramp, and he's happy with anything as long as his fluffy pillow is available.

Comfort is always more important than style. This house isn't our taste. Bubba doesn't like ranches. I think the boxy style is boring. But with no stairs, Freki can access every room without whining for someone to pick him up.

There's so much space—three times as much as my place in Hickory Creek—and I'm obsessed with having room for people to stay over. The house quickly feels warm and relaxed as we fill it with an odd mix of furniture and décor.

While I get my elephant tapestry on the wall behind the couch, Bubba enjoys his giant fucking TV. I mean, seriously, the thing is huge and nearly covers the entire wall across from the couch. I don't watch much TV, but he's used to winding down after work by staring at the boob tube.

I have all day to bask in the quiet house with my yoga and meditation. If Bubba needs to watch trash TV all evening, I'm happy to cuddle next to him and learn to appreciate what he loves.

Each compromise doesn't make us resentful. Instead, we grow closer. Negotiating becomes a game to see who can be the most creative by making the house fit us both. Like when Bubba manages to find a couch, loveseat, and chair that are all brown leather, yet different tones and styles. He's a man who fixes problems rather than ignores them. If I want something and he wants something else? Well, that's just a fun challenge.

Before moving in, we paint the living room and kitchen with burnished gold, sea blue, and rustic red. The rest of the house's walls wait for a weekend when a dozen Brotherhood families and my parents drive up. We make the painting party an event—tents out back, feasts, music, and swapping stories.

Many of the Brotherhood can't come up for family or work reasons. Others refuse to embrace my bad taste in men. After all, I gave up a good guy like Griff, only to turn around and settle for an outsider. I don't take their opinions personally. They don't know Bubba like I do. Hell, they haven't even seen Griff the way I have. Their views are based on limited knowledge. If they knew what I do, they'd no doubt fall for Bubba too.

Conroe is my home now. Lonely at times, I wish Bubba was with me constantly, but he has a ton of work. There's a lot of unfinished rental houses waiting to be put on the market. Butch obviously can't help, and the Dogs are useless. I sense Jack is either lazy, stupid, or both. Bubba claims his cousin is just easily distracted, and he'll grow out of that.

His uncle Jace keeps busy, and that overly muscled guy name Ron does fine. Overall, Bubba and Butch seem to be the real workhorses. Now one of them is on the mend, and the other fell behind on his projects while banging me in Tennessee.

To add to Bubba's stress, I open my big mouth about how the Johansson name needs to be more prominent in the town. This inspires Bailey and Sawyer to buy two empty storefronts with no idea what to do with them. I then make the mistake of agreeing with their plan to "do something." Now, I'm supposed to help them figure out the logistics of their expansion. It's not as if I can tell them no. They're family now. It might not be legal yet, but their needs are my needs.

Layla comes up for the weekend to talk about how we'll manage the sanctuary now that I no longer live in Hickory Creek.

"Do you want to quit?" she asks while curled up on my couch.

"Never."

"Then I do the manual labor, and you do the bookkeeping?"

Hearing her irritation, I point out, "You get to spend time with the birds."

"True," she says. "I win."

Layla isn't happy with my moving. She doesn't like Bubba. She hates Conroe. Nothing pleases her here.

That's on Friday.

By Saturday, she admits Bubba is very hot and probably the best I could hope for since I crave a biker like my dad. "Why not date a lawyer or a barista?"

"Why don't you date them?"

"I should. Bad men do bad things," she says as we hang out on my back porch. "I'm staying far away from bad men."

That's on Saturday.

By Sunday, she seems ready to rub up against Jack Johansson until I distract her by mentioning peppermint cookies. My cousin is amazing, but the chick's attention span is that of a small child.

Before returning to Tennessee, Layla and I brainstorm ideas for the storefronts I'm supposed to manage.

"Go boho," Layla says, stoned and giggling about Ula's dancing. "Sell a bunch of random shit. These rednecks won't get it, and it'll be hilarious."

"Scarlet and Phoebe make soap with their goat milk. Sissy said Lily likes to crochet."

"Yeah, sell that hippie shit to these yokels. I fucking dare you!" she cries, laughing so hard she needs to pee.

While Layla finds this concept hilarious—mainly because she's stoned—I think I could put together a little bohemian boutique with fresh farm products from Scarlet and Phoebe, quilts and blankets from Lily, and some other crap I'll need to figure out later.

None of that will happen soon, though. Lily is swamped with motherhood. Scarlet and Phoebe have twin infants and three school-aged daughters. These women also don't know me well enough to feel comfortable to sign on just yet.

But I can do this, and I'll be helping the Johansson family. If Bubba wants to be the king of Conroe. he'll need a queen who does more than sit around polishing her crown.

I'll help him make this little town the best it can be. My dream is for Bubba to leave a legacy to rival those of his uncles and grandfather.

THE RUNAWAY

Butch doesn't understand why we should waste money changing the name of Morty's Pub. Having never been to Hickory Creek Township, he can't understand the almost oppressive presence the Brotherhood and Hallstead family have in their town.

"Soso says we need to remind everyone who runs shit."

"Soso says," he mocks while cradling his gut after overdoing his exercise for the day.

I only smile at his taunt. What else can I do? He's recovering from a gunshot wound that I'm certain he wouldn't have if I remained in Conroe. This is the reason I don't tease him about his pastel house or the barrette stuck in his hair. Yeah, I'm just going to let that shit slide…for now.

"Is Johansson Pub the best name you could come up with?" he asks after glancing toward the kitchen where Sissy hums.

"It's the name people need to remember."

"Why not Davies?"

"Because there are more Johanssons than there are Davies."

"Did Soso count them for you?" he asks, smirking at his jokester shit.

Butch has been in a considerably better mood since ending Sissy's mom a week ago. Though I wasn't looking forward to offing a woman, he needed someone to help with the heavy lifting even if he was the one to finish her. Sissy's mother was a threat to his family, and Butch doesn't fuck around when it comes to his woman and kids. Having his back was the least I could do after bailing on Conroe weeks ago.

"We both fell for blondes," I say, pointing out the obvious, "and Mom is blonde. Do you think that means something?"

"Yeah, that you're weird, and I have good taste."

I warm up to this calmer side of Butch. He still does his silent routine when we're out with people. At home with his family, though, he's downright jolly. If this keeps up, I'll suggest he play Santa at this year's Christmas party. Oh, he'll fucking love that!

"So, Johansson Pub, it is," I announce.

"I like Whiskey Kirk's better."

"Yeah, but no one here knows who Kirk is any more than they know who the fuck Morty is. This isn't about honoring our family. We want to instill fear in everyone by constantly reminding them of our presence."

After Butch glances at Haydee dancing into the room to music only she can hear, his gaze returns to me.

"I'll be ready to work soon," he says before adding, "And to do other strenuous stuff."

"Hey, man, that's between you and Sissy."

"Asshole," he growls while I stand up.

"We'll have a party at the pub to celebrate the name change. I'm thinking about inviting Soso's dad and brother. Wouldn't hurt for us to create stronger connections to powerful people. We'll never get any respect if we always rely on Cooper."

I stop at the door and think of my uncle who's been in Conroe more lately because of Lily's new baby. "Cooper is always willing to get into a dick measuring contest with Hayes and the Brotherhood. There's no downside to him acting that way because Ellsberg is secure. Conroe isn't, and I want more allies."

"A party?" Butch grumbles, likely hearing nothing else I said.

"Yeah, and Mom's picking the new sign."

"Smart to let her have a little power now that you're swinging your dick around."

"That was Soso's idea."

His blue eyes twinkle with amusement. "Do you ever come up with anything on your own?"

"I came up with the idea of marrying Soso."

"Smart man."

While Butch isn't happy about the party idea, I promise he only has to show up and look scary. Plus, we'll have a family portion of the event located in the parking lot. Butch immediately approves of his kids enjoying themselves.

The party planning grows every day. Soon, Soso works with Scarlet and Sawyer on the non-club portions of the event. They organize food, inflatables, face painting, and music. She's really sexy when she gets organized, and I nearly break my dick from fucking her nonstop some days.

"I'm trying to work here," she whines while also positioning herself—on all fours, pussy at the ready—in front of her laptop to allow me some loving.

Possibly because of Soso's influence on me, I decide to get the Dogs involved in party activities. Pavel drives around town, putting up signs directing people toward the pub. Tolya and Andrei set up tables and chairs. Diak hauls cases of soda from Soso's truck. I even make Vlad inflate helium balloons.

Noticing how I've put them to work, Soso gives me a smirk. While they'll be talking shit later, none of them dare complain to my face. Not out of fear of me, of course, but they know about Cooper and Colton's frequent visits to see Lily and Byron. For now, they'll play along.

"Those dumbasses need to find a way to get rid of you without it pointing at them," Soso said the other night. "Having met them now, I sense it'll be a while before they come up with anything worthwhile. They lack brains and fear death. No way are they screwing with you for at least a few months."

I love when she talks business with me. Soso has a fuck ton of ideas about how to run the club. Things she learned from spying on her dad and uncle when she was a kid.

"I wanted to be like them," she said, giving me a sheepish smile a few nights back. "I was convinced I would be the first chick in the Brotherhood. That clearly didn't happen, but I learned some things. Now, you can use their good ideas and skip the stuff that failed."

One of her plans is for the club to track down every source of illegal product sold in the Conroe area and force the distributor to pay us a kickback. If they want to do business in our territory, we get paid. Seems simple, but the Dogs have long claimed to Cooper and my mother that no one sells anything of worth in the area except a little meth and the girls at the Rossiya Motel. Considering I spotted teenagers smoking pot at the park the other day, Vlad is full of shit. The Dogs were just too lazy to care, and we've allowed the criminal side of the business to slowly unwind for years. *That kind of thinking is over.*

A new name and a sign for the pub might seem like a tiny thing, but it's the first item in a long list of things I plan to get done. Most of which I haven't even shared with my mom yet. That part wasn't Soso's idea, but I'm sure she agrees. I need to make moves on my own or else I'll never earn respect.

Mom's quite proud of the sign at the unveiling. Around us, locals begin arriving for food and games. Later, we'll unveil a new menu for the pub, and the party will switch to adults-only.

"Dayton likes the sign," Mom tells me around three pm after the parking lot is full of people.

I spot Hart riding Butch's shoulders to avoid getting overwhelmed by the dozens of kids running and screaming around them.

"The horse rides are a cute idea," she says, fixing the collar of my T-shirt. I know darn well there's nothing fucking wrong with my clothes, but Mom needs to fret. She's worried Cooper will make an appearance.

Around ten that morning, Colton showed up at Mom's house where we were finalizing plans for the day. He immediately asked if Soso's blue-haired cousin was around.

"I haven't found my special woman," he explained to Mom. "I might need to open myself up to chicks with unusual hair."

"Stay away from Layla," Soso growled.

Colton smiled in a way that I felt was too flirtatious. Punches were nearly thrown until Buzz announced that Denny had shit in the toilet like a big boy, and we all had to stop fighting long enough to applaud.

A sick bird keeps Layla from driving up with her parents. While Colton might not get laid today, he's certainly a hit with a handful of ladies. Haydee and Scarlet and Phoebe's daughters—Janis, Yancy, and Cady—follow him around the parking lot as if he's a tattooed Pied Piper.

The family part of our day goes off without a hitch. Though I expect more families than we get, Conroe is weird. Even free shit makes them wary.

Eventually, the first part of our big day winds down. The bounce castle gets deflated and returned. Chairs and tables are folded. Pop follows Mom around while she organizes all this activity. Sawyer disappears at some point and returns with her shirt inside out. Her preteen daughter, Kiki, just shakes her head and walks away when she finds her disheveled parents.

"Nasty," she mumbles.

Sawyer shrugs. "One day, she'll understand how sexy those bounce houses can be."

I frown at her comment, now regretting how I never got Soso in there before it was deflated.

Scarlet and Phoebe take home their five kids while Sissy, Haydee, and Hart hang around a bit longer before leaving with Lily, Dash, and Byron. I don't know when Buzz, Panni, and Denny left, but it's likely related to the toilet triumph earlier.

The mood shifts as the adult portion of the day begins. Colton decides to have one drink before heading over to Sawyer's to hang out with our gram.

"I'm her favorite," he says, flashing me a smile. "Nice party, Conroe cousin."

"Thanks for spying for your father, Ellsberg cousin."

"Enjoy your woman," Colton says, just begging for me to take a swing at him again.

Soso changes out of her skirt and flowery blouse before dressing in a leather and jeans getup that makes my body temp rise. She's full biker chick tonight, and I appreciate the show she provides. A badass president needs his badass old lady.

"We'll make this official soon," I whisper while dancing to one of those pop-country songs that Mom listens to while working out.

"Why? Legal shit is for other people."

"Legal shit matters. If I die, I want you taken care of."

I know I'm saying something stupid before the words even finish leaving my mouth, but I can't stop. Despite smiling at my idiocy, Soso doesn't laugh.

"Okay, baby," she says and wraps her arms tighter around me. "Let's pretend this is a slow song."

I struggle not to kiss her into submission and then carry her out of the pub for car sex in our new, used SUV. Soso knows where my mind goes, so she helpfully suggests my mother's recent clinginess is likely caused by menopause. *Yeah, that info quickly throws cold water on my dick region.*

My mom and pop leave soon after Soso's comment. They pretend they want to check on Denny and his new pooping skills. Soso claims that's the weirdest code for wanting to fuck she's ever heard.

Butch hangs around long after I expect him to head home to where Sissy and his kids wait. I sense he's edgy about the Dogs sitting in the corner, watching us while speaking in Ukrainian.

I don't know why they stayed, considering there are no club bunnies around to fawn over them. Starting today, I instituted a new rule. If club women are on the premises, club bunnies can't be. No way do I want women I've fucked anywhere near Soso. Any more than I'd want to hang out with men she's fucked. Even if Griff settled down and acted normal, I'd never want him in my face.

Jack wasn't happy with the rule and left with his sister and mom. I assumed the Dogs wouldn't hang around either.

But they remain in their corner, speaking in a language they figure we can't understand. Vlad and his boys could sit right in front of us, making plans to spill our blood. We'd have no clue.

Or, at least, we wouldn't if it weren't for my old lady's savvy ways.

THE BOHEMIAN

THREE DAYS AGO

The women at the rundown Rossiya Motel near the highway are essentially sex slaves. Despite being "freed" by the Johansson family when the Reapers took over, the Midnight Dogs were allowed to remain in control of the motel where the immigrant women live and work. Many of the prostitutes were lured to the US with promises of work and given fake visas. Most don't speak enough English to gain normal employment, and all of them are conditioned by their owners—the Dogs—to believe their current situation is their only choice.

After moving to Conroe, I find myself often thinking about the women. I even consider inviting them to the party at the pub. Unfortunately, they'd just end up being abused by the Dogs.

The Johanssons are like most "moral" crime families. They react to what's in their faces and ignore the rest. These women arrived in Conroe prior to the Johanssons' rule, and they remain the Dogs' responsibility. Out of sight, out of mind.

But I plan to end this blasé view of the motel. I'm enraged at the thought of anyone whored out against their wills. It's not like they can save up their money and walk away either. They're charged for their rooms, clothing, food, and other essentials. It's the classic pimp modus operandi.

That's not how prostitution works in Hickory Creek Township. Maybe my uncle and dad changed stuff years ago, or maybe the system was always in place. I just know those women choose their customers, keep most of their income, and pay the club for protection. If they want to quit, they can. If they want to work in the club's territory, though, they pay a kickback. The women are essentially independent contractors. It's not a pretty life, and I wouldn't want to fuck to pay my bills, but prostitution is a business in Hickory Creek. Here, it's something else. For now, anyway.

With Lex Zaldo rotting somewhere, Diak and Pavel run the motel.

"We like to rotate the men to ensure there are always enough to help the Reapers," Vlad tells me after he hears of my visit and feels the need to supervise.

I think to question why he speaks of "the Reapers" as if he isn't the fucking vice president of the local chapter. Of course, I just smile and nod. Men like him are useless. They're dumb muscle to be molded by better men or tossed aside. Bubba already made a choice on these idiots' fates. No reason for me to argue with a dead man.

"I'm a bit of a feminist," I say, giving Vlad a sheepish smile. "My friend in high school got into prostitution and enjoyed her work. Do the women here enjoy their work?"

Vlad smiles at me and strokes his beard. If I had a buck for every man who stroked a part of himself while talking to me over the years, I wouldn't need to inherit my wealth.

"Not all customers are so good. Many can be, um, how do you say, rough?"

I remember how Bubba claims the Dogs forget how to speak in English whenever they don't want to answer a question. I notice how Diak and Pavel whisper in Ukrainian behind Vlad. They feel safe saying whatever they want because they know I can't call them on it. Keanu and I pull that same move by speaking Korean in front of assholes. I've looked people in the eyes before and said the worst shit without them having a clue.

And that's the main reason I'm here today. Not to help these women. Until the Dogs are dead, I can't do much. No, I'm here to find a translator.

Butch installed surveillance at the pub while Bubba was in Hickory Creek. He worried the Dogs were plotting something. Of course, those recordings are useless unless translated. This motel is full of women capable of telling us what the Dogs say when they believe no one is the wiser.

"I have people in Tennessee," I tell Vlad and then add just to be a bitch, "Do you know where that is?"

"Yes, yes," he bullshits. "It's a state nearby."

"Yes, and my father is part of a club there."

"I heard he is a very important man."

"Yes, and he has many friends looking to visit Conroe for relaxation. I would act as a liaison for my father's friends and the women here who could help them relax. Do you understand?"

"Yes," he says, smiling wider. I love how the asshole understands the word "liaison" but pretends to get hung up on "rough."

"I want to meet your girls. One at a time. Talk to them to see who might fit with what my father's friends seek. Like an audition, yes?"

Great, now I sound as if I don't speak English well. Vlad gets what I'm saying. He mutters something over his shoulder to the other men who nod in unison. They've decided they'll "let" me speak to the women.

"Are you sure alone is good, though?" Vlad asks, following me into the tacky as fuck front office complete with cheap red carpet and dirty gold chairs.

"Why wouldn't it be?"

"They can be temperamental."

Turning around to look at him, I smile widely. "My father is a killer, Vlad. My brother is too. They taught me how to handle temperamental people. Don't get me wrong. I'm not saying I plan to kill any of these women, but I don't need a bodyguard either."

His smile remains. The humor in his gaze disappears, though. It's quickly replaced by a realization that I'm more than Bubba's blonde bimbo. I can make a call and end this man. He might have already known I was connected, but he's just grasped that I'm willing to remove a problem. So, the question is: Will Vlad become my problem?

No, he won't. Living is more important than his ego today.

I talk with each girl for exactly twenty minutes, showing none any obvious preference. Most are blonde, very thin, and pale. A few women seem actually ill, and the newest girl looks barely legal. They all wear ratty babydoll lingerie and cheap heels.

After the first round of interviews, I zero in on Katya who knows enough English to translate for the others. I have the women return one by one except this time Katya sits with me and translates. I tell Vlad the girls are hard to understand and I don't trust their answers.

"I can't have them disappointing the men I bring here," I explain when he offers to translate. "Katya seems obedient. She'll help me figure out if the women are lying. I'll let you know if any of them are."

Vlad thinks we're on the same side again. He's so easy to manipulate. Just useless muscle. No wonder the income stream in Conroe is so pathetic. With Vlad in charge, there's no imagination or determination.

The blonde, emaciated Katya breathes faster whenever I praise her. She's older than me by a few years but almost childlike and desperate for praise. When I ask how she knows so much English, she tells me she watches TV and imitates what she hears.

"I speak good, yes?" she asks, craving my approval.

"Very good."

While waiting for one of the girls to arrive in the front office, I casually slip Katya a throwaway phone.

"This is from Bubba," I say in the low, inviting voice I use when my birds get agitated. "He is everyone's boss. If he calls, you answer and obey. If you do good, you'll be rewarded."

Katya's blue eyes flash to the door where the three Dogs stand outside uselessly.

"They work for Bubba, just like you," I say, taking her hand and noticing her busted nails. "They want to be in charge, but they aren't. My man is, and he will reward you for doing good. No punishments, just rewards, but you have to be smart, Katya. I think you are smart," I say, letting the compliment sink in and watching her expression change. "But I think you're also scared, and it's easier to be scared than smart. Which one will you choose?"

"They will get angry."

"Don't tell them what I said. I will explain you need the phone because I want you for a special man from Tennessee. If Vlad or his friends hurt you, that will fuck up my plans with that man, and I'll be angry."

"You are just a girl."

Channeling my inner Hallstead, I harden my gaze. "No, I'm a biker bitch with the phone numbers for a dozen professional killers who'd end those assholes outside. Vlad and the others work for my man, and I say you are protected. Do you want to be protected, Katya?"

She doesn't answer before the next girl—Anna—enters. I feel Katya struggling next to me. She stumbles over a few translations. I know she's worried. She should be. The Dogs are evil fucks, but they'll be dead soon. I can't tell her this part or even what Bubba will want from her.

Katya never verbally answers if she's more smart than scared. Instead, she slides the phone into the bra of her dress, and I know she wants to be protected.

I finish with the rest of the woman, asking them the same questions as before. Their answers don't matter. I'll be asking new ones once the Dogs are dead and I can change things here.

But I got what I wanted from this visit. If Vlad worries a little more about his safety now, that's a bonus. Whatever he hopes for the future doesn't matter. He's already dead, and I'd love for Katya to be the one who seals his fate.

THE RUNAWAY

At eleven, Soso and Keanu decide to have a dance-off. I sit at a table with Butch whose jaw is clenched tight enough to cause damage. I mention Sissy teaching Soso to cook, and my brother's entire demeanor relaxes. Voila! I've found the off button on Butch's bitchiness!

Focusing on my woman's dancing, I'm shocked by her and Keanu's lack of skill. Apparently, rhythm isn't necessary for success at yoga or karate.

The Dogs also watch the siblings' antics. Vlad leans over to say something to Diak, and the others laugh. Soso tells me nearly every day that I have better things to do than stressing over dead men. As much as I love when she talks tough, I can't stop wondering about their conspiratorial smiles. What the fuck are they saying? Are they plotting something?

No, they wouldn't dare fuck with me on a night when top members of the Brotherhood are in Conroe. Colton is in town too. It'd be suicide.

But I hadn't expected the move with Vigo. Then I was surprised by their sacrifice of Lex. Am I making another mistake tonight?

Leaving Soso and Keanu to their dance contest, I have no idea how they'll declare a winner. I think Dayton is the judge. Harmony left earlier with Camden and his wife, Daisy. Her stomach rebelled from today's food offerings, and I wonder if she's currently puking.

Unable to settle down, I leave Butch and head to the pub's back office. I'm such a nonthreat to the Dogs that they never glance in my direction as I walk by. Shouldn't they be more aware of my movements if they're planning something tonight?

In the tiny back office, I dig out a tablet hidden under the desk. Soon, I've pulled up the surveillance of the Dogs' favored table. I hear the men's words clear as day, but it's all gibberish to me.

Calling Katya feels like a mistake. My paranoia is based on nothing. The men are behaving the way they always do—talking shit in a language we don't understand and feeling superior for keeping us in the dark. It's all bravado.

But what if it's not? I remember my brother in the hospital, looking fragile like a child. I should have protected him. It's my job, but I hadn't dealt with the Dogs in time.

And I still haven't.

Stupid paranoia or not, I dial Katya's number. She answers in her heavily-accented voice.

"I'm going to play you something in Ukrainian. Tell me what they're saying."

Katya squeaks in agreement, clearly nervous as fuck. I let her listen to the men's current conversation for only a minute before asking her to translate.

"I don't want to."

Dread fills my gut until it's boiling over. "Why?"

"I can't."

"Katya, you work for me, not them. I can make your life better. They can make it worse. Why are you protecting them?"

"It's not that. I don't think you want to know what they say."

Realizing she's scared of my reaction rather than theirs; I soften my voice. "I need to know my family is safe."

Katya is silent for what feels like an eternity but is likely only a few seconds. She exhales unsteadily.

"They talk about Soso."

"What about her?" I ask in the calmest voice I can manage.

"They say what they want to do to her. I'm sorry."

"What is it that they want to do?"

After a short pause, she whispers, "What they do to me."

Katya isn't willing to spell out their vile fantasies, which is probably best.

I thank her and promise everything will be fine. She did good. Soso said we could trust her. I hear less fear in her voice when she says goodbye.

I stare at the camera above the men, studying their relaxed, amused faces. They're watching Soso goof around with her brother. Even surrounded by killers, they remain fearless. They think we're stupid. Or that they're untouchable.

Even after Lex and Vigo, they bold enough to imagine putting their hands on my woman. It's a joke to them. All women are only meat in their eyes. This isn't new information. I see how they leer at every woman they meet. More than once, I've nearly caught them giving my mother one of their nasty smirks behind her back. It's all a joke. It's not personal to them. Just locker room talk between men, who fuck like they breathe.

It's not fucking personal.

I leave the office and return to where everyone enjoys the late evening. Butch and Dayton remain at the table by the door. Soso and Keanu look to be wearing themselves out, though I don't know who is winning. The bartender talks with Roid Ron. The waitress is in the bathroom. The Dogs sit in their corner, leering at my woman.

The gun feels weightless in my hand. Both when I point it at the closest Dog and when I fire.

The first bullet ends Tolya. The other men barely have time to react. Diak suffers a shot to the face before he finishes gasping at the sight of his dead friend. Bullets tear into Pavel next and then Andrei. Finally, I fire at Vlad.

In an ideal world, he'd have more time to worry about his impending death. Fear it, fight to survive, beg even. But I don't live in an ideal world.

I empty the gun.

I count the five dead men before lowering my weapon.

Only then do I notice how Butch and Dayton are next to me. Guns out, they're both ready for a battle. My gaze slides over their startled expressions as they accept what's happened. I look at Roid Ron and gesture toward the door.

He gets the message and secures the pub. Keanu is on the move, past me and to the ladies' room. He'll make sure Embry doesn't see anything. The bartender continues cleaning the glass in his hand. I sense he's more interested in his next smoke break than the execution of the former owners of this pub.

"What the fuck happened?" Butch growls, still ready for a fight.

I think to explain to my brother, but then Soso approaches me. She's wary. Does she fear me?

Dayton shoves his weapon into his back holster and wraps an arm around his daughter. "Num-Num, let Keanu drive you home."

"I want to stay," she says, her gaze locked on mine.

"Things need cleaning up."

"I'm needed here."

"Your mom's sick. Bubba has business to deal with."

When Dayton nods at me, I realize I need to speak. The words refuse to come out. Again, I can imagine how Butch feels.

I look to my brother staring hard at Vlad's slumped body. "I couldn't wait."

Butch frowns at me and then nods. "I'll get Jack and Jace back here to help us make these five disappear."

Nodding, I look to Soso who stares with unreadable eyes. I need her to understand, but talking in front of everyone isn't an option.

"Wait for me at home," I finally say. "Please, Num-Num."

Soso's icy expression cracks, and she smiles at my use of her childhood nickname. I recall how Dayton claims his daughter was a noisy eater as a kid. She's soundless now. Chewing quietly improves her chances of stealing food, no doubt.

The dread and cold rage inside me is instantly gone once I see Soso's smile. Giving a quick glance to the dead men, I feel nothing beyond a desire to erase every bit of their existence.

THE BOHEMIAN

The only way Keanu or I can win a dance contest is for our parents to do the judging. They find our attempts so entertaining that they often requested a dance-off whenever the cable went out.

Tonight, I'm so overjoyed about life—Bubba, my new home, the chapter's fresh start—that I'm willing to embarrass myself with Keanu. For my brother's part, he thinks he dances well. Compared to Cap, yes, Keanu is Fred Astaire. But compared to anyone with the least bit of rhythm, he sucks as much as I do.

Our contests are never about who has the best moves. Or even who makes our parents laugh the hardest. It simply comes down to who can dance for the longest. That's why I usually try to wear Keanu out first like by asking him to show me some karate moves. There's no time for trickery tonight. Dad announces I should give swaying with Bubba a rest and dance with Keanu instead.

And here we go!

Keanu's been dying for distractions since Lottie left the US. He worries she won't come back, or will come back but won't want him, or will come back and still want him but realize they've both changed, or finally will come back and will want him and they will have stayed the same, but some unknown thing will break them up. For an easygoing guy, that's a lot of damn worrying.

Tonight, I do my best to distract my brother after he was nice enough to dress all in black to a party at a rustic pub as if he's John Fucking Wick.

I start off my dancing with classic moves like "1980s white girl" bouncing. Just like my mom and aunts perfected at every party they've ever attended.

Keanu embraces "Saturday Night Fever" finger-pointing. I fall into The Twist when all the New Wave bouncing stirs up the mojitos in my stomach. Keanu imitates me. That's when I start the Chicken Dance despite the overhead song being "As Good As I Once Was" by Toby Keith. Fortunately, my lack of rhythm means I can make any music fit my crap dance moves.

There's the Sprinkler. Then the Shopping Cart. Next, I try the Elaine dance where I nearly kick Keanu, and he flies into karate moves in response. My brother effortlessly slides off his black jacket while still dancing. Meanwhile, I nearly injure myself taking off my leather jacket while also swaying. Dad loses his shit when I try to be cool by tossing him my jacket and end up throwing it at the bartender. Hell, Butch even cracks a smile over that, and Bubba stops eyeballing the Dogs long enough to grin.

"Hey, I'm dizzy," I say when Dad laughs for too long.

"For fuck's sake," Keanu grumbles when "Red Solo Cup" starts playing. "Who keeps putting on Toby Keith?"

"Having trouble, big bro?" I taunt despite me just bouncing now.

"No, cool comes easily for me."

Laughing at his wink, I start doing the Running Man because our father loves this move.

Bubba walks away during this song, and I worry he's hit his limit of embarrassment for the night. Then I remember how tight my jeans are and assume he's just horny.

Another Toby Keith song starts up, and Keanu frowns at everyone. "Who is picking these fucking songs? Do you not see how I'm trying to dance here?"

I give my brother's arm a pat. "Don't blame the songs. You wouldn't be doing any better with K-pop."

"Cabbage patch, Num-Num," he sneers and starts swinging his arms. "I'm taking you down."

Laughing harder, I mimic his dance moves. We make a circle on the dance floor, gazes locked, dancing as well as two rhythmically-challenged people can dance, and singing along with "God Love Her."

I don't even see Bubba return. I barely hear the gunshots over the loud music before Keanu nearly tackles me.

Everyone's guns are out. Dad is on his feet, moving in my direction until he realizes Keanu has me covered. Stalking toward Bubba, Dad and Butch remind me of lions hunting their prey.

But they might as well be vultures because there's no one left to kill.

I shadow Keanu as he approaches the back table where the Dogs once joked around. Peering around him, I catch sight of the bloody mess Bubba left behind. Each man suffered a shot to the head, probably more than one.

It was over before the Dogs had time to realize what was happening. That makes sense. Bubba said Butch would be dead if Vigo had taken the shot when his brother's back was turned. He had the perfect drop on the stronger, younger man. Yet Vigo's ego demanded Butch know who was killing him. That was his mistake. Butch survived the gunshot; Vigo did not survive his crushed skull.

"Ambushes only work if you don't announce they're about to happen," Bubba taunted one night while we talked about how close he came to losing his little brother.

I'm desperate to rush to Bubba and check him for injuries that I know he doesn't have. Mostly, I want to hold him.

But Bubba isn't a baby, and he doesn't need another mom coddling him, especially in front of these men.

That's why I leave the bar when Bubba asks rather than demand to be at his side. Keanu drives me home where we check on Mom.

"I puked just a little," she says when we find her in the bathroom cradling a trashcan. "I'm getting too old for carnival food."

Mom, Keanu, and I decide to watch a movie until Bubba and Dad arrive. My aunt and uncle are bunking at Sawyer and Jace's house. There's a weird little bond brewing between the Johansson sisters and the Serrated Brotherhood club management. They're creating a friendly rivalry much like the one between Cooper and Hayes. I'm frequently amazed by how competitive the Johanssons are with each other.

By two a.m., Mom is asleep on the couch, mumbling about corn. Keanu sits like a ninja across from me. I think maybe he's taking part in a staring contest I'm not aware of. I finally get my brother to stop doing his cold motherfucker routine by unleashing Ula on him. He's done for as soon as she shakes the junk in her bird trunk.

By three a.m., Dad and Bubba arrive home. They say nothing before walking to separate bathrooms to shower. Dad reappears first to claim a half-asleep Mom.

"I dreamed I was attacked by a Chupacabra, but Freki saved me," she mumbles happily. "Kicked its fucking ass."

Smiling, I remain in the living room with Keanu. TV off, birds now resting. Just me and my beloved brother.

"I'm ditching you as soon as Bubba gets out of the shower," he says, tapping his fingers on the arms of the chair.

"Did you ever ask Lottie to marry you?"

"Yes."

"And she said no?"

"She said she needed to be successful without me, or I'd think she was using me."

"What did you say?"

"Nothing. I instigated foreplay to end the conversation."

"Smooth move, wiener."

Keanu smirks. "She chooses to listen to the lies in her head rather than the truth that comes from my mouth. How can I fix that?"

"What lies?"

"That we're too different."

"But you aren't really. You both live in White Horse and think bagels are a decent meal."

"True, but she doesn't feel like she belongs here. She also doesn't feel like she belongs back in Indonesia. She's lost. I offer to help her, but one fucking person one fucking time hinted that she was a gold digger, and she now worries that's what everyone thinks."

"I assure you that every woman, who's ever wanted you and lost out to Lottie, does indeed think she's a gold digger. No one who matters does. I've told her that too."

"But she's stubborn."

"Have you tried crying when you ask her to marry you?"

"No."

"Well, now, you have a new plan."

Keanu gives me a half-smile. "What if she doesn't want to marry me because she doesn't want to marry me?"

"How could she not want to marry Keanu Slater?"

"Women be crazy."

"That they are, but Lottie loves you. I have no doubt about that. If she knows that you're hurt by her holding back, I think she'll finally take the leap. Then when she visits her family in Indonesia, you won't have to worry if she'll come back."

"Are you going to marry Bubba?"

"Yes," I say immediately.

"When?"

"As soon as it won't cause Griff to go nuts."

Keanu rolls his eyes. "I should kill him for you."

"And I should let you kill him for me."

"But you don't like murder. Which is very odd considering you didn't bat an eye when you saw those dead fuckers tonight."

Shrugging, I rub Freki's head. "I already knew they would die. I just didn't know when. Now I do. Nothing shocking about it."

"What about Griff?"

"His mom loves him. Other people do too."

"I don't give a fuck about his mom, Soso," Keanu says in that icy voice of his.

"Griff needs time. He's not in love with the real me. He'll find someone hot and forget about me. Then he doesn't need to die, his mom doesn't need to be sad, I don't have to feel like the bad guy, and the Brotherhood won't have issues with the Hayes family. Everyone will be happy."

"Are you stoned?" he asks, grinning. "What's with the hippie-dippy shit?"

"I'm happy. I want everyone to be happy. Happy is good."

"Now, you're just a fucking fortune cookie."

"Stop cussing so much."

"Well, I didn't get to kill anyone tonight," he grumbles, exhaling roughly. "Plus, I never officially won the dance-off. I have a lot of pent-up fucking animosity."

"I declare you the winner."

"It's true that I whipped your ass, Num-Num."

"Only because I was wearing jeans. In a skirt, I'd have crushed you."

Keanu smirks. We both know I've only won a single dance-off in all these years, and I had to nail him in the balls to achieve my triumph.

"It was an accident," I remind him.

"Oh, I know."

We share a smile until Bubba appears from the hallway. Keanu says nothing before standing and leaving the room.

Bubba's green eyes study me.

"Are you okay?" I ask, standing up.

Nodding, Bubba walks to the kitchen where he sits in one of the non-matching chairs.

I stand behind him and lean his head back against my chest. Sliding my fingers through his thick hair, I smile down at his uncertain gaze.

"You handled a problem."

"I lost my temper," he mumbles and frowns. "But I wasn't even angry. Not like hot angry. It was colder."

"You still handled a problem. There's no reason to second-guess yourself."

"I could have fucked up everything."

"But you didn't."

"I told Butch I would wait for him and do it together."

"Yes, but you're the president and not just his big brother."

"Soso, I fucked up."

"No, baby," I whisper and kiss his forehead. "You showed the rest of the club how you aren't a pretty boy pussy. You took charge, killed those men, and ended their threat to your club and family. No matter what Butch says, he respects how you handled shit. I think maybe he thought you were soft too, especially after that thing with Sissy's mom. You proved otherwise."

Bubba's lips curve into a smile. "You make everything sound simple."

"Because I don't have to be the one to pull the trigger or take charge. Being your sounding board is easier than doing the actual work."

"You're perfect."

"So are you," I promise as my hands massage the tension from his shoulders. "You weren't planning what happened, and that freaks you out. But remaining in control is overrated. Camden is all about the rules until he gets pissed and fucks up someone. His erratic behavior keeps people on their toes. They never know which guy they'll end up with. Yeah, he's their friend, but then maybe he isn't. Creating that uncertainty with violent men isn't such a bad thing for a guy as young as you."

"I don't feel young."

Stroking his jaw, I smile. "The only way you could have sounded younger saying that was if you used a baby voice."

"I need cuddles," Bubba says in probably the worst baby talk I've ever heard.

Of course, his failure makes him even more irresistible. *I don't know how he does that.*

I crawl into his lap and nuzzle his throat. "You did good tonight, but it's okay to question why you lost your temper. While I don't want you kicking yourself over a good move, smart leaders don't accept everything and move on. You, Bubba Davies, are a smart man, so these worries are okay."

"Is there anything I can do that isn't okay with you?"

"Don't fucking cheat on me," I growl, grabbing his shirt. "I put up with that shit with Griff because he didn't own my heart. If you cheat, I will fuck everything up. You, her, me. I won't care."

"I'm blind to other women."

"Sure."

"No, seriously, those club bunnies were hanging around the other day. Their presence didn't register beyond me telling them if they showed up at the unveiling party that they'd be cut off from the pub completely. Otherwise, I only want to look at you, hear you, feel you."

I smile at his sincerity. "What happens if I get fat?"

"Don't even start. If I had a beer belly and man boobs, you'd be out the door in a second."

"Never doubt that I'd think up very sexy things to do to your man boobs and belly."

"Can I still walk around shirtless all the time if I get fat?" he asks, as his arms tighten around me.

"I'd insist on it. No one puts Bubba in a corner."

"I don't understand that reference because I'm a man and only watch manly movies."

Pressing my forehead against his, I smile. "It's okay to feel bad about what happened. Or feel happy or scared. Always remember with me that you can feel whatever you need to feel. I'll never judge you."

An emotion I can't quite pinpoint flashes across his gaze. He watches me for a minute and then sighs.

"I want to feel guilty about Butch's shooting. I shouldn't have run off and left him and the others vulnerable. I fucked up, but I refuse to regret the path that led me to you."

"That's how I feel about Griff. If I hadn't been hiding in the corner of Salty Peanuts and you hadn't fought with him, I might never have given you a chance."

"I should thank him, but no."

"No is right," I whisper and kiss his lips. "Are you feeling better?"

"I think so. Like I mainly feel weird about not feeling more rattled by the violence."

"Some people can turn off that part of them when necessary. Some people love violence, craving it even. Then some people are wussies like me."

"You're the badass bitch telling me to fuck everyone up."

Inhaling his clean scent, I smile. "Again, because I don't have to do the ugly stuff. I'm a pussy. When you fought with Griff that day in my front yard, and we got inside, you were mostly focused on getting in my pants. You barely seemed fazed. I was rattled, though."

"Because he nearly fucked you up," he sneers in the way he always does when he thinks of that day.

"Yeah, and because violence rattles me. I have no taste for it. I freeze up too easily. Even with the training from my dad and brother, I just can't react the way I want. You don't have that problem. You're prettier than sin," I say, and he bats his thick lashes at me. "And soft in a lot of ways. But when you need to bleed or make someone bleed, you can snap into attack mode without hesitation."

"I'm a badass," he says, standing up with me in his arms. "An alpha. A real man who only fucks hard and fast without any concerns for his woman's needs."

"Can I be on top?" I ask as he carries me down the hall toward our bedroom.

"Yeah, sure, baby."

I lean my head back and laugh at my hunky puppy's obedience. There's something beautiful about a man who just wants to get laid and won't let the specifics get in the way of him enjoying himself.

Of course, in my eyes, there's something beautiful about every damn thing Bubba does.

THE RUNAWAY

My day starts with watching Soso brew tea for her still queasy mom. Dayton and Keanu left before we got up. Harmony says they're visiting Sawyer's house. I can't help smiling at how our families are beginning to mesh.

Soso knows I'm having a meeting at Mom's with the remaining club. She's worried about me. Not that she mentions this fact. No, she pretends I'm the toughest guy around. Her thumbs-up makes me oddly erect, and I don't think my dick understands what she's signaling.

Pop is gone when I arrive. Jace and Sawyer are already here. Butch and Jack arrive just after Ron. Buzz wanders past us with Denny on his hip.

"Keep the stink down, boys," he announces. "My son and I are on vacation."

Ignoring my brother's taunting, I join Mom in her office. The group files inside, and we shut the door. The room is large, lush, and smells like bacon, but seven people are several too many. Buzz's warning makes a lot more sense now.

Sitting in her wide, leather chair, Mom holds my gaze and tries to converse with me telepathically. I have no fucking clue what she thinks she's saying, but I nod anyway.

"Last night got messy," I say, remaining at the door while the others get comfortable, "but it was always going to happen."

"Why did you fuck them up when people were around?" Jack demands.

"The waitress didn't see shit. The bartender doesn't care. The rest are our people."

"Dayton Rutgers isn't one of us."

"He helped clean up the bodies, didn't he?"

"Oh, so he's one of the Reapers now, huh?"

"He's an ally," I respond, refusing to lower myself to Jack's temper. "Those dead men were technically part of our club, but they were never allies."

"You should have told us," Jack grumbles.

"Sometimes, you'll know what I'm thinking. Other times, you won't. If you want to make a play for the top spot, then do it. If not, shut the fuck up."

Jack looks so much like his dad as he scowls at me. I don't know who I look like when I scowl back at him. Mom wants desperately to step in but defeats the urge. I wonder if Sawyer might be mentally controlling her right now. Jace keeps frowning at his wife, which makes me think someone said something to someone earlier.

"Are you done?" I ask when Jack just stares.

"I'm thinking about how to kick your ass without your brother jumping me."

"I'll help you out by explaining you can't. Now sit down."

As legacy members of the Reapers looking to prove our worth, Jack and I aren't so different. That doesn't mean I plan to coddle him.

"We need a new vice president. If you can follow directions, that'll be you," I tell Jack. "If not, we'll have new members in time."

"Dick," Jack growls, but his ass also hits the chair like I instruct.

"We're starting clean today. We have five guys, which sounds like nothing, but we have five loyal guys. Anyone new will have to jump through a lot of fucking hoops to join. I want absolute loyalty from whoever we let in, and I'll make the final decision. No more letting Ellsberg call the shots," I say and glance at Mom.

She's dying to speak up and take charge. We had a little chat the other day about how I needed to handle club business, and she needed to handle the legit side.

Crossing my arms, I look over the six people who expect me to make shit right.

"First off, we need to clean up the mess the Dogs left behind. Soso and I will figure out the motel situation. Jack, I want you to handle the two meth guys in the area. Ron, you seem to have a good grasp of the town's dynamics. It was you who knew about that abandoned park," I say, and he nods immediately. Ron is stupid and rude, but he's loyal. He wants to prove his worth here like he didn't in Ellsberg. If I give him that chance, he'll ride with me to hell. Or at least, that's what Soso claims.

Continuing with my speech, I explain, "I want you to figure out who is selling what under our noses. Pot, booze, sex, even fucking counterfeit Blu-rays. Anything that's not legal in Conroe is our business. When we have the muscle, we'll start pulling those distributors under our control."

"The Dogs said…" Mom blurts out, but I wave off her comment. While she hates losing power, she wants me to succeed. It'll take time to establish a balance between us, but eventually, she'll see a man when she looks at me rather than just her boy.

"We can't trust anything the Dogs said. They were likely siphoning cash off everything from the motel to the drug sales. They hoarded booze from the pub and never paid their tabs. Butch thinks they were the ones stealing shit from the worksites."

I see Mom's expression freeze as she realizes both the Dogs were fucking with her and that we didn't inform her of this fact. She'll give me hell about that later no doubt.

"We don't know anything for a fact, though. We might have enemies in Conroe. The Dogs could have allies we never knew about. Nothing should be assumed. We'll need to learn the backgrounds of every person in this town. I want to know who is a snitch, a bootlicker, or has a thief in their family tree. Everything about the citizenry is our business. It'll take time, but we start building today."

"What about the legit businesses?" Sawyer asks.

"You and Mom have that organized. Sissy and Dash are picking up the slack from Lily being on maternity leave. Soso will help more as she settles into Conroe."

Before my speech becomes too tedious, I open the door and thank everyone for coming. Then I leave before anyone can get chatty.

Mom and Sawyer remain in the office while Ron and Jack leave immediately. I hear them talking about meeting at the pub tonight. As far as I can tell, Jace disappears into thin air. Only Butch joins me in the kitchen.

My brother was quiet last night while we disposed of the Dogs. While his silence might have been related to that mutism thing, I sensed he was processing the situation.

Now I hope he'll express himself verbally, so I can stop guessing about what's on his mind. Instead, he sits at the island and stares at me.

"Last night wasn't how I wanted shit to go down," I explain to him. "I saw them on the video and knew they were talking about Soso, and I just snapped inside. There was no more waiting."

"I'd have done the same."

"Trust is important. Last night didn't help prove my word means anything."

"You fucked up," Buzz says, entering the kitchen.

"I did what I felt I had to do."

"Yeah, and that's why I'm not in your stinking club," he says, leaning his head into the fridge.

"What does that mean?"

"It means," Buzz says, closing the fridge once he locates a juice pouch, "I'd be flying off the handle every damn day."

"You are impulsive," I admit as soon as I realize he isn't pointing fingers at me. "But I still wish you'd join the family business."

Buzz walks over to me and smiles. "I'd never listen to you. I'd do whatever I wanted and talk shit behind your back. Do you still want me in your club, big bro?"

"No, I'm good. Thanks."

Grinning, Buzz pats my back and starts to leave. "I might one day decide to do the legit side of the family business, but even then, I suspect I'd just push everyone's buttons."

I consider asking if he behaves that way with his current boss at the RV sales lot. Buzz is gone, though, and I figure it doesn't matter. He has never wanted to be in the Reapers, and my brother should live his life how he pleases.

Butch studies me for a long time. I'm used to him not talking and assume he's just stuck in his head. Then he remembers to speak.

"You fucked them up," he says.

"Yeah, so?"

"I didn't think you were capable."

"I beat you up."

"I let you beat me up."

We share a smile. "This is a chance for us to get out from under Cooper's control and prove we deserve to be in charge."

"You're afraid you'll fuck it up," he says, being helpful as usual.

"No."

"Good."

"Think Jack will be a good VP?"

"No."

"Seriously or are you worried he'll boss you around?"

Butch stretches, hesitates while waiting to see if the movement causes him pain, and then accepts how his body works better these days.

"He already bosses me around. The difference is I'd need to listen to him if he was the vice president."

"Do you want to be the vice president?" I ask, already knowing the answer.

"No."

"Ron isn't an option."

"He likes drugs too much."

"Jace claims he's too old to give a shit about what happens."

"He's forty," Butch mutters.

"Yeah."

"Then I guess you have to give it to Jack, but make him beg first."

We share a smile again and then glance in the direction of our mother's very loud entry.

"My sons!" she declares. "Could a mother be any prouder of her boys than I am of mine?"

"Even me, Mommy?" Buzz cries out from somewhere in the house.

"You're my favorite!" she yells back while winking at Butch and me.

Mom gives Butch a hug and pats his belly. Then she lunges for me.

"My boy is all grown up," she says, stroking my head and making me worry she'll try to put a diaper on me soon. "You're a man with a woman and a house, and I'm so proud."

I stare at Butch over Mom's shoulder and find him smirking at my predicament. Breaking loose from her grip will be impossible without someone getting hurt. Relenting, I let her cuddle me. Minutes pass—so many minutes—and she just keeps holding on.

Finally, Pop enters the kitchen and tells her that summer break makes him lonely. Lunging for him, Mom latches on and refuses to let go. They're still attached when Butch and I flee the house twenty minutes later.

Yes, Mom will need time to accept our new power-sharing situation. Fortunately, Pop still has plenty of summer vacation left.

THE CHAPTER WHERE NOTHING'S REALLY OVER
THE BOHEMIAN

Conroe is full of gossips, and I often feel uneasy as if being watched. They routinely spy on the Johansson family, looking for more dirt to tell at their tea parties—that last part might just be my vivid imagination. The disappearance of the Dogs likely gave them more evidence of wrongdoing by the newcomers.

Or I could be completely paranoid.

I never catch anyone looking at Sissy and me as we walk around the grocery store. No one even makes that move where they glance away quickly. Yet I still feel watched.

But I don't tell Sissy. She already suspects everyone has a negative view of her. Mentioning how people are watching will make her more self-conscious. Lottie is the same way in Hickory Creek, though she seems less uncomfortable in White Horse. Again, I've always believed much of her concern is in her head. People aren't nicer in White Horse. Since she believes they are, that's how they seem.

Just as being watched is probably in my head. Ignoring the hunted sensation, I pay for my groceries. Behind me, Sissy hums a song I don't know. She's excited about Butch feeling better and them having sex soon.

"He makes me happy," she says while we walk to her SUV.

I find Sissy and Butch's relationship fascinating. They both forget to talk sometimes. She just spaces out, and he seems to lock up. I assumed they'd be a very quiet couple. Instead, when together, they seem to fix those bad habits in each other and speak normally.

Since moving to Conroe, I'm always analyzing other people's relationships and imagining what they're like when no one's watching. Is Nick a super dominant alpha while Bailey giggles and swoons? That one I can almost believe. Scarlet and Phoebe are the two I have the most trouble analyzing. I keep thinking Scarlet is the dominant one because she's louder, more Johansson-like. But Phoebe tends to be the one who gets her way.

What do people think about Bubba and me? Do I seem like a pushover? Am I one? I did give up my home to chase after a man I'd known for less than two weeks. No, that clearly makes me a romantic, not a weakling.

Leaving Sissy at her SUV, I push my cart to my truck. Bubba and I have an SUV now, but I still prefer to run errands in my clunker.

For every bag I rest inside the passenger seat, I stop to look around. The hairs on the back of my neck are standing at attention. The parking lot isn't empty. Gossips could be watching without me seeing them.

I'm likely paranoid, but I dig around in my purse for my switchblade just in case. With no pockets, I stick it in the band of my skirt. It's dumb, but I'm nervous.

Mom says people have a sixth sense about danger. She claims its leftover from our caveman days. I always assumed mine was broken. I hadn't felt in danger at the party where a guy nearly raped me. I never sensed anything particularly fucked up about Griff. The day he destroyed my garden and stole my birds, my spidey senses didn't go off.

But I'm struck by foreboding now.

Or I've worked myself into such a mental frenzy that I'm noticing things that aren't there.

I dial Bubba. Hearing his voice will calm whatever crazy I've caught from a routine visit to the grocery store.

Before Bubba answers, I turn my head and realize I haven't imagined anything.

Diving into the truck, I try to climb into the driver's seat and away from Griff. He moves too fast, nearly running. His hand grips my shirt and yanks me from the truck. I feel the fabric tear.

Without thinking, I shove my phone down the front of my skirt and underwear, keeping it out of sight.

As I fall backward, Griff does nothing to keep my ass from crashing down on the asphalt. I don't look up at him.

Instead, I see past his huge build and into my truck where my purse and gun sit inside.

The bag is too far away. I flip onto my knees and start crawling. So startled, I nearly forget to scream. Layla mocks girls like me in horror movies.

"If she screamed, her friends would hear, and they'd live, but she was too stupid!" Layla yelled at the TV more than once.

I do think to cry for help, but it's too late. Griff is on top of me, his hand over my face, covering my mouth and nose. I can't breathe as he effortlessly carries me to a nearby black SUV.

My hand reaches for my switchblade before realizing it's fallen into my underwear with my damn phone. Before I can fetch the weapon free, Griff body slams me into the side of the SUV.

Even stunned, I enjoy a momentary reprieve and can breathe while he opens the door. Then he tosses me like a ragdoll into the passenger seat. I plan to run as soon as he walks around to the driver's side.

Clearly un-fooled by my momentary docility, Griff slaps me across the face.

I'm shocked by the pain. Despite freezing, I still plan to go for the door once he's out of range.

Griff reads my mind, climbing over me rather than walking around the outside.

"You make everything so fucking difficult," he grumbles and starts the SUV.

Escape is all I can see. Sissy is still in the parking lot. I don't know if she heard my short-lived cry. Someone probably did. They might have seen the struggle. Help is coming, but I need to remain here.

Despite feeling as if I'm moving lightning fast, I never get the door open. Griff grips my hair and slams my face into the window. I see stars, tears blinding me.

"Either I can have you," Griff growls, yanking my face closer, "Or I can make it so he'll never want you. How badly do you want the day to go, Soso?"

I can't see him through my tears. Is he smiling at my fear? Frowning at my silence? I don't know what he expects me to say.

"Sit still and keep your fucking mouth shut, and we'll do fine," he mutters, pulling the SUV out of the parking lot.

I wipe my eyes just so I can see. Is there anyone watching us? Are the police on the way? Will Sissy tell Bubba? I think of my parents and wish I'd taken my mom's warning about trolls more seriously. I could have shot Griff before he ever put his vile fucking hands on me.

"Shut up!" he screams when I cry louder.

Thinking of my parents was a mistake. I need to stay calm. Be cool like Keanu. He never shows his hand. He's icy. I can be icy too.

Steadying myself, I study my surroundings. If I get the chance to jump out, where's the closest safe place?

"I know where I made my mistake," Griff says, driving with his left hand on the wheel while his right remains free in case I need to be hit again. "You rich bitches get bored easy. All women do. They need something to keep them entertained, so they don't get stupid thoughts in their heads."

While he babbles, I don't waste time trying to convince Griff that I understand. I used up all that capital when I played him to get back my birds. He knows I don't want him. He might think he can change that, but there's no reason for me to pretend we're at that point. I need to save my lies for when he might actually believe them.

"I should have knocked you up day fucking one," he grumbles while turning the SUV down a road I don't recognize. "The best way to keep a woman in her place is to breed her. Give her a kid or two to mind, and she won't have time for fancy ideas. That's all your bird shit is. You want to be a great savior. Your fucking rich aunt thought the same way. Bitch never had any kids and wasted her life. Went through husbands out of boredom. She needed someone to breed her. That was my mistake. I thought you were a Rutgers, but you're a Hallstead. Those women only know their place when they've been bred by a powerful man."

"I miss Hickory Creek," I whisper.

Griff flashes an angry scowl at me. "You should have thought about that before you ran off with that fucking rapist," he sneers and shoves my head toward the window.

This time, I keep my skull from making contact. "I thought he was the one."

Griff hears my regret. I'm having second thoughts about Bubba. Moving here was a mistake.

I keep my gaze on my lap, only making quick glances up at him to see if my words affected him.

Uncertainty is written all over his face now. I'm no longer a lost cause. I can learn from my mistakes. He can teach me to make things right.

In my head, I remind myself to remain calm and wait for my chance to move. Griff isn't smarter than I am, but he is stronger. I just need the chance to get away from him and then it'll be over.

Griff can't walk back what he's done today. He had to know he was sealing his fate when he took me. This man is on the edge. Either he makes me understand, or we're both dead.

I'm sure he believes he can kill me and go on the run, but deep inside, he knows there's nowhere he to hide. Griff loves his mom and knows my family will tear her apart to find him. It's the way the world works in Hickory Creek.

But now I've given him a chance to fix things between us. He doesn't have to kill me or die. Life can be good again.

With enough time, he believes he can redeem me.

With enough time, I know I can escape.

Soon, we'll learn which one is right.

THE RUNAWAY

Sawyer instructs Butch and me to organize the work schedules now that we've "fired" over half of the club. We still have plenty of projects left open, and we were behind even before I ended the Dogs. However, rather than focus on worksites, I've spent the last day designing the specifics for the atrium.

"Other shit matters," Butch grumbles at me when I say I need to spend tomorrow picking up supplies for the enclosure.

"Yeah, I see how you spend all your fucking time working rather than playing Mister Mom here," I growl back at him and gesture toward Hart drawing next to us at the kitchen table.

"What's your point?"

"I didn't have one. I just wanted you to shut up."

Butch narrows his green eyes. "People bitch when I don't talk. Then they bitch when I speak up."

I fight a smile since I can't tell if he's serious or not.

"Do you want to help me build it?" I ask when he stares at me with his grumpy expression.

Butch suddenly smiles. "Do you have your design sketched out?"

We skip the work schedule part and focus on how best to incorporate the atrium/enclosed porch into the house while also providing a secluded area for the birds.

As quiet as Butch, Hart draws Ula and Bjork in the atrium we're designing.

"You're a dad," I mumble to my brother. Frowning instantly, Butch assumes I'm talking shit. "That makes me an uncle to three kids now," I add before he hurts himself from frowning so much.

Butch's smile returns. "Hart is excited about homeschool."

The boy looks up at the sound of his name and smiles at Butch. There's already a trust built between them even after a short time. Maybe that's how Davies men roll. We all fell fast and hard for our women and raced to build lives with them.

Twenty minutes after Butch and I finish with the atrium design and finally start figuring out the work schedules, my phone rings.

I smile at the sight of Soso's number. This morning, she told me that she decided to give our future children "place names" in honor of her father. I suggested Charlotte for a girl and Austin for a boy. Soso's laughter indicated those names would never be unique enough for her tastes.

Answering the phone, I hear muffled sounds but no voices. I nearly grin at the thought of Soso butt dialing me. Then I remember she's wearing a skirt with no pockets. It's possible she hit the wrong button while reaching in her bag, but I know in my gut that she's in danger.

"I have to go," I say, jumping up and running for the door.

"What's happening?"

"Soso's in trouble. I don't know where or how, but I need to find her."

Butch frowns darker. He doesn't know why I'm panicking, and I'm not sure how to explain why I know Soso's in trouble. She isn't flighty like Sissy. Soso doesn't accidentally dial people.

Butch hurries after me as I exit his townhome. "What should I do?

I stand on the front porch and realize I have no clear idea where I'm headed. My brain recalls her plans for the day. She wanted to cook dinner together tonight. Enchiladas maybe. Plus, she mentioned Freki was low on his special kibble. At breakfast, I asked if she wanted me to pick up food, but she said she would do a round of shopping with Sissy instead.

"Soso and Sissy went to the store together," I tell Butch, who instantly calls his woman.

Panic easing, I remember the app on my phone that allows me to track her location. She agreed to sync our phones since she still doesn't know the town well and might get lost. She also wanted to spy on me.

"I get nosy too," she said, wearing a devious smile as we installed the app.

The thought of her in danger makes my blood run ice cold. Conroe is a quiet town except for the Dogs. Or maybe not. We worried there might be people pissed about the Dogs' disappearances. Is that why Soso is in danger?

I'm halfway to my Harley before Butch calls out to me. "They finished up shopping and were packing up their groceries, but Sissy can't find her. Soso's truck is still in the lot. The door is open, and her purse was left behind."

Butch knows what he's saying, but he doesn't dare utter the words, "someone took her."

I study the map on my phone. A small red dot moves along a winding road in Conroe. Soso's on the move, and the speed indicates she's in a vehicle.

"Call the guys and get them out looking for her. Put out feelers to everyone in town. We need to find her."

I climb on my Harley and race in the direction the app says she's headed. Though it's possible Soso is nowhere near her phone now, my only option is to chase down the moving dot on the phone map.

THE BOHEMIAN

I quickly lose track of where we are in Conroe. Woods on both sides of the road, no homes or businesses in sight. Griff doesn't check his phone for directions. Does he even know where we are going?

"I couldn't fucking believe those assholes came up here to paint your damn house," Griff grumbles as we turn onto a winding road. "Where's their fucking loyalty?"

"My dad made them come up."

Griff gives me a quick glare before returning his blue-eyed gaze to the road with its many curves.

"Your father is a bitch," he says. When I don't answer, he grabs my wrist. "Wouldn't you agree?"

"I'm not trash-talking my dad to feed your ego."

"But you'll trash talk your fucking rapist man."

I fight the urge to argue with him. Griff always did this crap. He would claim he heard something about someone and then bring it up again and again to make an issue. Like he once claimed "someone" told him that Layla was a thief. Then every time I misplaced anything even for a few seconds, he'd mention how she probably stole it.

I'd point out how she couldn't have stolen it, but that was my mistake. There's no arguing with Griff. I can never give him enough evidence to prove he's wrong. It's just an exercise in frustration. Even if he never convinces me either, he still wins by having me argue. His behavior wore down my resolve, making me easier to bully in other ways.

I'm not falling for his tricks today. I will remain calm. When we stop somewhere, even if only at a light, I'm making a run for safety. The problem is we're in the middle of bumfuck nowhere with no lights or stop signs. Even if I jump out, I won't find a sanctuary out there.

But I still plan to escape the SUV when I get the chance. I'm aware that Griff never lets down his guard. Meaning, even if I escape the vehicle, I'll have him right on my ass. Timing will be everything.

That's why I don't waste time arguing with him. I need to keep sharp. Except my body hurts from him smashing me against the SUV in the parking lot. Pain also radiates from where he backhanded me.

But I refuse to focus on anything except the road. Sooner or later, he'll need to stop, and I'll make my move.

"You're so fucking stupid," he says, chuckling angrily. "You have stars in your eyes for that rapist as if he's special, but you looked at me like that when we started dating. You thought I was fucking everything. What happened to that, huh, Soso?"

His voice rises until he hollers my name. I rack my brain for the right response.

"What do you want me to say?" I yell, and he looks ready to hit me again. "I made a mistake, okay, but it's too late to change anything now. I moved here. People helped us move in. I can't just go back home. It's too late."

Griff growls full of frustration and bangs on the steering wheel until he nearly loses control of the SUV and sends us into a ditch.

"You fucked up everything!" he screams. When I don't react, he shakes his head. "I've had so many hotter women than you. Better in bed too. You're a lousy lay, but I loved you anyway. Loved you more than you deserved."

"If I'm shit, why are we doing this?" I ask quietly.

"Because I love you, bitch!" he says, shoving me against the door.

Again, I prevent my head from bouncing off the window. Griff glances at me, looking disappointed.

"What you need is a strong man to keep you in line. I was too soft. I thought you'd whine to your daddy if I put you in your place, but deep inside, that's what you want. That's why you're in love with a rapist."

I want so badly to yell at him or, at least, roll my eyes as he claims our relationship would have been better if he smacked me around or raped me when I said no. Griff is fucking ridiculous, and I want to scream at him. I always wanted to put him in his place, but he doesn't listen, and we'd go in circles until I got tired and he won.

Today, I hide in my head and stare out the front window. I watch the road, curving this way and then that way. With the thick woods, I have no idea if we're close to anything until we're on top of it.

"Watch out!" I cry when Griff starts grabbing at me and stops paying attention to the road.

Crashing into the fender-bender in the road might have been a better solution than warning Griff. Except I saw the women in the road and knew they'd get run over if his SUV shoved their sedans forward.

The road's twists and turns led these older drivers to clip each other. Rather than move to the side, they left their sedans resting in the middle while they argue over fault.

My warning allows Griff to hit the brakes in time. The SUV screeches to a halt, only clipping the car on the right side of the road. The women jump at the sound. The impact isn't enough to push their cars forward, though.

Despite suffering a scare, they immediately start yelling at us. Griff frowns at the women while holding his breath. He's startled by how close we came to smashing into the cars and killing the women.

His distracted mind offers me a chance to escape.

I've been side-eyeing that door handle for ten minutes. My hand's been aching to touch it. Now, I have my chance.

I pull hard at the lever and throw myself against the door, hoping gravity will ensure I get away from Griff before he can grab me.

My shoulder takes the brunt of the fall onto the asphalt. Scrambling to my feet, I don't wait to catch my breath. I run toward the woods, knowing the women offer no help. They're old and likely not packing a weapon. Griff no doubt has one in his jacket. He'd end them long before they pulled a weapon from their granny purses.

The woods are my only escape.

I seek the clearest path, avoiding brush that might entangle me. I don't dare look back. I steady my breathing.

My sandals are horrible for running, but there's no time to take them off. I can only keep moving forward.

Behind me, Griff gives chase. I don't need to look back to know he's catching up. I feel him closing in.

I won't be able to outrun him. His long legs dwarf mine. I had hoped the thick brush might slow down his larger build.

But he's right behind me, and I don't have much time. I know I'm taking a risk, but I slow down enough to jam my hand into my skirt and panties. Ignoring the phone bouncing around in my underwear, I search for the switchblade and pray it hasn't fallen out during the run.

Griff tackles me as my fingers brush over the metal. I go sprawling on the ground. The wind bursts from my lungs as his body lands on mine. The jolt stuns me. I can't breathe for a few seconds. Then he yanks me by the arm and flips me over onto my back.

When I was little, my mom warned me that monsters were real. "They're out there, but don't be afraid," she said, wearing the most beautiful smile. "Just be smart and stay ready to deal with them."

I don't know if I believe in Bigfoot or trolls, but I know monsters are real, and I invited one into my bed months ago.

Now, he's going to kill me.

I see the realization in his eyes that he's taken things too far and can't rewind the clock. His ridiculous breeding plan is out of reach. There's no scenario where he survives. If Bubba doesn't kill him, Dad will. No one in the Brotherhood will care about a dead Griff. The second he grabbed me from the parking lot, he burned through all his goodwill.

With nothing to lose, Griff chooses to go out in a blaze of violent glory. He tears open my shirt, scratching my chest in the process. I can't freeze. Not when he's about to rape and kill me. There's no running away or talking him down either. I have to fight, but I only have the one shot.

The switchblade clicks open. I hear the sound, but he's too busy bitching about how I ruin everything to notice. His powerful hands shred my bra, leaving me exposed.

Despite my fear and panic, my mind focuses only on my target.

When his hands move down to my skirt, I see my opportunity. The blade feels so small in my hand. Such a tiny blade can't do enough damage. I'll only make him angrier.

But I have to do something.

The tip disappears into his left eye. I shove the blade as deep as possible, quickly hitting bone. In my head, he'll drop like a rock. I'll survive to see Bubba. Everything can still be okay.

Griff lets out a roar of pain that I feel through my entire body. Clenching, I know he won't drop. I've hurt him, but it's not enough. Should I have aimed for his throat? Is it too late?

I never get another chance to strike. His left hand seizes my right one holding the knife. He squeezes in the way I imagined him doing to Freki or the birds. My bones snap under the power of his grip.

I scream in pain, and my mind goes blank. Nothing registers beyond wanting to go home. Rather than returning to a place, I want to go back to a time before I agreed to date Griff. Or farther still to when I was a kid. Back when my dad scared away the monsters, and my mom kissed away my ouchies.

I don't want to be here in the woods, tits out, hand broken, waiting to die.

Griff is speaking, but I can't hear his words. I want to cradle my hand and crawl out from under him. I'm suffocating under the weight of his body.

I wish I could disappear, but I'm all Griff sees.

Holding his eye with his left hand, he brings his right fist down on my face. I hear the bones crack. I see bright stars and feel as if I need to vomit. My mind swims, and I wish it were over. Now, I want to die because I'm afraid of how much more he'll do before he ends me.

I crawl into my mind and hide there, deep inside my happy place. There's no pain here. No fear either. I'm at the

A-frame with Bubba. Freki sits next to him, always wanting to be close to the big, kind man. I know the feeling. Ula makes Bubba smile, and he rubs Bjork's belly. We're safe here, back in a time before Butch was shot and I ended up broken in the woods.

My happy place is where I want to be when Griff kills me. Not with him as he takes out his disappointment and rage on my body.

I want to be with Bubba, where we first fell in love.

THE RUNAWAY

The dot on the map stops moving on a small, rural road. I arrive only a few minutes later to find two old women squabbling over their fender-bender. There's an idling SUV with Tennessee plates behind their crashed sedans. In my mind, everything clicks. Griff came for Soso.

"He just left!" yells one of the women as if it's my fucking fault.

"Where did he go?"

"That way after his girlfriend!" the other woman screams.

I don't know if they're deaf or pissed, but they do point me in the right direction. Driving my Harley into the thick woods will likely just slow me down, so I jump off the bike and begin running.

I'm barely past the tree line when I hear Soso scream. The pain in her voice inspires me to run faster than I think possible. I hear more noises, echoing in the thick brush. I don't deviate, running instead through the clearest path. Soso would have wanted the quickest route away from Griff.

She didn't waste time asking for the old women's help. If Griff is unhinged enough to grab Soso, he's willing to kill a few bystanders. My woman hoped to hide in these woods, but he was too fast, and now he's hurting her.

I hear her cry out again. First in pain and then her voice shifts into desperate sobs. She sounds so hopeless.

My rage nearly blinds me. All that register are Soso's screams.

I see Griff ahead of me in the woods. He's crouched down. His back is to me, but the crunch of leaves and tree branches under my feet alert him to my arrival. Griff turns around to reveal a bloody left eye. Good on Soso for fucking him up, but it's not nearly enough.

He lifts a gun, but there's no time to aim. The bullet tears through my right arm. I feel the heat of the contact, but my pain disappears into the void. I only see a man who needs killing.

Tackling him, we fall next to Soso.

I don't dare look at her.

My heart aches to hold her and know she's alive.

But I can't give into that softness.

Every part of me must focus on the death of this man.

Griff and I know the routine. We are evenly matched in size and skill. We always end up at a stalemate with Soso breaking the tie.

Not today.

I pin his right arm to the ground, above his head. The gun in his hand fires pointlessly as he tries to break free.

My free hand digs into his open eye wound. Griff screams, drowning out the sounds of Soso's sobs and the gun firing. His cries invigorate me, and I shove my hand deeper. Tearing away flesh, I return for more.

The gun clicks empty. His other hand scratches at my face before punching me. He's desperate to live now. Seeing me through his good eye, Griff begs to go back in time. I revel in his terror, pain, and panic. I think maybe he cries out like a child, begging for mercy.

I let go of his right arm and shove my other fingers into his good eye. His body convulses under me. Blood gushes around my hands. I feel him fading as I break bones.

I've lost control of my bloodlust. Driven by the fear of learning what he did to Soso, I refuse to stop.

If Soso's dead, I won't be able to survive. I realize I can't hear her any longer over Griff's weakening cries. I'm terrified to know her suffering.

Soso owns my heart, and I failed her.

Even when Griff is long past dead, I can't stop. Punching his destroyed face, I refuse to look away from what used to be a man. I'm too afraid to let go of my rage and feel the full agony of failing Soso.

Then her fingers caress my jaw, and everything demonic inside me shuts off.

I reach for Soso, seeing only her.

Griff's corpse doesn't exist.

The world outside of her in my arms is a mirage.

THE BOHEMIAN

Bubba is the man I love. I believe I know him. But he's not the man I see tearing apart another man's face. This creature is a stranger to me.

I'd vomit at the sight of his violence, but my body is in shock. My mind isn't much better. I spin even when remaining perfectly still. I continue waiting for death despite watching Bubba destroy my attacker.

The sounds Griff makes as he dies are like nothing I've heard before. They're inhuman, much like Bubba's violence.

My eyes swell from where Griff hit me. My nose is broken. I spit blood while covering my bare chest.

The physical pain barely registers. I'm overwhelmed by that noise Griff makes. In contrast, Bubba is eerily quiet as he rips flesh from the man that I once shared my life with.

I don't know either of them anymore.

Looking in the direction I came, I want to crawl to safety. Away from the madness next to me. I want my brother to appear to lift me up like he always did when I was a kid.

But I'm alone here with two monsters.

Griff, thankfully, stops making that horrible high-pitched scream. The woods fall silent.

I don't know this Bubba. I can't imagine him ever touching me again.

I'm ready to flee, as fearful of him as I was when Griff attacked me.

Then I hear a noise. A whimper maybe. Bubba saying my name. He's lost in a fit of violence and rage, but there's some part of him that's still my hunky puppy.

My mind returns to him drunk from the Korean Kickass. He was vulnerable, wanting to be better but not knowing how. I fell in love with him a little that night. I wanted to believe he was a big strong man with a big soft heart. He proved I was right to have faith in him.

He's lost again. Instead of booze, he can't let go of the anger and fear. I see in his eyes how he's gone deep inside and let out a part of him that he can't control.

I don't know how to bring him back to me. The fingers on my non-broken hand reach out. I stroke his face in the same way I did when he dream-ranted. I hope to soothe this beast until my Bubba can retake control.

And he's suddenly in front of me. The man I love, the one who holds the birds so carefully, the guy still growing up but already amazing. That Bubba wraps his arms around me and cradles my chilled pained body against his stronger one.

I search his eyes for reassurance. He looks back at me with the same need.

"I knew you'd come," I lie.

I hadn't believed he would find me, but somehow, he did. My truth won't help Bubba. He craves lies to help him look at me without feeling as if he failed. I know what kind of man he needs to be.

In his mind, he should have the power to shield me from all danger. It's the unrealistic aspirations of a man still learning. I don't need to be a mature woman to know he isn't ready to hear ugly truths.

I force my numb face to smile and provide Bubba with what he needs. That's what love really is anyway. It's not great sex and joyful times. Love means you don't look away even when it'd be easier. Love means also embracing the monster capable of doing what he did to Griff. That violence is a part of the whole man. I can't just have the good stuff any more than Bubba can just have me belly dancing naked day and night.

I promise myself we'll be okay.

Even in the eerie woods with a dead man nearby, I try to imagine only the best for Bubba and me.

THE CHAPTER WHERE THERE ARE NO EASY FIXES
THE RUNAWAY

I'm on autopilot for the next few hours. I take off my jacket and wrap it around a shivering Soso while making calls to Butch and Mom. He sends Jack and Jace to clean up the mess.

Too busy screaming at each other, the old ladies didn't hear anything. Their sole focus is on getting their cars towed. The cops never show up despite them both apparently calling for someone to arrest the other. I don't know what Roid Ron tells the women, but he removes Griff's SUV before the tow trucks arrive.

Dumping Griff's body isn't an option. Neither is reporting his death. He'll lead the cops to the Brotherhood. I decide to have him put on ice until Dayton decides what he wants done.

Mom paves the way for Soso and me to receive medical treatment without the cops getting wind. The doctor on our payroll is waiting for us at the hospital. Weeks ago, Soso suggested we get something in order after Butch's shooting brought a lot of police attention.

Today, I'm the one with a bullet wound. Nothing serious like with Butch. Just a flesh wound. An x-ray and a few stitches later, I feel fine. No doubt it'll hurt more once the shock and adrenaline wear off. For now, my mind is numb, and only my heart hurts.

Soso's nose is broken. Her right hand too. The doctor can't do anything about her face until she heals. Then he'll know if she needs anything reconstructive done. He applies a cast to her right hand and prescribes plenty of pain meds that she refuses. Tylenol is all she'll accept.

The doctor doesn't ask for specifics about the incident. Though he does whisper a few questions to Soso regarding STD tests and emergency contraception. With her face swollen, speaking proves difficult, and she only shakes her head.

While we wait for Pop and Mom to drive us home, I take off my shirt and switch it with her tattered one. Soso cries when I discard her top in the trash. I remember her saying once how it was one of her favorites. Now, the shirt's a rag, but I take it from the trash, and her whimpers stop. She cradles the shirt in her arms and stares at the floor until we leave.

Soso's parents are on the road, headed this way. They aren't coming alone. Keanu, Camden, and several members of the Brotherhood on driving up too.

"Are you in pain?" Mom asks Soso once we enter our house.

Soso mumbles something, and Mom looks to me to translate.

"They gave her Tylenol at the hospital."

Mumbling again, Soso hands me her phone. I read a message from Sissy suggesting Dash bring over pot from their Ellsberg stash.

"It helped more when I got hurt," Sissy types.

Considering Sissy spent most of her life getting pounded on by her asshole father, I'm sure she knows what's works best. I text back a thank you.

Likely in shock, Soso stands confused in the middle of the living room for nearly five minutes before I guide her to the couch. Freki immediately joins her.

I start to remove Soso's shoes, but Mom waves me off. "You need to rest too. Let us help."

Soso stares at my mother, not really seeing her. I don't think she even realizes Freki is next to her. The sound of the birds draws her attention but gains no emotional reaction.

I study Soso while my parents do busy work in the kitchen. Someone is bringing her truck over. The groceries are mostly salvageable. They'll replace what isn't. There's talk of casseroles being cooked by friends to ensure we don't have to worry about food for a few days.

My aunt Sawyer is organizing a schedule for the family to help out until we're back on our feet. Jack messages to say he'll handle our lawn. Butch promises he'll help with the atrium. Buzz plans to come over once Panni finishes a spaghetti bake she's making for us. Even the women at the Rossiya offer to clean and take the dog for walks.

Everyone rallies, just like they would back in Ellsberg.

And I'm thankful for their support.

Yet, as Soso sits inches away from me, I can't feel her. She's lost in her head. I suspect she wants to shower, but I'm afraid to ask. She's barely made eye contact with me since I stopped fucking up Griff. I get the distinct impression she's angry with me. Or fearful.

I ought to give her space, but I'm tired now that the adrenaline tapes off. The pain of nearly losing her makes me hurt all over. Inching closer on the couch, I need her to help me even if my presence makes her feel worse.

Soso notices me scooting closer and glances up at me. Her face is unreadable between the swelling and the blank expression in her dark eyes. Finally, she mumbles something I can't understand. She says it again. Then I realize she's asking for her mom.

I take my phone and text Harmony. "They're less than thirty minutes out."

Tears spill from her swollen eyes, and she nods. Looking away, she shrinks next to me. I think to ask if she wants the girls. I'm desperate to reassure her, but the birds aren't toys. Bjork especially gets startled by new people coming in and out. During our painting party weekend, the birds remained under their cover whenever the house wasn't quiet.

Worried now, I leave Soso and cover the cage. Ula sees me and makes her head roll move. I can't help smiling when she flirts that way. As Bjork chatters, I pretend she's promising everything will be okay. *Soso's strong. She just needs to rest. Don't worry, Bubba.*

I cover the birds, planning to let them out later when the house is quiet, and they're safe. I might not know the right thing to do for Soso, but I understand our girls.

Returning to the couch, I'm afraid to look at my woman. Soso tries to smile when I finally glance down at her. This small gesture reinvigorates me. I'm not a monster in her eyes. I think I'd be fine if others saw me that way. Even my parents can think I'm a vile fuck but never Soso. She saw me at my weakest that first night, and she still wanted to know me. A lot of women would have been turned off. I don't care what women claim about craving a man with a good heart, they usually want men like me to be hard inside.

With Soso, I can be me. That's why I can't handle her thinking I'm a monster. If that's what she sees when she looks at my face, how can she still love me?

THE BOHEMIAN

I don't feel like me. The house I sit in isn't mine. The people around me are strangers. The man at my side is someone I don't know. My body doesn't do what I want. When I try to smile for Bubba after he covers the birds, I don't know if my face even moves. Half of me is in pain, the other half is numb.

I stare at Bubba's right hand during its slow journey over to my left one. He's hesitant to hurt me. I'm not sure I want him touching me anyway. He likely thinks I look awful. I'm afraid to look in a mirror. Everything is jumbled in my head.

Griff might be dead—torn apart by the same hand holding mine—but he left me forever changed. The doctor said I might need physical therapy after the twelve broken bones in my hand heal. He also warned surgery could be necessary in the future for both my hand and my nose. Griff is dead, but he remains burned into my future.

What I need is my mom. Though Bailey offers mothering, she's mostly a stranger. I want my mom's arms around me. I need my dad to look at me and promise it'll be okay. I wish Keanu was breathing the same air as me. If I'm surrounded by my family, maybe I'll remember how to be me again.

I've never been a badass, but I'm not used to feeling this weak. I need something to click inside me and reclaim what Griff stole.

Bubba is a ghost next to me. I feel him wanting something—to speak, to run, to hold me, to push me away. I doubt he knows what he wants, but I can't give him anything. I'm barely holding on. The tears keep breaking loose, pushing Bubba close to the edge.

When I stare at his fingers wrapped around mine, it's almost like before. We'd spend time on the couch, casually affectionate until we finally needed to be completely connected. These little finger dances led to sex, but I can't imagine anyone ever touching me like that again.

Opening the door for my parents, Bailey seems nervous. She takes everything that occurs in Conroe personally, and today happened on her watch.

My attention leaves Bubba's mom and focuses on mine. Seeing her flushed face and wet eyes make me hurt with guilt.

Bubba helps me to my feet so I can get to my parents. I sigh at the feel of her arms around me. I find Dad's gaze over her shoulder and find he's embraced cold rage. That's how he'll cope, but I see cracks in his rough shell when he sees my battered face.

"I want to take a shower, but I don't know how," I whimper to my teary-eyed mom.

"We've got this," she reassures me.

I don't look back at Bubba before my mother guides me out of the room and toward the master bathroom. My mind is on washing away everything that happened today. I smell like blood, dirt, and Griff. Nothing matters more than getting clean.

Then I imagine Bubba miserable in the living room, kicking himself for not getting to me sooner.

Sighing loudly, I leave Mom and shuffle down the hall to the living room where Bubba is, in fact, sitting like a lump with a pout on his face and regret in his eyes.

"You can take a shower after I do," I tell him.

Bubba knows what I'm saying, and the melancholy lessens in his expression. He even manages a smile once he realizes that's what my face is attempting.

I leave him and return to Mom, who washes the tears from her red cheeks. Dad follows me back and stands in the doorway.

"I need to get undressed," I say.

"I'll make sure no one bothers you."

Like Bubba, Dad needs reassurance. These are powerful, scary men accustomed to fixing problems with violence. But there's no one to punch anymore. They're left with only dark thoughts and ugly feelings.

I hug him before joining Mom in the bathroom. We strip me out of Bubba's shirt and my dirty skirt. I stand naked except for the wrap around my cast. Mom gets naked too. I don't know why the two of us undressed cracks me up. The giggles start soft, and then I laugh so hard that I can barely breathe. Mom steadies me as I step into the shower and relax under the hot water.

I rest my head against the wall and let the heat ease my tension. A momentary reprieve from my battered body and disturbing memories. I ache to sleep and wake up with that foggy feeling where I can't be sure if what I remember is real or a dream.

Instead, I'm right back in the woods as soon as I step out of the shower. The cold air hits my naked body, and I feel exposed. Breathing faster, I imagine myself on the ground, tits out, at Griff's mercy.

Mom wraps me in a towel and calls for Dad to bring me something warm to wear.

"He wanted to rape me," I whisper to my mother. "I couldn't stop him. He tore open my shirt. I was out there, and anyone could see. I couldn't stop him."

Sobbing, I don't even know what happens in the next few minutes. I try to reach for my mom, but I only see Griff over me. I feel his nails scratching at me as he ripped off my clothes. I can't find my way back to where I'm safe at home.

Then I'm dressed and in Dad's arms. We're sitting on the bed. Mom is nearby, still damp. I inhale my father's familiar cologne. In the background, I hear Bailey talking to someone. She can't see us. The door is shut. I'm relieved by the privacy, but also hearing Bailey's voice reminds me that I'm not in the woods. I'm safe at home. Griff is dead. I'm alive.

The tears stop, and I can breathe again. Only then do I realize my father's shaking. His expression doesn't reveal the anger he's clearly fighting. I tell him I love him, and it'll be okay. He says the same back to me. Mom finishes dressing and joins us on the bed. She says the words too.

I'm okay now. My nightgown is thick flannel. I'm no longer exposed. This home is safe. Dad is here. Mom is here. Soon, Keanu will be here.

But Bubba is the one who needs the kind of reassurance my parents provide me. I don't know if he can share with his family how he feels. Worse still, I'm not sure I'm strong enough to help him either.

THE RUNAWAY

I take a shower in the hall bathroom when it becomes apparent Soso's family isn't leaving the master. Mom rounds up clothes from the laundry room. Then I go through the motions of getting my shit together.

After dressing in faded jeans and a gray T-shirt that Soso likes, I return to the living room to find Camden and Keanu. The other Brotherhood men don't enter the house, choosing to watch from outside. Do they resent me for killing their club brother?

No, they're on edge because one of them crossed a line with someone protected. Griff and Soso are family to them. Their tension has nothing to do with me or the Reapers.

But I feel judged.

Not by my parents. Pop tells me I did what I needed to do. Mom says I killed the bad guy, which makes me a hero.

Or by Keanu who shakes my hand and thanks me for saving his sister from the sick fuck.

"I owe you," he swears, holding my gaze.

Camden then thanks me for cleaning up the club's mess. The Brotherhood owes us for this.

"What about Griff's body?" I ask.

"We'll take it back and handle shit with his mom," Camden says, stroking his lumberjack beard and making me think of Soso's reaction to it. Her uncle lowers his voice. "This clusterfuck today makes Conroe and Hickory Creek tight. We were obviously on good terms since you and Soso hooked up. What I'm talking about now isn't that. You're a small chapter, low on muscle. Just remember that if you need numbers, you've got them with us."

Any other day, I'd be fucking stoked to know I created an alliance with a larger, established club. Sure, Cooper would send in the troops if necessary, but this bond between Conroe and Hickory Creek is my doing. Not something my uncles or grandfather accomplished while I lazily reaped the benefits. This shit is mine.

But today isn't any other day.

Soso hiding in our bedroom steals away any sense of my triumph. I want to see her. Hear her voice. Know if she's crying. Is she in pain? Does she need anything?

She's mine, but I'm out here, and I don't think I'm wanted in there.

Keanu disappears into the room I feel locked out of. Camden finishes making chit chat with my mom and heads over to where Jack stashed Griff's body.

Sawyer arrives with food. "More's coming," she promises as Jace enters with the casserole dish. "Scarlet and Phoebe are cooking up a storm."

"We don't need so much food," I mumble while Mom looks over the dish.

"Her family is here," Sawyer says, cupping my face like she did when I was a kid and needed a talking-to. "Your family is here. People will be coming and going until you're back to normal. People are pigs and will eat all your crap. This way, you won't have to worry about keeping them fed."

I stare into my aunt's bright blue eyes and nod. She makes good points. I hadn't thought about how long Soso's family might remain in Conroe. They likely didn't have time to pack, and I suspect they drove up on Dayton's Harley.

There are questions I want to ask, but the people with the answers are hiding in the bedroom.

Dash arrives with a casserole dish and primo pot. "This shit is heavier," he says, showing me how he's organized the pot in a small metal tin. "Basically, this hash is good for when you want to chill, and these others are for when you really need to chill. Don't overdo the second one if you'll need to drive any time soon. But if you're in a world of pain, the second one will be a lifesaver."

I nod, despite not understanding anything he just told me. I've smoked pot since I was a teen. Never before did I think about safety precautions. I lit up, got stoned, laughed at stupid shit, and craved chips. I never paid attention to how there was more than one kind of pot.

"I'll write it down for you," Dash says when I stare dumbly into his gray eyes for too long.

"Do you want to run our local pot business?"

"Not really, but I'll help out if you need it. Just relax."

"I am relaxed."

Dash gives me an odd frown "You look ready to punch me, and you're cradling your injured arm."

I look at where he's gesturing and, yes, I'm holding where Griff shot me. Tired now, I shrug. "I didn't get there fast enough," I blurt out. "That's why she isn't letting me close."

Pop appears next to me, and I wonder how loud I'm talking. He leads me into the kitchen where we sit down.

"You're fine," he says.

"Soso won't let me in the room."

"Did you ask?"

"No."

"Bubba, you're tired and in pain, and she's just down the hall with her family. Let her parents take care of her for a little bit."

"I want to take care of her."

"You will."

Shaking my head, I sigh. "I don't know what I'm supposed to do."

"Turn on the TV and stare at something stupid. If you're hungry, eat. If you're tired, close your eyes. Soso is right down the hall."

My hand reaches for my arm again. The pain is getting worse. Or I no longer have anything to distract from it. The wound has a heartbeat, and each one gets more painful and accusatory. I ended up with only a flesh wound, but Soso is likely black and blue.

I didn't save her fast enough. Or I should I have known Griff would pull this shit. Something should have been done differently, and now I can't be with Soso.

"Try a doobie," Pop says, waking me from my thoughts. When I chuckle at his word choice, he adds, "It'll settle you down at least."

"What about Soso?"

"She also wants you to settle down. She and I spoke spiritually."

Grinning, I nod. "Maybe someone can offer her a joint to see if it helps. The Tylenol will be wearing off soon."

Pop realizes I'm asking him to do it. I'm afraid to go to the door. If Soso reacts badly, I'll probably cry like a bitch. I really, really don't want to get teary-eyed in front of all these people. Only Bjork wouldn't judge me, and she's hiding under the cover.

I walk out back to smoke a joint while Freki runs around the yard. He's hyper with so many people in his house. He acts the same way at Butch's place when the kids are loud.

"Someone's getting a taste for killing," Dayton says, walking outside.

"How is Soso?"

"Alive."

With his dark gaze reminding me so much of Soso's, I feel judged when he just watches me. "I'm sorry."

Dayton sighs. "I don't know why you're sorry when I'm the asshole who almost got my baby girl killed."

Not wanting him to blame himself, I turn rational. "The only one to blame is Griff."

"True, but I read him all wrong. Even after the crap he pulled with the birds and that day at the house, I didn't see him as a real threat. Like I looked in his eyes and told him to back off or else, and I thought he was reasonable enough to listen. I didn't see anything in him that said today would happen. I always thought I was a good judge of character, but now…" He pauses and sighs again. "I don't know what's what now."

"Maybe he just snapped," I lie.

Dayton walks farther into the yard. His regrets make him sheepish about talking around others.

"When Soso and Griff started dating, I never worried about violence. Or even that nagging bullshit he did until she finally dumped him. My first thought was she needed a strong man in the life to understand her," he says and then mutters, "My second thought was if Griff could keep it in his pants. Some men will always cheat. My father is that way. I couldn't tell which way Griff would go, but I knew they wouldn't last if he was running around with other women. Not once did I think he'd hit her, let alone try to kill her."

"And you worry that you misjudged me too?"

Dayton gives me a little frown. "Griff would have been at the bedroom door, knocking and whining about coming in. Then he'd come back and ask again and again and again until either we gave in or he threw a fit. He couldn't see outside of himself."

Dayton leans down to give Freki's head a rub. "You're out here pouting because Soso's feelings matter more than yours. That's not something Griff would do. I know you're not him."

"Does Soso?"

"She's all jammed up in her head. I think she's scared of you," he says, and I feel as if I've been slapped. "But she keeps talking about you. 'Bubba eats a lot of ribs. He doesn't like hickory sauce, only honey.' She's just rambling, but she's rambling about you."

"Do you think she'll talk to me today?"

I flinch at Dayton's laughter. He sees my expression and looks guilty. "Kid, she's only been away from you for like an hour, and she asked me to come out and check on you. Don't worry so much."

"She nearly died."

"Yeah, and then you fucked up the asshole. She'll heal, and you'll heal, and he'll still be dead. That's how things worked out. Maybe you two can't see that right yet."

Everything that happened in the woods is a blur in my mind. I ran on pure emotion. Soso needed to live, and he needed to die. Nothing else registered.

"It's only been an hour?" I ask, blowing out smoke. "It feels like longer."

"I think Soso hopes something will click and she'll instantly feel better. That's not going to happen. It'll take time for her body and mind to recover. She's lived a charmed life for the most part. Shit, look at how things played out with you. How many women take home a drunk biker and end up with a man who puts up with her little dog and birds?"

I look at my hands and flash back to the woods when I tore apart Griff. "I don't know why I didn't beat him to death. I ripped him to shreds. That's why Soso thinks I'm a monster."

"Killing is ugly, no matter how you do it. Soso is still in shock. Her fear of you is part of her fear of everything."

Dayton is suffering from a bad case of regret with Griff, but I don't think he'd lie to save my feelings. His words calm me, and I ask, "How long will you stay?"

"Tonight, at least. We didn't bring anything. Got that call from your mom and dropped everything. We'll be back, but Harmony works at a demanding group home and finding replacement staff can be tough. Let's just say we'll be back and forth unless Soso can't handle us gone. If we cramp your style, we can stay with Bailey and Nick. She's been asking for us to hang out."

"I don't know what to do."

"There's nothing to do. Sit back and let everyone do the work. Like when Harmony gave birth to Soso and her sisters were all over us to help out. At first, I was annoyed by the constant company, but then I decided to stop bitching and enjoy the extra pairs of hands. You should do that now. I told Soso the same thing. Her new home is filled with people, and she's overwhelmed, but she needs the help. Being alone won't make her feel better. She needs to suck it up and appreciate how people care enough to be here."

I look back inside where Mom and Sawyer discuss cleaning the house. They want to schedule everything. When the yard is mowed, who cleans out the birdcage, which of them will run errands. It's busy work for women uncomfortable with feeling helpless.

"I'll see if Soso is willing to come out of the room," Dayton says, walking back to the door.

"I can come in if she's not ready."

"Hiding isn't the answer. She has nothing to fear and even less to feel ashamed over."

The pot takes the edge off my pain and unease, but only intensifies my lost feeling. "I don't know what to do with myself."

"Sit on the couch, turn on the TV, and comfort the dog," Dayton says, talking to me as if I'm his kid rather than another man. "Soso will be out soon."

I obey him. What the fuck else am I going to do? Freki joins me on the couch and cuddles close. He's a sensitive little guy, and I'm his security blanket right now. I smile at the way he looks at me.

Mom joins me for a few minutes, fixing my hair and telling me how proud she is of how I handled today. I smile at her words.

I feel calmer thanks to the pot, but a gloom lingers because Soso feels a million miles away. The last time we shared a room, she was covered in blood and dirt. I imagine her clean now, surrounded by her family. Has she smoked her joint? Is she calmer? Is the pain more bearable?

Time is a blur. I think none has passed and then I notice everyone around me moved. Mom is with Pop. Sawyer and Jace are in the backyard. Keanu walks out the front door while taking a phone call. Then I blink, and Mom is gone, and now Dash is talking to Pop.

Did I smoke the wrong joint? Am I tripping balls? Why can't I track what's happening?

Then I blink, and Soso is next to me with Freki in her lap. Wearing a blue and red flannel nightgown that reaches her ankles, she looks snug. When she studies my face, I think I smile.

"I smoked too much pot," I whisper.

Soso's battered face struggles to smile. She looks around before returning her gaze to me.

"You're talking too loud," she whispers, and we share a chuckle.

Then my laughter dies, and I say, "I'm sorry."

Soso wipes something from my cheek and strokes my forehead. "You can never go wrong being you."

I open my mouth to say something, but I don't know if I do. Soso takes my arm and wraps it around her shoulders. Sighing with relief, I hold her against me. She rests her head against my chest and stares at the TV that I just now realize is actually on and playing a baseball game.

My mind is a mess, and I'll need to be more careful with the pot. Still, I'm calmer, and Soso is finally back in my arms. If I can work on my volume control, everything will be perfect.

Well, at least, until the pot wears off.

THE BOHEMIAN

Even dead, Griff torments me. I'm haunted by his screaming even when I'm wide awake and surrounded by people. Sometimes, his terrified cries are all I can hear.

The first night isn't horrible. Then my parents have to drive back to Hickory Creek. They promise to return.

On my second night home, I wake up to Griff screaming that high-pitched, panicked cry. I try to calm myself and be rational, but the sound echoes in my mind. His fear infects me. I'm overwhelmed with guilt as if I'm the reason he died. Finally, I scream just to drown out his.

Bubba must think I'm crazy. He holds me in his arms and promises to protect me. His words help for a short while, but then I hear Griff again in my head.

I can't sleep. In my dreams, Griff's on top of me, inside me, his face hollowed out, his eyes gone. Even awake, I see him hiding in the shadowed corners of every room.

Bubba prowls around the house, holding a gun, worrying over how I cry and shrink in fear. He doesn't understand.

"It's not real. I'm afraid of what's in my head. The bad memories of him and you and me and what happened. I can't stop hearing him. What I fear isn't something you can shoot! It's not something you can kill!"

My yelling hurts Bubba. He wears a pained expression. I don't know how to explain that the quiet is driving me crazy. It makes no sense to me, so how can any of it make sense to him? But I say the words anyway. Bubba sees what I'm blind to. He understands what I can't.

He puts away the gun and turns on all the lights. The TV too. I start to say I don't want to watch anything, but he's creating noise, distractions, something besides the memories to occupy my time.

I crawl into Bubba's lap and marvel at how he doesn't push me away even when I do the same to him.

"I want to learn to belly dance," he says when my fear returns and I require a distraction.

I can't focus on my memories of Griff when Bubba says such silly things. He knows how to keep my mind from replaying the past. Firmly in the present with him, I don't know how Bubba remains so strong when he must be stressed and in pain too.

"That night you were drunk, I told you to do you and not be someone else. I didn't know you then. I had no clue who I was telling you to be. I'm happy to report you're better than I could have imagined."

Bubba might be a rock, but he exhales with relief at my words. He's still my hunky puppy wanting to impress me. I try to focus on reassuring this man right here rather than thinking about the one in the woods. I need those memories to fade until I can eventually doubt that they're even real.

In Bubba's arms, while we watch dumb comedies and he laughs at the silly antics, I only feel us.

THE RUNAWAY

Soso nearly breaks me when she won't stop screaming. I don't understand what she's reacting to, and I don't know how to erase her fear. Eventually, I somehow calm her panic.

But I'm rattled.

The next morning, I can't leave her alone, but I need time away from her to get myself in order.

Soso claims she's fine alone, but she also agrees quickly to hanging out with Lily and Sissy at their place. Freki comes along to play with Hart.

Soso pretends to be okay with me leaving her. Then I catch her staring out the front windows of Sissy's townhome as I prepare to leave. I don't know if I should go back inside. Even with her swollen face, I can see her terror. Someone must speak to her because she leaves the window.

I'm afraid to go to my parents' house where Mom might want to help me. Her tendency to fix things will likely make them worse. I'll step back and let her take charge because I'm terrified of fucking shit up.

Pop agrees to meet me at The Bean Hut for a cup of coffee. I'm relieved by his expression when he arrives. He knows I'm fucked in the head. There's no need to dumb things down and explain anything.

"I should have kept her safe," I say as soon as he sits down.

Pop exhales softly and hesitates before speaking. "I won't waste time saying you did all you could. Or that you shouldn't feel guilty. That's a cross you'll bear no matter what I tell you."

Having expected him to provide soothing advice, his harsh truth cuts deep. Pop gives me a sympathetic smile and says, "Lies won't help you or Soso."

"I thought ending him would make her feel better. That probably sounds stupid, but I thought seeing him die would provide her relief."

"Trauma doesn't always make sense. The reason she's afraid is gone, but the fear remains. It'll never go away completely. I still hear my father's voice sometimes. The asshole's been dead for longer than he was in my life, but the old fear returns at the oddest times. I've learned to deal with it. Soso will too, but it takes time."

"I wonder if she'd be better off in Hickory Creek with her family," I say, unable to control my words. "Like they'd know what to do, but I can't leave Conroe again, and I can't be away from Soso."

"Does she want to stay with her family?"

"I don't know."

"Does she tell you what she wants?"

"Yes."

Pop's green eyes remain perfectly calm despite my edginess. "Then if she hasn't asked, assume she wants to be here with you."

"What if I make things worse?"

"Why do you assume you would?"

"I let her down before."

"Ugly shit happens," Pop says and adds when I frown, "The world is fucked up. People do bad things. You can't keep your woman or your future kids locked away from the world. If you try, you become the bad thing that happened to them."

"Then what do I do?"

"I don't know Soso well. I know you, though. It's your nature to watch out for people. I think you have all the skills to take care of her. If she says she needs to be in Tennessee with her family, you'll adapt. If she wants to stay here, you'll help her through the dark moments. Time will heal a lot of what's hurting her right now."

I think of Soso screaming last night. Her big brown eyes stared at me in horror. Her terror made no sense. We were alone in the room, and she was wide-awake. Was I the monster she feared?

"Bubba, we can help you," Pop says when I feel myself choking up. "You're not alone."

"I just wanted him dead. I didn't think about how I might seem to her. Now, I think she hates me. I know she fears me. I see her watching me like I'm the scariest thing she's ever seen."

Pop studies me for a minute and then nods. "Think of what happened as having the flu. At first, when you start feeling bad, you can make plans for how to deal with the symptoms. Then the sickness overwhelms you until your plans feel impossible. None of the medicine helps enough. You're miserable, and you believe you'll feel that way forever. You're too sick to be rational. But, eventually, you wake up feeling a little better. Still bad but there's a change. It gives you hope. But if you rush back into normal activity too soon, you can backtrack and feel worse. However, if you take your time recuperating, you'll get past it."

"So, I just have to wait for her to work it out?"

"You keep her comfortable. If she needs something, you give it to her. If she feels crappy and doesn't want you around, you give her space. But don't be surprised if she turns around and wants you close because you gave her space. It's like how your mother kicks off the blankets when she's sick and then complains that she's cold. Soso won't act like herself, and some of her reactions might seem bizarre. She'll fear you and then want you to make her feel safe. But you just do what she needs and remember it's not forever."

Nodding, I feel tired in a way I never have before. Pop reaches across the table and pats my hand.

"With you and Soso hooking up so fast, you're not equipped to deal with this stress. But love isn't a fairytale. Just remember that you don't always have to say the right thing to Soso. Sometimes, you'll be a dick. I'm a dick to your mom, and she acts like a raging bitch to me. Not all the time, of course, but we have bad days. Good marriages can handle the bad times. Rocky marriages have trouble with even the smallest problems. If you and Soso are meant to work, you'll find a way. Just do your best with her. If it's not enough, you can't force it to be enough."

"I feel like I can't breathe if I don't have Soso."

"Good," Pop says instantly. "She gave up a lot to be here with you. I want you to need her like that."

"I do."

"And you'll still fuck up sometimes, Bubba. Don't get so focused on not fucking up that you don't do anything at all."

"Like how I was when I first became president?"

"Exactly," Pop says and sips his coffee. His calm infects me, and I want to settle down too. "All your life, you only heard about your uncles' success or how great your grandfather was, but they fucked up too. No one talks about that crap, but it happened because it happens to everyone. The difference is they didn't stop when they failed. They adjusted and kept going. That's why they found success. That'll all you need to do with Soso and as president."

"What if I can't give her everything she needs?"

"Bubba, I see in your eyes how you want me to promise you that everything will work out. But you didn't call your mom despite knowing she would have promised. You called me because you wanted to hear it straight."

"Soso is the best thing I've ever known," I say, tensing again. "If I lose her, I'm not sure how I keep going."

"Stop thinking about what happens if you fail. Just focus on getting through this single day. Help her with what she fears today. Then tomorrow, you work on tomorrow's fears. Every day will be different, and you'll take them as they come. Then one day, you'll either be back in a good place or you won't, but you'll know you did everything you could."

Nodding, I realize I needed to hear the truth. I wanted to know if Soso can't love me in the same way and returns to Hickory Creek that I'll survive. I'll go on, and it won't kill me.

Once I face my biggest fear of losing Soso's love, I can see more clearly. I know she won't leave me, and I know I'll never walk away. I just needed to know I could survive if she left me. For years, the fear of failing as president kept me from being president. Soso built me up to face that, but she's in no condition to be my cheerleader today.

Pop gave me the straight truth. My honeymoon period with Soso is over. I can't run from our fears. I'll probably do the wrong thing more than once, but better men than me have fucked up and fixed things. I'll manage because Soso needs me to be strong, and I need her to feel confident again.

THE BOHEMIAN

Bubba wants away from me. He doesn't say that, of course, but he's hit a limit on the amount of drama he can process. That's why he ditches me at Sissy's Victorian townhome. He claims he needs to work, but I know he's lying.

I sit on the pale blue couch in the pastel living room and feel like I'm at Disney World. Everything is festive and kid-friendly. Well, not the brown monstrosity Sissy bought for Butch. Otherwise, the house feels decorated using only cotton candy colors.

From the room entry, Hart stares at me. I try not to feel self-conscious, but I know I look like shit. My eyes are swollen and bruised. My nose is twice it's normal size. My upper lip is huge. Griff's giant hand managed to nail me square in the middle of my face.

"It's okay, baby," Sissy says, picking up Hart when he starts crying.

Haydee climbs on the couch next to me. "Mama got beat up in Ellsberg. Our grandpa was bad. He's dead now."

"I'm glad he's dead."

"Me too," Haydee says, leaning closer. "Does it hurt?"

"Yes."

"Do you want medicine?"

"No, thank you."

Haydee looks at where her mother and brother now sit on the floor with Freki. My dog distracts Hart from his tears.

"Dad says we can have a cat soon."

Despite how much it'll hurt, I still smile at her comment. Not the cat part, but how she calls Butch "dad" already. I couldn't picture how Bubba's mute brother was supposed to fit into a family, especially one with a background like Sissy's. When it works, it just does.

I thought that about Bubba, but now I worry he isn't ready. In the span of three months, he dated his brother's dream woman, fought with Butch, left town, fell in love with me, dealt with his brother's shooting, moved in with me, gunned down a group of men, and now killed his rival with his bare hands.

Anyone would be overwhelmed and need a break.

I shouldn't cry over something I understand. Things have changed between Bubba and me. We're not in a good place. He should want distance. I just hope he doesn't make our separation permanent.

"Can I braid your hair?" Haydee whispers. "I've been practicing, and your hair is straight, and that's easier."

I really don't want anyone touching me, but how do I tell this child no? She wants to make me feel pretty so I'll stop crying.

Lily kneels down next to the couch and asks if I need anything. Her dark eyes offer such compassion, but I just shake my head.

My mind wanders as Butch's family takes care of me. Haydee creates many small braids in my hair. Sissy bakes cookies. Hart lets me pick the movie we watch.

They all want to help me stop crying, but the tears won't end. I go to the bathroom to clean up and feel worse after seeing my reflection. I feel ugly and ashamed.

I put down the toilet seat and hide in the bathroom. Closing my eyes, I breathe slowly and center myself.

I'm not dead. I didn't lose any teeth. My nose will heal. It's only been three days. When Odin attacked me, I was in pain for at least a week, and my shoulder wasn't completely healed for much longer. I didn't let myself fear him.

Why am I allowing Griff's actions to destroy my confidence? Or keep me from feeling close with Bubba?

And if my broken nose and black eyes do repulse Bubba, it's better to learn he's shallow now while we're starting out rather than down the road when I get a fat ass from having his kids.

Hearing his voice, I wipe my tears and leave the bathroom. Bubba stands in the living room, listening to Haydee who tells him about the cat her dad says they can have.

"Your cat better not eat my birds," he says, leaning down until their noses are nearly touching. "Or I'll sic Freki on it."

Haydee laughs and looks at the dog. "He too little to do anything."

"Well, then I'll sic Frenchie on your cat."

"I promise I won't let my kitty eat your birds."

Bubba pats her head and then notices me watching them. His expression turns weird for a few seconds, and I realize he's reacting to my hair. I shrug while he hesitantly moves toward me.

"I have only one question," he says.

"Me too."

"You first."

"Do you want me less because I look like this?"

Bubba sighs deeply. "Oh, Soso, don't you remember what I told you at the sanctuary?"

"No."

"You asked if I'd still want you if you lost an eye to Grinch and I said I'd want you more."

"Because everything makes you want me more," I whisper, recalling his words. "Now ask your question."

Bubba kneels down and wraps his arms around my waist before resting his cheek against my stomach. His expression reminds me of a little boy's. "Will you teach me to braid your hair so we can be like your parents?"

Bursting into laughter, I run my fingers through his thick locks. "But yours isn't long enough to make a good braid."

"I'll grow it out for you."

"Um, no, thank you."

"Don't you think I'd look good as a dirty hippie?" he asks, batting his long lashes for me.

"I don't want you to change for me. Only change if you want to."

Bubba stands and covers my lips with his. He's been wary about kissing me. Though there's nothing sexy about my puffed out and bruised face, I taste a hint of heat. Bubba still wants me. Sex would likely help us both, but I'm scared.

Just the thought of taking off my top and feeling exposed makes me want to push him away. I don't, though, because I need to get stronger, and keeping Bubba at arm's length is a weak move.

"Are you done with work for the day?" I ask when he thanks Sissy and Lily for Soso-sitting.

"Yeah, I just wanted to talk to my dad about feelings and stuff. It was all girly, and we cried. Real embarrassing shit, but I'm fine now."

Smiling, I take his hand. "I'm going to walk out of this house with my head held high," I announce before whispering, "Even if my hair looks like an eight-year-old went braid crazy on it."

Bubba hugs his cousin, shakes his soon-to-be sister-in-law's hand—to avoid pissing off Butch—and then showers his niece and nephews with high-fives. Seeing him tap his finger against Byron's tiny palm heals something deep inside me.

Since the woods, I haven't stopped thinking about his hands tearing apart Griff. I couldn't picture them caressing me or rubbing Bjork's belly or carrying Freki. They only represented violence.

But then his pinkie taps Byron's tiny palm, and I only see Bubba.

That's how healing works, and I need to remember to be patient with both Bubba and me.

THE RUNAWAY

Lily doesn't want me to take Soso. My cousin worries I'm still an arrogant dick. After all, I dated Sissy despite not wanting her. I ran off when shit didn't go my way. That's all true, but I've changed.

Not that I'm in the mood to prove anything to my cousin. Soso is the only one who matters. I hadn't been certain I knew how to help her. I'm still unsure, but Pop helped me realize that it's enough to try. Soso wants me to be the one at her side.

And she makes that clear again when she dares me to admit I'm turned off by her battered face. Based on her smile, my answer hits the sweet spot.

We tell everyone goodbye and promise to bring Freki back over to play with Hart soon. Soso smiles during the drive. She smiles when we walk through the door. She smiles when I ask if she wants to watch a silly movie. She smiles when I undo the many braids in her hair.

We sit on the couch where she holds my hand with her unbroken one and stares at me.

"My parents will be here tonight," Soso says, studying my face as if waiting for something.

"Good because we have more food than we can ever eat."

"But we won't have much privacy."

I hear an emotion in her voice that draws my attention away from "Airplane."

"Privacy for what?"

Her brown eyes reveal fear. She looks nearly ready to scoot away from me. Instead, Soso straddles my lap and exhales unsteadily. "Do you remember our first time in my truck?"

My fingers brush away the hair from her shoulders. Soso shivers, but she's waiting for my answer.

"I replay that day in my head regularly," I whisper as my hands slide down her arms to her waist.

"Bubba, stop coming onto me and pay attention," she says and cups my face. "I might freak out while we fuck. I could scream or jump off your dick or do all kinds of insane shit. I need you to understand that whatever happens isn't personal. I'm not completely in control of myself."

"Then we should wait," I mumble, removing my hands.

"I don't want to wait," she says and exhales deeply. "Sex with you makes me feel beautiful and relaxed and hopeful. My body hurts, and I look terrible, but I want to celebrate that you and I are alive. But you still need to be ready for me to lose my shit halfway through."

The last thing I should do is laugh, but the image of her jumping off my dick and running away stirs something stupid inside me. I fight my chuckles, but then Soso starts laughing, and I can't help myself.

"I'll be gentle," she says, running her fingers over my injured arm. "Can you be gentle?"

Her question is accompanied by a soft roll of her hips against mine. My dick has been stuck in the depressed mode for days. The pot hasn't helped either.

Her little thrust and the warmth in her gaze are all the prompting my dick needs to cheer up.

"I want you to touch me, but I can't take off my shirt. Do you understand?" she whispers just before her lips brush against mine.

"Do I have to keep my shirt on too?" I ask, and Soso bursts into teary laughter.

"You and your fucking shirt," she snickers before sighing. "You never, ever have to keep on your shirt. After all, if you've got it, why not flaunt it?"

I love the humor in her voice, and I'm dying to make her moan. Yet my lips on hers cause Soso to wince.

"We'll need to try different spots to avoid our tender ones," she says and lifts herself up, so her tits brush against my lips.

Soso takes a few tries to get the hang of touching me without banging her cast. Finally, the fingers from her good hand slide through my hair.

The feel of her intoxicates me. My lips graze her nipples, finding them hard under her shirt. Soso exhales in the familiar way I've missed the last few days.

I get creative as I work her body into submission. Her lips are too tender, but kissing her soft throat makes Soso moan just right. My fingers find her back too sensitive, but her thighs shiver at my touch.

Then out of nowhere, Soso freezes in my arms. She stares at me with wide, terrified eyes. "I told Griff that moving here was a mistake. When we were in the SUV, and I wanted him to lower his guard, I said being with you was a mistake. I said that, but I didn't mean it."

Soso awkwardly cups my face with her hands. "I'm still homesick for Hickory Creek and my family. That's true. And I haven't gotten completely comfortable with your family and friends yet. That's all true. But I don't regret moving here or being with you. That was a lie. I know you know it's a lie, but I needed to say out loud how it was a lie. I love you more than I could ever think possible and I want to be here with you. I didn't mean what I said to him."

My hands cover hers as I hold her gaze. "That was really smart how you played him."

Looking relieved, Soso nods. "I never loved him. He said I did, and he said I told him I did, but I never loved him. You're the only one, and I think that's probably obvious, but I still needed to say the words."

"You were so smart that day," I whisper as my fingers stroke her battered shoulders. "I don't know what would have happened if I found the SUV with you two inside. But you saw your chance and ran. That likely saved us both."

The fear fades in Soso's wet eyes, and she nods. "I lied a lot with Griff. Just to make him stop nagging or to keep him calm. I don't want to be that way with you. I want you to trust me because I trust you. Today, I thought maybe you didn't want me because of how I looked. I was making excuses for things to end. I was weak, but you weren't. That's why I trust you, and I want you to trust me like that too."

"I do trust you, but I'm a dumb guy and sometimes forget."

"And I'm a dumb girl, who sometimes forgets too."

"We're perfectly dumb together."

Soso winces when she smiles big for me, but my woman's too joyful to let a little pain ruin this moment. She also returns to wiggling her ass on my lap to reignite what we created so easily back in Hickory Creek in her rusty truck.

Our first time together seems like an eternity ago. We were strangers then. I felt lost. She feared letting another man close. But we were both what the other needed.

Stars aligned for us to meet. Soso went against her better judgment to give me a shot. I should have avoided becoming an "us" when I didn't even know how to be me. We moved way too fast, and Soso gave up her home for me. I don't know if I can ever repay her for such a gift.

But we have a long life together for me to try.

THE CHAPTER WHERE THE STORY ENDS
THE BOHEMIAN

I never enjoy a eureka moment where I suddenly let go of the day in the woods. It's a slow grind of day-to-day choices to feel more secure. By the end of the first week, I don't waste as much electricity by leaving on all the lights. My nightmares aren't so vivid. I no longer smoke so much pot to deal with the pain and anxiety.

Mom and Dad return to Conroe after she gets a replacement trained for the group home. She has some vacation time saved up and uses almost two weeks of it to take care of me. I don't really need physical help. My broken hand doesn't cause too many problems, and Bubba's family handles cleaning and cooking.

Emotionally, Mom is my lifesaver. Each day in the backyard while draped in the soothing summer sunlight, we spend hours talking about everything from my move to Conroe to what happened with Griff.

We go over some of the stuff a lot. Every time I replay what happened in the woods, the vivid fear from that day fades a little more. Talking about it with Bubba isn't really an option. He suffers from too much guilt despite having done nothing wrong. Hearing more details about that day will only dump my pain on top of his.

Plus, he will never understand why I feel tremendous guilt over Griff's death. There's no rational reason to pity the man. Bubba might even worry I cared more for Griff than I ever did.

How can I explain to him that my ex-boyfriend's final cries of pain and fear haunt me? Bubba shoulders too much responsibility for my happiness. It's the way he loves and how he views his worth as a man. No doubt sharing my guilt, confusion, and fear about Griff will only create more of a burden for him.

Talking with Mom is the best kind of therapy. I can't exactly see a real shrink anyway. Physician-patient privilege doesn't mean crap in the real world. How can I trust a shrink not to rat me out to the cops about Griff or anything that might seem illegal? No catharsis is worth risking Bubba's freedom.

But I can say anything to Mom. A few times, I give a play-by-play about that day only to go through it again as soon as I finish. I share what I wish I did differently. I cry over how scared I felt and how terrified Griff sounded and how frightening Bubba looked. She never judges me.

Mom shares too. About how depressed she's been since I moved away and how much she resents both Bubba for stealing my heart and Dad for needing to stay in Hickory Creek. Mom knows she can't move to Conroe even if he could. Her work, her friends, her life is in Tennessee, but she misses me more than she thought possible.

I notice how the more she shares with me, the warmer she acts around Bubba. Getting honest about her feelings helps Mom accept this new reality.

I suspect Bubba notices, too. When she pats him on the head one day after dinner, he gives me that little boy pleased with himself grin. I swear Bubba's irresistible at times. If we ever have a real argument, I doubt I'll have a shot in hell of winning once he flashes one of his smiles at me.

During the two weeks, Dad goofs around with Bailey while Bubba works with Butch on the atrium. Mom and I just talk and talk.

Slowly, my panic attacks lessen in both frequency and intensity, but going topless without agitation takes a lot longer. Bubba and I have sex every day, sometimes more than once, but I can't do it with my top off. Even if his hands go exploring, I need to remain covered up.

"Fucking is good," Bubba grunts whenever I apologize for needing to keep my top on.

His caveman horniness truly helps me. I feel ugly whenever I think of my face. The swelling diminishes, and the bruising fades, but I don't look like me. Bubba hinting for sex whenever we're alone for five seconds certainly feeds my ego.

Soon, my parents must leave, but they promise to return the following weekend.

Though sad, I focus on meditation and yoga to keep me calm. I also accept that Bubba does not get the latter. He treats yoga as a mating call and swoops in whenever I begin stretching. However, he keeps it in his pants the day I decide to do yoga in my bra.

"I'm training myself to be a nudist again," I say, nervous already.

"Jack loves to run around naked."

"I know."

"Don't look at him naked," he mutters, frowning possessively at me. "I don't want to cut off my cousin's dick. How awkward would family dinners be after that?"

I pat his cheek. "Your cousin is barely a man to me. I mean, I know technically he probably has those parts, but I only see a blob with hair."

"What do you see when you look at me?" he asks, wiggling his brows.

"Save the horndog routine for after my yoga."

"I'll be respectful."

"No jacking off while I exercise," I say, flashing my sternest look.

"What if I do it in the bathroom?"

"Well, what's the fun of you jacking off if I can't watch?"

Bubba leans down and kisses me gently. "I'm going to fuck you so good later."

Nudging him away from me, I walk to the bedroom where I take off my shirt.

"I'm in my house with my man," I say to the scared chick in the mirror. "I am not in the woods with a psycho. I can do this."

Still, I cover my chest with my balled-up shirt. Bubba relaxes on the couch, waiting for the show. Next to him sits Freki. I hear the girls chattering in their new atrium. I am safe here. No one will hurt or judge me. I've got this.

"I'm in my bra!" I announce for really no reason. "This is my bra!"

I toss my shirt on the chair and force down my arms. Bubba glances at the dog for support and then shrugs.

"Can I applaud?" he asks.

"Knock yourself out, hunky puppy."

Bubba pants for me and continues making doggy whining noises while I bend into a Downward-Facing Pose. Freki decides to bark since he thinks Bubba is hogging all his moves. I ignore them both and stretch.

"I am in my home with my man," I say when I start flashing back to the woods. "I am safe."

"And hot, Num-Num. Don't forget that."

Bent forward, I twist enough to look back at a smiling Bubba. If I designed my dream man back in Hickory Creek, I never would have imagined anyone half as amazing as the now shirtless hunk admiring my butt. Bubba winks at Freki as if they're in on a joke, and I realize yoga isn't happening.

Like most days, I'll get my work out with a naked Bubba.

THE RUNAWAY

Soso doesn't just steal my heart. She takes control of my brain too. I hear her even when she's not around. Like when I'm mowing our front lawn one day and glance at the park across the street. Soso's voice pops in my head to suggest we change the name.

"Kirk Johansson Memorial Park," I tell Mom. "We can petition the city council and donate funds to have the signs changed."

"The plan is to name half of the town after our family, huh?" she grumbles as if she doesn't love the idea.

"The Hallstead name is on half of Hickory Creek. Do you think their residents ever forget who runs shit?"

Mom lunges for me in the way she's prone to do lately. "You're such a good boy. Such a smart, sweet boy."

"Thanks, Mom," I mumble while she finger-combs my hair.

Soon, Sissy's pregnancy announcement allows my mother to focus her crazy clinginess on someone else. Soso falls into the background of family functions, edgy around people. The swelling around her nose is mostly gone, but her cast will be on for another few weeks.

Despite being still on the mend, Soso doesn't hide from the world. She decides to take charge of the motel, believing the young women will respond better to her than any of the Reapers. Soso sets them up with clinic visits and educational videos. After a few visits, she decides to upgrade their living quarters. Plus, she adds surveillance in the rooms that'll allow the women to turn on the cameras whenever they have customers.

"For their protection," she explains when Jack wants to know about costs. "Besides, we never know when one of their clients could be someone prime for blackmail."

Jack likes that last part and immediately signs on to do the upgrades. Layla visits Conroe to help find cost-efficient ways to make the motel more livable and stylish. Though

Soso gets along with the women in my family, she still relies heavily on her mom and cousin.

My contribution to improving the Rossiya Motel is to hire two local guys to take turns playing security there. Neither of the men is particularly badass, but they look scary. Both are vets and ex-cons. Both know how to keep their mouths shut. Both quickly become dependent on their new income to support their families—immediately buying newer cars and upgrading their homes. Soso likes to show up unannounced to make sure the men are actually around, playing guard and keeping their hands off the women.

"No one fucks for free," she insists. "Just like no one drinks for free at the pub. Everyone carries their weight and pays their due or the club should take it personally."

Man, Soso's hot when she embraces her inner bitch.

Layla does more than help with design ideas. She also bird-sits for us while Soso and I join my family on our yearly RVing road trip. This year is special for many reasons. All three of Cooper's daughters bring along their new babies. Plus, Sissy, Haydee, and Hart have never traveled before. And, of course, Soso and I enjoy our my first RVing experience together.

It's a tight fit in the Bailey's Badass Bus—aka my parents' RV. Technically, we're on our second "Bus" after Buzz got Mom and Pop a good deal on a newer, larger Class A motorhome last year.

"It won't fit all of us soon," Pop says during a pit stop in South Carolina.

I follow his gaze to where Butch rubs Sissy's still flat belly. Nearby, Soso walks around a grassy area with Haydee, Hart, and Freki. Frenchie lounges nearby, watching the smaller dog. They still have their tiffs. Like with the rest of us, they're learning to bond as a family.

"I know a guy that'll help us find a second one," I say, and Pop grins.

"Do you think you'll have babies soon?"

My gaze returns to Soso, who squats next to Freki and smiles when the kids mimic her.

"No idea. She's given up so much to be with me. If she wants one tomorrow, I'll say yes. If she doesn't want them ever, I'll say yes to that too. Soso makes everything feel like the right answer."

Pop gives me a look somewhere between pride and embarrassment. I mean, yeah, I'm whipped, but who's he to judge? *Hasn't he seen him and Mom together?*

I don't ask Soso about babies on the trip. We have time to talk privately once we're back in Conroe. For those two weeks, we focus on sightseeing and family time.

Occasionally, Mom and Soso butt heads. This is new territory for the former. After all, Panni and Sissy are pushovers who crave a mother figure. Soso has no problem disagreeing with Mom or taking charge.

"Too slow, lady," she says one day when everyone meanders in a multi-restaurant parking lot without a clue where to eat. Mom doesn't choose a place quickly enough, leaving my woman to step up.

"Your father might be the best twin, but you are not his best child." Mom mutters at Soso who nods.

"Keanu really is better."

The women agree on that much. Oh, and that I'm the best of the three boys—as long as Butch and Buzz aren't close enough to overhear. Mom has to keep things fair.

As much fun as the trip is, I'm relieved when we return to Conroe. I miss my house and the girls and even the town itself.

Soso and I go riding on our first day back. I love the feel of her arms wrapped around me as we speed along the long rural roads. At every stop sign and light, I glance back to find Soso smiling. She feels what I do that day.

Conroe is where our heart belongs and where our future begins.

OH, BY THE WAY, FROM THE BOHEMIAN

My near-death experience lights a fire under my beloved brother's butt. Lottie returns to the US to find a man obsessed with knowing their future.

Days after she settles back into her life in White Horse, Keanu throws a party at The Glenn to celebrate. He hopes to propose too. His uncertainty about her answer keeps him on edge. Despite not wanting to visit Hickory Creek and possibly run into people—namely Griff's mom who was told he died doing club business—I know my brother needs me to attend his party.

The restaurant is closed for the private event. The entire Hayes family shows up, including the babies. Cap hangs close to Keanu, giving him pep talks about the big moment. Lottie must realize something's up because she goes to the ladies' room and remains there.

Inside, I find her sitting on the counter and staring at her hands. Her face is hidden by her green shag cut. When I enter, she glances at me and then sighs.

"Everyone probably thinks I'm an ungrateful twat," she mutters.

Leaning against the counter, I nudge her with my knee. "Don't worry about everyone. Just tell me what's happening with you?"

"I got a lot of mixed messages in Bandung," she blurts out, clearly desperate to tell someone. "My grandmother said I should marry Keanu. My other grandmother said I shouldn't marry him. My mom worries people here think I'm a gold digger. My father still doesn't know why I want to live in the US. They made me think I shouldn't even return."

"What do you want?"

"I'm not sure. I mean, I feel like no matter what I do that I'm letting someone down. Whatever choice I make will be a mistake, so I can't choose at all."

"Lottie, clear your head," I say, and she gives me a half-smile. Worrying I'll go full hippie on her, she probably

263

wants me to back off. However, with my face still a little swollen, making me cry isn't an option, so she chooses to play along.

"Okay," she says and takes a deep breath.

"Now, imagine you and Keanu break up. You and he remain friends. No one is mad."

Lottie's gaze turns uneasy, but she nods.

"Now imagine you find a man from Indonesia here or maybe you return to Bandung. Imagine you are dating this new man. He comes from your culture, and your grandmothers are both happy. He's nice and handsome and appreciates you. Do you feel hope when you imagine that man? If so, then I don't think other people are confusing you. I think you know what you want, but you're scared to tell Keanu goodbye."

Lottie says nothing. Her gaze flashes to the door before returning to me. It'll break my heart if Lottie ends things with Keanu. My brother loves her, and she's my friend. They both deserve to be happy, though. If Keanu isn't the one for her, they're just wasting time together.

"It's okay to say you want out, Lottie."

Looking like a cornered animal, she wears the same expression she did when a lady at the grocery store yelled at her to go back to Mexico. In her element, Lottie is a super calm hip chick. But put her on the spot, and she freezes up. Suffering from the same habit, I don't want to be the reason she feels attacked.

"My brother loves you. He wants a life with you. But what you need matters too," I say and hold her hand. "You've been dating for a while now, and you know everything there is to know about Keanu. If you think another man would be better for you now, then you'll feel the same way next year or in ten years. Why waste more time on someone that doesn't give you what you need?"

Lottie stares at me with terrified hazel eyes and blurts out, "Keanu is everything."

"Because you think that's what I want to hear or because that's what you really feel? You have a right to be happy, Lottie, even if it upsets other people. So, what do you want?"

"I want to be with Keanu," she says, tears falling down her cheeks.

I hand her a paper towel. "Then that's it. Just be with him. Don't worry about what your family thinks. If you're happy, they'll be happy. If they aren't happy about you being happy, well, then, no offense, but fuck 'em. Life's too short, Lottie. There's no shame in wanting to enjoy yourself rather than being miserable to fit the needs of other people."

Lottie can't change how she was raised, and her mind will always wonder if she's doing right by her family.

But the idea of being with someone besides Keanu makes her realize no other man will do.

I felt the same way when I thought about Bubba returning to Conroe without me. Sure, we could do the long-distance thing and take things slowly. But when I imagined losing him, I knew the risk wasn't worth it. Leaving my hometown was nowhere as painful as life without Bubba.

Lottie cleans up in the restroom before we return to the dining area where she takes my brother's hand and asks, "Will you be my husband?"

Keanu answers by marrying her twice—once in White Horse that August after I return from the Johansson family road trip and again in October in Bandung, Indonesia.

Bubba travels with my family and the entire Hayes clan in a private jet Angus insists on renting.

"I want to survive twenty fucking hours of flight time with all my grand-spawn," he growls when Dad taunts him for being a rich prick.

Angus fires back by calling my father a RUB—aka a rich upscale biker—which is a term he learned from Cap. The men's bickering is the only negative part of the entire trip.

Otherwise, Lottie is a vision in her pale pink dress, and Keanu is dapper as always in his sleek black suit. I cry a lot more than I should, but I'm overjoyed for my brother.

While Keanu doesn't cry at my wedding, I have no doubt he wants to. Remaining dry-eyed is a struggle he fights all day. One that Mom easily crumbles under, and Dad has varying success at.

Before the day in the woods, Bubba and I planned to have a sizable wedding in Hickory Creek. We wanted to invite all of his family and friends along with mine. The only holdup was waiting for Griff to find a woman to distract him from his obsession with me.

Then he died, and I felt too insecure about a crowd of people staring at me. Plus, I still didn't trust all of the people in the Brotherhood or their families. *Do they view Griff as a victim pushed over the edge by my selfishness? Would just questioning their loyalties ruin my wedding?* Not inviting them to a big wedding wasn't an option unless I hoped to create a ton of grudges. Planning a ceremony seemed like too much stress for too little payoff.

I'm ready to put aside getting married. After all, life with Bubba is going so well. I'm finding my place in Conroe. He's taking charge of the club and building respect with the people who matter to him. My family visits often. His family accepts me. Why do we need a ceremony or a piece of paper?

"It's not the legal part," Bubba explains one night while Ula climbs in my hair and Bjork flirts with my man. "I don't care if we have a piece of fucking paper. I just want something, I don't know, ceremonial to prove you're not any woman to me. Does that make sense?"

Whether it makes sense or not, I can't tell him no. Bubba loves me so much, and I need him to be happy.

Getting married at the bird sanctuary is his idea. We keep everything intimate, casual, and stress-free. I love being surrounded by the birds, including Odin, who rides around on my shoulder most of the evening.

Bubba promises he isn't jealous of my first love, but those two possessive guys eyeball each other all damn night. Their rivalry never stops being funny to me either. Bubba eventually even takes off his shirt just to flaunt what his parents gave him. Grinch then calls him a whore, and I nearly pee myself laughing. The night is both the funniest and most romantic wedding I could have imagined.

We marry four months to the day after we meet. For some, our relationship moved too fast.

But for Bubba and me, waiting was never an option.

A FINAL WORD FROM THE BOHEMIAN

Motherhood doesn't interest me right away. Not when I babysit Byron or after Sissy gives birth to a son named Hopper. I love watching Scarlet and Phoebe's kids, and I frequently hang out with Hart and Haydee. But I just don't feel the urge to have a kid of my own.

Bubba doesn't seem in a hurry either. Bailey frequently hints for more grandbabies. She's addicted to all the attention and cuddles being a nana affords her.

"It's up to Soso," Bubba says whenever anyone asks.

To some people, it might seem as if he's passing the buck or doesn't care. But he knows what Griff wanted to do. Rushing into "breeding" panics me, and that panics Bubba.

"We'll know when we know," I reply when everyone invariably turns to me.

Life is great that first year. I settle into my oddball group of friends. Sissy is the gentle ditz. Lily is the organized badass. Panni is the shy hugger. Phoebe is the easygoing artist who never wants to plan shit. Scarlet is the hothead farmer who also never wants to plan shit. Bailey expects everyone to do what she says. Sawyer wants everyone to ignore Bailey. I'm not entirely certain of my role, though.

"You're the sexy one," Bubba says when I ask his opinion. "The hot one. The cool one. You know, the best one."

Taking Layla's suggestion, I open a small boho store. We sell "hippie food" like lettuce wraps and wheat germ. Lily produces crotched blankets and quilts. Scarlet turns her goat milk into soaps, skincare products, and cheese. Her Cajeta is a hit, and she buys more goats to keep up with the demand.

A few of the women from the Rossiya Motel work at the store part-time. Plus, they learn how to waitress at the pub. I also personally train Katya to be the motel manager. She cries when I buy her a language program to help improve her English skills.

"I said you would only get rewards, not punishments," I tell Katya. "You are brave, and you are smart. Nothing in your past will keep you from succeeding in the future. Do you understand?"

Katya knows she can always call me. Whatever the problem—from a customer bothering her to not understanding the meaning of the word—I will always listen. That's what loyalty means in Conroe now.

Katya and the other girls learn quickly, and they rarely complain. One day, I hope many of them will use their new skills to find legal work. I want them to know they have options, even if they don't seem willing to give up the safety and familiarity of the motel yet.

I'm able to do most of my work from home, using my laptop to oversee the stores, motel, pub, and even the sanctuary in Hickory Creek. That flexibility pressures me to think I should have a baby now. Plus, Lily and Sissy want more, and my baby would have instant friends. The timing is right, but the urge for a child escapes me.

Until one day when I'm at Bailey and Nick's house. I wander down a hallway near Buzz's section that I've never visited before. On the wall are pictures of Bubba and his brothers. There are tons of adorable photos, but one catches my eye.

Bubba, Butch, and Buzz sit in an inflatable pool. The brothers are probably between the ages of seven and three. The three wet boys stare at the camera wearing matching "huh?" expressions.

That picture inspires me to make a little Bubba. I can't explain why, but I need to be a mother, and I need him to be a father.

Bailey cries hysterically when Bubba and I announce we're having a girl.

"I knew you were the best one!" Bailey declares, eliciting groans and complaints from her other sons.

Panni doesn't take it personally because she knows Bailey's full of shit. Sissy doesn't seem to even hear the comment because she's mesmerized by her son's tiny toes.

Once Malibu is born, I understand the fascination with baby feet. Our daughter is terribly tiny, and Bubba worries she didn't cook long enough despite her being a week overdue.

He's even afraid to hold her until I remind him how he cuddles the much smaller Ula and Bjork. Once Bubba takes Malibu in his arms, he never wants to let her go.

Growing up to be a hardcore daddy's girl, she's basically me as a kid. Though I craved my mom when I was sick and scared, I always wanted to know where my dad was and if I could go with him. Now Bubba enjoys his own shadow.

When she's three, our dirty-blonde, dark-eyed daughter decides we need to shorten Malibu to "Bubu," so she can sound more like her dad. My parents and I get a kick out of her doing the same to her name that Mom did to mine.

Her devotion to Bubba makes me so nostalgic that I find myself calling Dad daily, just to say hi.

He and Mom drive up every other week. More often, when I'm nearly ready to pop with their newest granddaughter.

Venice isn't an independent tomboy like her sister. My daydreamer prefers sitting on my lap and listening to a story rather than learning how Daddy's chopper works.

Two is enough. I've always thought one child per parent was the best scenario. It's how my parents did it.

Plus, space is always an issue, and I don't want to move from this ranch. Bailey sold us the house cheap, and we could conceivably add on down the road. For now, I can't find a flaw with it.

After all, this is the house where Bubba calmed my fears after Griff. Where I lingered when Malibu's labor took forever. Where I nearly gave birth to Venice, who decided to show up early and with minimal warning. Where my pets feel comfortable. And where Bubba and I built our life together.

Bubba's already made improvements. After the atrium, Buzz and Butch help him build a workshop out back. He added a carport where the club guys can hang out and drink beer.

Often, Bubba, the girls, and I walk across the street to play at the Kirk Johansson Memorial Park. My man staked his claim on Conroe in the same way he did with my heart. He's become as fiercely protective of our town as I am.

For our frequent visits to Hickory Creek, we buy a small three-bedroom place near my parents. The A-frame isn't an option with such a tiny bedroom and no privacy. Three chicks and one bathroom is also Bubba's biggest nightmare. He endures enough of that during our summer road trips.

Both girls love the sanctuary and learn to respect the birds' power. Every time we're in town, we spend hours visiting, getting to know newcomers and spending time with old friends. Back in Conroe, Venice often pulls up the camera feed from the sanctuary on my laptop and checks on her feathered buddies. Venice's love of birds reminds me of Keanu as a kid when he'd watch the fish in his aquarium.

Life is perfect. I know people roll their eyes when I say that, but there's no other word to describe how I feel. Bubba is the best man. My daughters are the best kids. Our house is the best home. Our extended family meshes together perfectly.

Not everything was ideal on our way to this current perfection. We struggled. We suffered. We persevered. Just like his parents did, and my parents did, and our kids will do one day.

And every day together is my reward for choosing to follow my hunky puppy rather than settle for what was safe, easy, and expected.

A FINAL WORD FROM THE STALWART

At the age of twenty-two, I ran away from Conroe. At thirty-two, I'm the king of this fucking place.

These days, my club gets a piece of everything illegal in this county. When Cooper claimed Conroe, he only wanted a buffer town near the Kentucky border with Missouri and Illinois. I doubt he ever figured we'd amount to anything more than a weak satellite chapter or a vanity club for his sisters to run. Without a doubt, we floundered for a few years, but running away like a bitch proved to be a turning point for me and the local Reapers.

Somehow, Soso manages to get more beautiful every year we're together. She never stops being patient with me either. I can tell her anything, fuck up like an idiot, whine like a baby, and she always helps me get back on track. I like to think I'm everything she needs too. Not a day goes by that she doesn't smile as if the sun itself is shining through her. I might not be the only reason she's happy, but I pray I'm a big part of it.

We're blessed with two brilliant little girls. Malibu wants to be just like me. By the time she was six, I had her riding with me around Conroe. She'd wear her baby blue helmet and "Lil Reaper" jacket. When I'd cross my arms and frown at someone, she'd mimic me completely.

Even now when she's nearing puberty, Malibu dreams of riding a chopper and beating down anyone who messes with the family. I hope she gets to be that tough chick one day. Of course, if she hits fifteen and decides she wants to be a princess or a scientist or a belly dancing, bird-loving bohemian, I'll be prouder than shit too.

Blonde, blue-eyed Venice loves animals, traveling, and books. I get the feeling she'll have trouble finding happiness in a small town when she's older. Her need to roam is infectious. When she's seven, we buy our own RV—The Sobu—and start taking trips throughout the year.

The four of us love the road. With the club stable, we can be gone for weeks without worrying about putting anyone in danger. The girls are part of the local educational co-op, meaning they can study anywhere. Ula and Bjork come along in the special cage we had built to fit in the RV, and Freki usually hogs the master bed.

The plan is for only two kids. It's not a set deal or anything, but we're happy with our daughters. However, since Soso's broken nose, she suffers a sinus infection at least twice a year. We're careful during every round of antibiotics because they can make her birth control wonky. Well, we are for the first nine years, but then someone suffers a condom failure—no blame assigned—and we end up with a beautiful baby boy.

Tripoli is a shy, timid child who wants to live on his mom's hip and hide his face in her hair. The older he gets, the more he reminds me of Butch. The sandy-haired boy talks easily enough, but the world would quickly pass by Tripoli if his big sisters weren't watching out for him.

"He was what we didn't even know we wanted," Soso says one night as we cuddle in our new master bedroom. "Just like how you were for me."

Our ranch house grows before Tripoli's birth, and then we add an in-law suite after he's walking. With the amount of time Dayton and Harmony spend in Conroe, they ought to buy a place of their own here. But we prefer them to stay with us. Soso is at her happiest when she's surrounded by her family.

At first, Keanu and Lottie bunk with us during their visits. Then when their son Farrell is born, they decide to rent a place a mile away from our house. He eventually opens up a steakhouse called The Glenn.

"I need to eat well even when visiting Bumfuck, Kentucky," he explains after announcing the purchase.

Over the years, Conroe grows both in the number of residents and in the local flavor. The old-timers don't like the changes one bit, but the opening of a local factory infuses the town with fresh blood. The club organizes yearly events as a way to give back and to remind everyone who really runs Conroe.

I'd be lying to claim I could have come up with any of these ideas without meeting Soso. If I stayed in Conroe after my fight with Butch, I don't know what would have happened. The Dogs might have killed us. Cooper could have installed a new president. We likely would have limped along for years. Eventually, I'd have married a woman that made me happy but never inspired me. My life wouldn't have been fulfilling. Only Soso knows how to inspire me to be my best. She's the magic ingredient I was missing.

Finding her saved me, my club, and likely my family. Falling in love with Soso happened fast. Loving her every day since has been easy.

THE END

Manufactured by Amazon.ca
Bolton, ON